Kätchen's Story

A German Girl Like Me – Book 1

by
Joseph R. Costa

In memory of my Mother (Kätchen) and
Grandmother (Margarete) who are dear to me
and of my Aunt Ruth and
Grandfather (Gustav) who I never knew.

Many thanks to my wife Kathy
and family and friends for their
support and encouragement.

ISBN-13: 9781520367675

Contents

Chapter 1
The Parade

"GIRLS! PAY ATTENTION to the music! March in step with the beat of the music! March like good soldiers, not school girls!" shouted our frustrated youth leader from her position at the front of us.

We were probably making her look bad, so she wasn't very happy with us. She hurried over to a girl in the front row and sternly corrected her marching.

Thankfully, I was in the middle of the sixty girls in our formation of eighth graders and not near the front. Many other student formations, some made up of boys and some of girls, marched in front of and behind ours. All the schools in our area were participating.

In places along our parade route, small crowds had gathered while in other places only a scattering of people stopped to watch as we marched by. Some onlookers waved and clapped, but many just eyed us curiously.

We could hear the music of the marching band up ahead in the distance. The commands being shouted up and down the parade line and the music resonating among the buildings were a new sensation for us.

We girls swung our arms and stepped stiffly as they had shown us. It was only our second parade though, so we weren't very good yet at marching in unison. I glanced over at my friend Marika marching beside me, and she looked back with a slight smile. No talking was allowed, so we didn't say anything.

Fortunately, the weather in Hamburg was nice that day, the kind of spring day when birds could normally be heard chirping. But with the noise and activity of the parade, they were chirping somewhere else. It was late April of 1933.

The weather that time of the year in northern Germany might get chilly later in the day, so we wore our sweaters.

We had pinned the arm bands with the swastikas on the outside of our sweaters. In our first Nazi parade earlier this month, some onlookers had booed us as we marched. In a few places along the parade route, we had even been pelted with potatoes by unhappy onlookers. Afterward, I told my teacher I didn't want to march in these parades anymore, but he told me that voluntary participation was expected, which meant it was mandatory.

Looking ahead along the line of marching formations, the large number of Nazi flags presented a swaying, moving forest of red, black, and white. I glanced to the side at the men in brown shirts walking along with us. These men escorting our marching formations were members of the SturmAbteilung (storm troops), known as the SA.

The SA was like a private army of the Nazi party. These brown shirted men had not been with us during the first parade. As they paced along beside us carrying their nightsticks, they menacingly eyed the crowd. Local Nazi officials wanted no repeat of the dissent shown at the first parade. The storm troopers had already confronted and silenced a number of people who had booed at us.

Up ahead we heard someone in the crowd call out, "We need work! And the Nazis give us parades of children!"

Several storm troopers rushed toward the crowd with their nightsticks poised to strike. One of them screamed, "Who said that! Who said that!" No one in the crowd answered as the storm trooper pushed his way through them.

"If I find out who said it, they'll have work all right! Plenty of it! In a labor camp!"

He glared around at them as they stood silent, looking away. With a threatening look, he then pushed his way back into the street, where the other scowling storm troopers were watching. After another dark look backward at the crowd, he and the others returned to their places alongside the groups of marchers.

Farther along the route, a crowd of people were cheering and clapping as we passed. A good many others like them seemed to be enthusiastic supporters of Hitler and the Nazis. I myself preferred to be back in school rather than marching in a parade. The weather was pleasant enough for it, but we were on our way, like the last time, to a Nazi rally at the sports field, where we would be standing for hours listening to boring political speeches. Not something a German girl like me, a fourteen year old eighth grade schoolgirl, looked forward to doing.

As we continued to march, I scanned the onlookers and the second story windows along the street. I still recalled dodging potatoes in the last parade. But our storm trooper escort seemed to have successfully discouraged any potato throwing.

"Hey you two! What are you doing there!" we heard a storm troopers shout. Off on the right, he burst through the crowd and surprised two young men who had been quietly passing out anti-Nazi leaflets in back of the crowd.

One of them surprised the storm trooper in return by punching him in the face and sending him sprawling to the ground. Both young men then flung their leaflets into the air above the crowd and ran for it down a side street.

"Halt! Halt!" yelled several other storm troopers rushing after them and blowing their whistles, which we could hear moving off in the distance.

"Girls, pay attention to your marching! Don't look at those hooligans! Keep your eyes forward!" our youth leader furiously shouted when she saw we had all turned our heads to watch the excitement. Even after her shouts, some still craned to look.

"Girls! Girls!! Eyes forward!" shouted the youth leader even louder, which brought everyone back to rigidly marching and looking straight ahead.

The leaflets thrown into the air were caught by an updraft of wind blowing between buildings. They fluttered up and about, eventually floating down onto the crowd and the street where we marched. The storm troopers were there furiously picking them up and threatening nearby people to stay away. After being screamed at by our youth leader, we rigidly looked straight ahead as we marched, trying to ignore the leaflets as they fluttered down among us.

"Girls! Keep marching! Ignore that trash! Don't touch any of them!" our youth leader commanded.

Unfortunately, one of the leaflets landed on me and somehow got stuck in my collar. I tried to keep looking ahead, but it was difficult not to notice the youth leader hustle over between the marching rows of girls and furiously snatch the leaflet from my collar. After glaring at me as if I were to blame for it, she finally returned to her place at the front of the formation.

As I continued to march, I thought to myself, "All this marching and armbands and yelling and potato throwing. What has happened? I don't understand. I want my old life back."

So went my second Nazi parade as a young girl growing up in Nazi Germany. It's one of many things I remember from those times, which seem like a previous life to me now. My life under the Nazis was very different from my life there in Hamburg before the Nazis took over.

I can remember those times too, my "old life," as I called it. They may have been turbulent times within Germany, but they had been happy times for me, back just two years earlier.

Chapter 2
On an Errand

I CAN STILL clearly see myself walking happily down a tree-lined street in Hamburg in the spring of 1931, when I was nearly twelve years old. Although it was an overcast afternoon, I was happy to be taking a break from homework and outside on an errand.

I was a girl of average height and weight with my dark hair in long braided pigtails. I suppose I had a pleasant enough face, but I never considered myself pretty. My parents only had modest incomes, so my shoes were fairly plain, and my dress was practical and made by my mother.

A friendly cat meowed and walked in front of me on the sidewalk, and I bent down to pet it.

As I scratched its back, I had no idea of the terrible political struggle going on in Germany at the time. A political party called the Social Democrats was in power and struggling to run the government and maintain order. Two other political factions; the National Socialist German Workers' Party (known as the Nazis) and the Communist Party were in violent, bitter conflict trying to gain power. The Nazis were gaining popular support as they promoted German nationalism, cultural superiority, and dissatisfaction with the surrender terms ending World War I (as it became known later).

Meanwhile, the Communists promoted their ideals and tried to organize workers into unions to increase their numbers. Their clashes often resulted in pitched physical battles with clubs and fists. The German government, already hampered by the war reparations resulting from Germany's surrender, was further hampered by the Depression, which had caused widespread unemployment in

Germany. They were times of turmoil, uncertainty, and dissatisfaction within Germany. And all the while, the Nazis struggled ruthlessly to tap into this dissatisfaction and gain power.

I gave the cat a last scratch and walked on underneath a row of linden trees where I heard the chirp of a finch above me. Looking up, I spotted it on a branch and waved to it. The little finch was telling me to "wave" with its "vink" chirp, which sounds like the German word for "wave." So, after a few more waves to my little friend up in the tree, I continued on my errand.

The street, where I walked, was an urban scene of multi-story apartment buildings, shops, and businesses. Despite the turmoil in the German government, life where I lived seemed normal. Shops were open. The streets were clean. People were friendly as they passed on the street.

I was on my way to a sewing shop to get my mother a spool of red thread. She was a seamstress and needed it for the dress she was making.

Soon I arrived in front of a store with a large front window with displays of cloths and yarns. Written in large letters above window were the words "Johanna Zöllmer Sewing Shop." Going inside, I walked, past the bolts of materials and other displays, to the counter where Frau Zöllmer was standing. She was a pleasant lady and my mother's friend. She smiled as I approached.

"Good day, Frau Zöllmer."

"Good day, Kätchen."

That's me. My name is Kätchen. Let's talk a little about my name. First, the umlaut (two dots) are there over the "a" to give it a different sound in German. The German pronunciation of my name is something like "Kāch-yen," with a German "ch" like in "Achtung," that German word from all the movies. Anyway, my name is difficult for English speakers to pronounce. It might be easier to think of its pronunciation as "Kā-chen" with an English "ch" similar to the English word "kitchen." The " ö " in "Zöllmer" is even harder to pronounce, so think of her name as Zullmer. Now let's get back to the story.

"What can I do for you today?" Frau Zöllmer added cheerily.

"My mother needs a spool of this thread, please," I said pulling a sample of thread from my pocket and showing her.

"I see she is still working on Juliet's dress," she noted.

"I think she's almost finished."

After getting the thread from a rack behind her and handing it to me, she asked, "Is your mother's cold doing better, Kätchen? She came in the other day with a bad cough. I made her some tea with honey and plum brandy. It's an old family remedy. It seemed to help her cough."

"Yes, she's doing fine now," I told her. Then with a grin, I added, "Tea with honey and plum brandy. That sounds like yummy medicine. I think *I'm* feeling a cough coming on." I added a few weak coughs into my hand for effect.

"Oh, you little faker," she said playfully. "That will be five pennies."

Grinning, I paid her and waved goodbye as I left.

As I walked back, I looked up at the sky and noted the sun was starting to peek through the clouds above our city. I wasn't born in Hamburg, but had spent most of my life here. So I considered it my hometown.

Hamburg is a large beautiful city on the Elbe River. People say we have more bridges and canals than Venice, a famous city in Italy. Our city has a long history of being a busy and important seaport. Along the way home was a store with a "sailing ship in a bottle" displayed in their show window. I always stopped to look at it. I would inspect the amazing minute detail of the ship and, of course, wonder how they got the ship in there.

Many years ago in the days of sail, huge wooden ships with many sails, like the little one in the bottle, would depart from Hamburg to all corners of the world. The sailors onboard sang songs to help them work together and to take their minds off their toil. In one of these songs called *Hamborger Veermaster* (*Hamburg Four-Masted Sailing Ship*), they sang the verses in our northern German dialect, but sang the chorus about California in English. It must have given them something to dream about as they worked. The chorus was as follows.

> "Blow, boys, blow, for Californio.
> There's plenty of gold, so I am told,
> On the banks of Sacramento."

I was staring transfixed at the ship in the store window, when someone passed nearby, bringing my thoughts back to the streets of Hamburg and my errand.

On my way home again, I turned a corner and found myself on a street with a number of restaurants along it. I could see a number of nicely dressed people seated inside by the windows eating, drinking, and enjoying themselves. I wished I could be like them. My family didn't have money for going to restaurants, even though my father, Gustav Thielke, was a waiter at an expensive restaurant, one much better than these restaurants along here.

For several years, my father had been a waiter at a well-known ferry house where wealthy people dined. Every day, he bustled about serving his well-to-do customers and putting up with their eccentricities. He had one stuffy gentleman with a monocle, who ordered a bowl of soup for lunch every day and always sent it back.

My father would take a steaming bowl of soup to him and wait politely as he took a taste.

"Not hot enough! Bring me another!" the gentleman would declare, motioning to take it away.

"I'm terribly sorry, sir. I'll get you another right away."

After taking the bowl of soup back into the kitchen, my father would give it a few stirs with a spoon, wait a moment, and then return with the same steaming bowl of soup to the gentleman, who would then dramatically taste it again.

"That's better," he would haughtily proclaim for the benefit of the people at nearby tables, who looked on approvingly.

"Very good, sir," my father would reply, then move on to another table. To us kids, it was another one of those unexplainable adult things.

Farther along, I stopped at the doorway of a tavern to listen to the men inside singing one of our many drinking songs. Germans love to drink and sing. My father would stop by a tavern, like this one, nearly every day after work. He called it his club. He didn't sing very much, but he enjoyed having beers with his friends before coming home.

A short time later, I arrived at our apartment building where I lived with my mother, father, and sister. The five story structure of concrete and stone was not a particularly new or beautiful building, but I was fond of it. An end apartment on the top floor had been our home ever since I could remember. With stairs being the only way of getting up to it, the stairwell echoed my footsteps as I quickly climbed five stories to the top floor. When I turned into the hallway, I could hear a baby crying in another apartment.

Upon entering our apartment, I said, "Hello Mutti, I'm back." I called my mother "Mutti" (rhymes with "footie"), which means "Mom" in German. Similarly, I called my father "Vati" (Remember, a German "v" sounds like an "f", so it is pronounced "faw-tee"), which means "Dad" in German.

Mutti was sitting by her sewing machine, sewing a seam on the red dress by hand.

"Oh good, did you get the thread?" she asked, looking up expectantly.

"Yes, here it is," I replied, bringing it to her.

"Thank you, Kätchen. How is Johanna today?"

"She's fine. She asked about your cough, and I told her you were better. She wouldn't give me any of her medicine."

"It was pretty tasty," Mutti said with a smile, "and better yet, it worked well on my cough."

My mother did sewing and dressmaking work to help pay our bills, and because she enjoyed sewing. She had a foot-peddled sewing machine set up in one corner of our living room. When she was working, elaborate dresses or suits in various stages of completion would be draped across the nearby furniture, while pieces of cloth and thread would litter the floor.

Much of her sewing work came from a local theater company. They staged a new play every three or four months and she would make or alter the costumes for them as needed. Based on a picture or drawing, she would get the material from Frau Zöllmer and make their costumes at home. She was now working on Juliet's dress for a famous Shakespearean play called *Romeo and Juliet.* I suppose there are many interesting things to know about the play, but all my mother knew about it was that one

Italian family wore red and orange colors, and the other family wore blue.

She would make a number of visits backstage at the theater for measurements and fittings in order to get them just right. My mother probably met some famous stars of German stage and screen, but she would not have known it, since we didn't go to plays or movies.

Poor Mutti, she had such a good life when she was a girl growing up. Her family owned a dry goods store and had money. When she was a girl, she had nice clothes, and probably attended plays and concerts. She would have gone to see movies in movie theaters, but movies hadn't been invented yet. Years later when I was growing up, she lived modestly in our apartment.

With my errand finished, I made my way back to our kitchen table where my homework was laid out and patiently waiting for me. As Mutti worked on Juliet's dress, my sister Ruth sat on the floor in the living room drawing with a pencil on a paper. She was four years younger than me, and was slim with a pretty face and light brown hair. She looked up at me, smiled, and resumed her drawing.

As a cute younger sister, she had always gotten more attention than me. At four years old, I had been my parent's center of attention. Suddenly, their attention seemed to shift to this new cute little intruder. They were making a fuss over her, while I was feeling left out. It seemed to me that she was their favorite child. I'm sorry to say that I became very jealous of her and wished I had no little sister.

But it all changed one day, several years later, when Ruth was four years old. Mutti, Ruth, and I had been walking in a park along the Osterbek Canal. Mutti had just turned to stroll over to sit down at a bench when Ruth saw some ducks along the canal bank. She pointed excitedly and took off at full speed as Mutti called for her to be careful. I walked toward the ducks too and watched without interest as the spoiled brat streaked through and scattered a group of them. But when she fell headlong into the canal and thrashed about in deep water screaming, I did not think, "Good, I hope she drowns," or anything else for that matter.

Without thinking, I ran and jumped in after her. I was only eight years old at the time and too little to swim with my flailing and choking little sister in tow back to the bank. I had to go underwater and push her toward safety. After a number of pushes, she was close enough to the edge of the canal for Mutti to grab her.

We got her onto the bank, and Mutti quickly had her over her knee pounding her back frantically to drain the water from her. By this time, other people had come running to help too, but Ruth was already recovering.

She was fine afterward, and for some reason, I wasn't jealous of her anymore. She and I got along together much better afterward, and my parents seemed to pay more attention to me.

Chapter 3
Family

THAT EVENING after clearing my homework away from the kitchen table, Mutti, Ruth, and I sat eating soup for dinner. Not very enthusiastic about the soup, both Ruth and I were playing with it more than eating it.

"Come on, girls. Eat your soup," Mutti said getting impatient with us. We both took a bite.

Ruth was about to ask a question when she was interrupted by a noise in the apartment hallway. We all suspected it was Vati coming home. Ruth and I started to get up, but Mutti gave us a stern look and motioned for us to stay where we were. The door opened and my father walked in with a hand behind his back.

"Hello, everyone," he said cheerfully.

"Hello, Vati!" said Ruth and I enthusiastically.

"Gustav, we got tired of waiting and started dinner without you," said Mutti with less enthusiasm.

"I'm sorry, my dear. There was so much political talk going on down at the club, that I regrettably lost track of time."

"And did you solve all of our problems, Gustav?" Mutti asked indifferently.

"Unfortunately not, but I did bring you something for dessert, a couple of fancy torts from work. I had a hard time keeping them from my friends at the club."

He brought a small bag from behind his back and put it on the table.

"Oh, boy," said Ruth and I, excitedly starting to get up to look in the bag, but Mutti put an end to it.

"Stay there and eat your dinner, girls. You can have some later if you finish your soup."

Vati gave us a quick hug and went to wash up. Ruth and I looked at each other, and we suddenly had more enthusiasm for our soup.

Vati periodically would bring home food from the restaurant. Too much of a dish was prepared, or food was no longer fresh enough. Instead of throwing it away, employees were sometimes allowed to take it home. We were able to sample many interesting dishes and desserts. It was almost like going to a restaurant, but not quite.

Mutti and Vati occupied one bedroom of our modest two-bedroom apartment while Ruth and I occupied the other. Our bedroom was not very big, with only enough room for one bed, which Ruth and I shared.

That night, Ruth and I were in bed lying awake. Mutti sat on a chair knitting by a light on the bed stand beside our bed. I couldn't sleep and, after watching for a while, asked Mutti what she was knitting.

"It's a sweater for Ruth. Both of you are growing out of your sweaters. I'll start on yours when this one is finished."

"Mutti, aren't you going to bed?" Ruth asked.

"I can hear your father snoring from here. It wouldn't do any good to try to sleep in there."

We paused to listen and could hear the loud snoring. This seemed to me to be one more instance of Mutti being less than happy with Vati.

"Mutti, why did you marry Vati?" I asked.

"What? Why did I marry your father? Why do you ask that?" she asked, a little surprised.

"I was just curious," I said, avoiding my reasons.

She matter-of-factly related, "I met your father after the war (World War I). He was the brother of a girlfriend of mine. We went out on several dates, and he asked me to marry him, so I said yes."

"Was he the first man to ask you to marry?" Ruth asked.

Mutti stopped her knitting and stared vacantly down at it for a moment before she replied, "No. Before the war, I knew a fine young man named Frederick. We were planning to someday get married. Unfortunately, the war started, and he was called up right away. He wrote me fond letters from the front, and I wrote often to him. But Frederick was killed in the trenches during one of the many battles, and I cried for weeks."

As we quietly watched, she continued to stare sadly for a few moments then began knitting again.

"Your father," she continued, "was in the army on the front too, but he was luckier and made it back. My mother was eager for me to get married, because I was almost twenty eight, so she gave me a good dowry of money from the sale of the family's old store."

"What's a dowry?" Ruth asked.

"It's like a wedding gift or a promise of one. A bride's dowry is added encouragement for a man to marry her. Your father had been a waiter before the war. After we married, we used the dowry money to buy a small inn, which your father ran. But the inn didn't work out, so here we are."

"Why didn't it work out?" I asked, but Mutti was tired of our questions.

"No more questions. Go to sleep and sweet dreams." She got up to give us a kiss on the cheek. After we said good night, she sat back down and continued to knit. Ruth and I turned over to face away from the light and tried to sleep.

The next morning, Ruth and I were at the kitchen table eating a bowl of cereal for breakfast. We were already dressed in our best dresses for school. Mutti had packed some lunch for us and was putting it in our backpacks.

"Mutti, what are we having for dinner tonight?" Ruth asked.

"I was thinking of potato pancakes."

"With applesauce?" I asked excitedly.

"If I can find apples that aren't too expensive."

"Yum," Ruth said as we finished our cereal and put on our sweaters. Mutti put the backpacks on us, and we gave her a kiss on the cheek as we bustled out the door. As we hurried down the hallway, Mutti watched and shut the door.

In a few moments, the bedroom door opened and a half-dressed Gustav groggily emerged.

"Good morning, my dear. Where are my other dears?"

"Morning, Gustav. They just left for school."

"Ah yes, I guess I did hear them leave, didn't I. Hmm. Too bad," he mumbled as he went back into the bedroom. When he came back out shortly, he was carrying a coat, tie, and fresh shirt. As they spoke, he put on the shirt and tie.

"Gustav, do you have some money for me today, or did you drink up all your pay last night?"

Gustav grunted, reached into his coat pocket and pulled out a small wad of bills. He examined the wad, pulled off a bill and handed the rest to Mutti.

"And coins too if you haven't drunk them all up," Mutti said holding out her hand.

Gustav raised his eyebrows, slightly offended. He fished into his pants pocket, pulled out some coins and gave them to her.

"Are you finished shaking me down, woman?"

"Yes, thank you. I need the money for the rent and some food. Do you want breakfast?"

"No, I think I'll get something at work."

Gustav was fully dressed now as he picked up his outer coat and took his hat from its place near the doorway.

"I'm off to work. Did I overhear something about potato pancakes for dinner tonight or was I dreaming?" he asked. Mutti looked at him with a slight smile and nodded.

"Well then, I most assuredly will be home on time for dinner tonight." He gave her a kiss on the cheek, put his hat on his head, and walked out with his coat.

Meanwhile, Ruth and I were on our way to school, which was several blocks away from the apartment. We were enjoying the nice spring weather and happy at the prospect of seeing our school friends again. A number of other boys and girls could be seen on the street walking to school individually and in small groups.

As Ruth jumped around avoiding sidewalk cracks, I asked, "Is anything special happening in your class today, Ruth?"

"A policeman and his dog, a German Shepard, are visiting our class."

"That should be fun. Our class has music with Frau Holtz today. I'm looking forward to it." I replied.

"I wish we could have a dog," Ruth said.

"Even if pets were allowed in our apartment, which they aren't, I think Mutti wouldn't want to spend the money feeding one."

"I could get a job to pay for its food," Ruth offered.

"Don't be silly. Oh, here comes Gitta," I said, as one of Ruth's classmates came running up.

Soon, they were talking excitedly as they jumped around avoiding sidewalk cracks on our way to school.

Chapter 4
Grade School

WHEN WE ENTERED the busy main entrance of the school, Ruth and Gitta quickly disappeared down the hallway headed for their classroom. I headed in the other direction toward my classroom. The hallway presented a lively scene of girls chatting before class.

I don't know if all grade schools were like it, but ours was divided into separate boys and girls sides. Inside the building was a doorway between the two sides, but it was always closed and not for our use. A high brick wall outside separated the two sides of the school yard. We never saw boys during school.

Uniforms were not required, so girls wore blouses and skirts or dresses of various colors and styles. I joined several of my girlfriends talking in the hallway and heard the latest news. Marika's bike has a flat tire. Heike's older brother has a new girlfriend. Annemarie was wearing a new pretty barrette in her hair.

It was my sixth year of an eight year grade school, in which a class of students has the same teacher and classroom for the first four years and then a second teacher and classroom for the last four years.

Herr Rimkeit, an enthusiastic young man with glasses and fluffy brown hair, had been my teacher in my first four years. He was kind but business-like in his lessons, never authoritarian or mean. He read many stories to us and would take us in the summers on field trips to the forest or a farm, bringing his wife along to help. We had fond memories of those years with him.

We were expected to behave in class and show respect for our teacher. When we first started school, we only knew the informal German that we spoke at home where we addressed each other with the informal "du" form of "you." But after several years at school, we transitioned to using the formal form of German speech, with its respectful "Sie" form of "you", when addressing our teachers.

As I was saying, we students knew to be well behaved. Very seldom did Herr Rimkeit need to scold any of us girls. I'm not sure what it was like for the boys, but we girls looked forward to school each day.

As the time for class neared, we stopped our chattering and made our way to our classroom. Our second teacher, Herr Stock, was seated at his desk in his coat and tie. Each of us greeted him as we entered and went to our desks. He was a congenial middle-aged balding man, and a capable teacher, who had taught at this school for many years.

I had already grown to like him very much, which was a lucky thing since he would be my teacher for another two years. He taught all of our lessons, except for a few special subjects during the week such as music or physical fitness.

Later in spelling class, Herr Stock was calling on girls to spell our weekly words. The thirty students in our class were all from working class families in the nearby neighborhood. I didn't know any girls from upper class families. They attended other grade schools, which cost money.

The work and lessons at our school were designed to educate us for working class lives and jobs. Only the children of families with money had the opportunity to attend schools leading to a university education and professions. It's the way our system was. But at the time, I was a happy sixth grader, completely unaware of and untroubled by such social economic thoughts.

I got along well with my classmates. During a break later in the morning, I was outside with Marika. She was probably my best friend. While the other girls played tag and other games, she would tell me the latest things her brat brothers had done.

Being very young, I had not had much interaction with normal boys my age. Ruth and I enjoyed being with my cousin Fritzi, but I didn't consider him normal. The boys in my neighborhood seemed preoccupied in their games and interests, so most of my knowledge of boys came from Marika who told me what brats they were.

In the afternoon, Herr Stock was conducting a grammar lesson and looked up at the clock.

"That's enough grammar for now. Put your books away. It's time for your music class. Everyone line up single file and we'll march quietly down to the music room," he said closing his book.

I was more than happy for a break from grammar. In the German language, every noun has gender (either male, female or neuter) and its gender is important in German sentences. One would think that an inanimate object would be neuter and living things would be either male or female, but not so. It was not readily apparent to me why, for example, a spoon was male, a fork was female, and a knife was neuter. Meanwhile, a living breathing girl like me was neuter and not female. Anyway, I happily put my grammar book away and lined up at the door with the others.

When we filed into the music room, Frau Holtz, our music teacher directed us onto the chorus stand. She was a young pretty woman, who played the piano well and sang with an excellent voice. That day, instead of filling the first, second, and third rows of the chorus stand as usual, she put us on the second, third, and fourth rows. One of the girls asked her why we were leaving the first row empty.

"Because," she said with a smile, "I have a surprise for you today." A murmur of excitement rose among the girls.

"I have permission from our principal to do something very special today. The sixth graders in this school, both sides of it, are such good singers that I've asked some of our sixth grade boys to join us today."

This announcement was received with a squeal of surprise and giggles. Frau Holtz clapped her hands and got everyone's attention.

"Girls. We are not going to do this if you aren't well behaved young ladies. So settle down. That's better. And so, are we ready?"

Though excited, we girls managed to stand quietly in our places. Frau Holtz went to a side door and opened it. Ten young boys looking uncomfortable filed in followed by a male music teacher, Herr Krauss, who carried an accordion. Frau Holtz directed the boys to the first row of the chorus stand. We watched them as they filed in and a few stifled giggles were heard.

Once the boys had taken their places, Frau Holtz continued, "Good morning boys. We're very pleased to have you with us today. You boys and girls are such good singers in your individual classes that Herr Krauss and I wanted to hear you sing together. We thought you could sing a few of our old folk songs, starting with *Schwarzbraun Ist Die Hazelnuss*, (*Dark Brown Is The Hazelnut*), which you all know well and have sung many times."

As an aside, the German word "Schwarzbraun" ("dark brown" in English) not only means "dark brown" as in the color of the nut, but it is also a German term meaning "dark-haired." My mother told me that the dark hair of "dark brown" Germans is probably the result of the many past French invasions, but she wouldn't explain what she meant. Being a "dark brown" girl myself, I naturally liked a song where "dark brown" girls are preferred over blonds, who usually get more than their fair share of attention anyway.

"Oh good. That's my favorite song," I whispered to Marika, standing next to me on the chorus stand.

"Mine, too," she whispered back as she brought a lock of her brown hair under her nose like a mustache, which made us giggle.

Frau Holtz, looking the boys over, said, "Hans, you sing the first verse. Helmet, you sing the second. Let's see. Gunther, you sing the third." The three boys all looked pleased by the honor and nodded.

"Altos, sopranos, you remember your parts?" All nodded in reply. "Herr Krauss will play for us. Are we all ready? Are there any questions?"

There were no questions and Frau Holtz stood in front of the children with her hands raised in preparation to start. In the meantime, several teachers and staff had come into the back of the room to listen. Frau Holtz nodded to Herr Krauss, and he began playing an introduction. At Frau Holtz's cue, Hans sang,

> " 'Dark brown' is the Hazelnut.
> 'Dark brown' am I too. Am I too.
> 'Dark brown' must my girlfriend be,
> I want her just like me."

Several "dark brown" girls innocently stroked their dark hair and eyed the boys as he sang, then it was time for all to sing the chorus.

> "Holdri-o, juvi juvi di, ha ha ha,
> Holdri-o, juvi juvi di, ha ha ha,
> Holdri-o, juvi juvi di, ha ha ha,
> Holdri-o, juvi juvi di."

At his cue, Helmet sang the second verse,

> "A girl gave me a kiss one day,
> And I, of course, was miffed. I was miffed.
> I gave the kiss right back to her.
> You see, I don't take gifts."

A few more looks were exchanged as he sang, then we sang the chorus a second time. At his cue, Gunther sang the third verse,

> "My girl has no dow-er-y.
> My girl has no gold. Has no gold.
> But she means more to me than,
> All riches in the world."

This verse caused quite a stir of excitement that resulted in a strong performance of the chorus a third and final time.

When Herr Krauss finished playing an ending, all the onlookers burst into enthusiastic clapping and cheering. All of us boys and girls beamed and started to cheer too.

When the uproar died down, Frau Holtz said, "Wonderful, children, wonderful. You sang beautifully. I'm very proud of you. Now let's see. What song shall we sing next?"

After school, I was happily humming the song as Ruth and I walked home together.

"What are you so happy about?" Ruth asked.

"I don't know. Today they invited the boys to sing with us in music class. It was fun."

"Thank goodness, we don't have boys in our class."

"How were the policeman and his dog?" I asked.

"They couldn't make it today and are supposed to come next week."

"Oh, that's too bad."

Ruth piped up, "During a break, Gitta and I put our ears against the classroom wall and could hear the boys in class on the other side. Boy, were they dumb. They couldn't answer any questions right."

"Did you recognize any boys from our apartment building?"

"No, but the ones there are pretty dumb too," she replied. We laughed and kept walking.

A few days later after dinner, Ruth and I were at the kitchen table playing a board game. Vati was reading his paper in his chair. Mutti was sitting on the sofa knitting as she chatted with her longtime friend Ilse.

Ilse and her husband had lived in an apartment just down the block. I used to love to watch them together. They were such a sweet couple. She adored him, and he adored her. But two years ago, he had been killed in a freak accident at the train station where he had worked. Now living in the apartment by herself, she had somehow kept going without losing her sweet disposition.

I had rolled the dice and sent one of Ruth's game pieces back to "Start." She was just beginning to fume at me when we heard several sirens nearby outside. We both jumped up and hurried over to the window to look down on the street.

The adults looked up, but remained seated. Ilse said, "Oh dear. I hope it's nothing serious."

After peering up and down the street, I said, "It must be on another street. I can't see anything."

"I can't either. Do you think someone's in trouble?" asked Ruth.

Vati looked up from his paper, "Whatever the trouble is, it's nothing compared to this country's trouble. I overheard people at the restaurant today saying the banks are about to collapse."

"Goodness," Mutti said.

"Bank buildings are going to fall down?" Ruth asked in amazement.

"No, Ruth. It's not like it sounds. It means people lose the money they have in the bank," Vati said.

"That would happen if the buildings fell down too," Ruth said.

"Do we have money in a bank, Vati?" I asked.

"No, but it might be bad for business at the restaurant. It isn't a good thing."

"I have a little money in a bank," Ilse said. "Maybe I should withdraw it. But then where would I put it? Under my mattress like they say?"

"Since the war," Mutti said with a sigh, "I can't think of any time when there wasn't some kind of crisis. This is just the latest one."

"How true, Margarete," Ilse said, "how true."

No matter how much we might fret over it, there was nothing we could do about banks collapsing. We would find out in the weeks to come that wealthy people somehow continued to dine at expensive restaurants like my father's, even when banks were collapsing.

Who could explain or understand such things? All I understood was my own small world of family and school. I was expected to be a good girl and a good student, to do my homework and get good grades in school.

Mutti came over to the window with us and gazed down on the street. Below, she saw a man carrying a camera bag and tripod walking along on the sidewalk.

"Oh Ilse, come over here. I think it's the street photographer you talked about earlier."

Ilse hurried over to the window and peered down.

"Yes, that's him. Herr Ziegler, I think is his name. He took a wonderful family picture for my neighbor."

"Quick, Kätchen. Go down and ask him if he would come back tomorrow night and take one of us," Mutti said grasping my shoulder.

"Why do we need a family photo?" Gustav protested. "Do you think you are royalty now, Mutti?"

"Oh hush, Gustav. Every family, even us, needs a family photo occasionally so the girls can remember growing up. Our last professional photo was the one of them posing with that little fence. That was six years ago!"

After a moment of reflection, Gustav said, "You know, Mutti. You're right. I agree."

Then with a devilish grin and giving Ilse a wink, he started in again, "As a matter of fact, Mutti. I was going to recommend it myself. In fact, I insist. It's important for the girls. I don't care what you say. We are going to do it!"

Now with his finger wagging in the air, he declared, "Yes, I insist. We are going to get a family photo taken, and that's the end of it!" With that, he quickly buried his head behind his newspaper again.

After a look of annoyance at her husband, Mutti turned back to the window and pointed down.

"Kätchen, you see him there, the man with the reddish hair. Give him our apartment number. Tell him to come up tomorrow night at this time. It seems your father wants a family photo! Now go!"

"Okay," I said, looking down and spotting the man.

"I'm going too," Ruth said as she raced out ahead of me, and I rushed to catch up with her.

The next evening, the photographer came back with his equipment. Ruth and I were well scrubbed and in our best dresses, with hair combed and braided by Mutti. The photographer got his equipment set up and took his time getting us situated just right. Finally he seemed satisfied with what he saw. He talked to us lightheartedly as we posed. At just the right moment, his flash went "poof."

We got a copy of the photograph several days later. Mutti was happy with it and ordered a large one for the wall and several smaller ones for the album. She paid Herr Ziegler his money while Ruth and I studied the new family photo. Little did I know at the time how I would treasure this picture years later.

"Mutti, why do I look different in this picture than I do in the mirror?" Ruth asked.

"I don't know, Ruth. I think it looks just like you. Now stop admiring yourself, wash your hands, and set the table for dinner," Mutti replied.

"All right," Ruth said, "but for some reason, Kätchen looks the same as always, but I look different."

Chapter 5
Summer Vacation

THAT SUMMER of 1931, Ruth and I were delighted to be sitting on a train on our way to visit Oma (Grandma) and my favorite aunt Rosa. They were Mutti's mother and sister, who lived together in a small town in the hill country of central Germany where Mutti grew up. We weren't able to visit Oma and Aunt Rosa every year, but Mutti had set aside enough money over time to be able to afford the train tickets that summer. She knew how much we liked going and thought we deserved it.

The month-long vacations at my aunt's house in a small town were an interesting and welcome break for us from our life in the big city. We sat and watched out the windows of the train as the towns, forests, green hills and farms passed by. That year's trip was even better because Cousin Fritzi also came with us.

His father, Uncle Fritz, was my mother's brother, but they were not close. He and his family lived only kilometers away on the west side of Hamburg, but we didn't get together very often. Uncle Fritz was a big-bellied, pompous, humorless, self-important man with a large mustache and bald head. That might have something to do with it. I never understood how his thin, handsome, amusing son Fritzi could be so different from him. And our lively sandy-haired cousin knew so many interesting things.

"Look!" he said pointing out the window. "You see that farm there with all the low buildings. That's a pig farm. You don't want to live downwind of it! Cow manure smells bad, but pig manure smells the worst. Believe me!" Fritzi exclaimed.

"How would you know, Fritzi?" Ruth asked, laughing.

"I am quite familiar with the smell, thank you. You might even call me an expert on the subject. My class once visited a pig farm, and the smell was just atrocious!"

Saying this, he clutched his throat and hung his tongue out on one side of his mouth in mock agony as he slumped over. Ruth and I watched and giggled.

Later in the afternoon, we arrived in the train station near Leimbach where we hurried off the train with our small suitcases. Aunt Rosa greeted us with open arms, a big hug, and a kiss. She had a kind pleasant face, wore round spectacles, and never seemed to change or grow older. Although she loved children, she had none of her own. Her husband had come back from the war a different person, abusive and a heavy drinker. After their divorce, she hadn't remarried.

As we walked the mile or two back to the little town of Leimbach where she lived, we looked about at the open spaces. A small river, the Werra, wound through the middle of the small valley rimmed on each side by high hills. Any field or hill that wasn't plowed for farming was verdant green. A few modest towns of two story houses and businesses dotted the open countryside. It was very different from the urban big city scenes we were accustomed to.

Leimbach was in Thuringia, an area of Germany with its own long history of dynasties, rulers, wars, and culture. In the last century, it was consolidated with many other German kingdoms into a unified Germany. The local speech, dress, foods, songs, beer, you name it, were all somewhat different from those in Hamburg, even though it was part of the same country.

When we reached the house in Leimbach, we rushed inside to see Oma. We found her sitting in her large wicker chair out back in the garden, where she happily welcomed us with open arms. For some time, she had lived with Aunt Rosa, who took care of her. She was a kind old lady who loved children and looked forward to our visits. She and Aunt Rosa always marveled at how much we had grown since the last time they saw us.

Oma, who was 83 years old, had difficulty getting around. Still she wanted to be with us in the house and participate in our activities as much as she could. At night, she would read to us from a large old storybook and tell us what it was like when she was a girl.

German towns take great pride in their local festivals. One town there had for many years in the summer held an annual rifle competition for veterans called a shooting festival. An elaborately decorated chain with medallions was presented to the best shooter, who was allowed to keep and wear the chain around his neck until the next year's competition. Considered a great honor, it was proudly worn by the winners when socializing.

While the shooting competition was the main event of the festival, it also had parades, local costumes, local crafts, music, food, and lots of beer. We went with Aunt Rosa and enjoyed watching the people having a good time. It seemed to me that the partying and beer drinking was the main interest of the festival and not the shooting.

One day Fritzi, Ruth, and I were exploring along the Werra River, which lazily flowed nearby through the farmland of the valley. It was only about fifty feet across and overgrown in many places with bushes hanging in the water.

As we walked along the banks periodically tossing rocks in the water, Fritzi spotted a raft and pole hidden under the overhanging bushes. He immediately pulled it out, and we gathered around to look at the crude raft, apparently made by local boys.

"Do you think it floats?" I asked.

"Let's find out," said Fritzi, and before we knew it, he had it in the water and was on it propelling himself along with slow deliberate strokes of the pole.

"Da Volga Boatmen. Da Volga Boatmen," he started droning with a Russian accent.

The raft was shaky and the pole too short. Fritzi looked like he was going to fall in a couple times.

"Be careful, Fritzi," we yelled to him. He managed to keep his balance, get it turned around, and headed back.

"Don't worry about me. I know how to do this. Someday I'll do this on the Volga and the Nile. And on the Amazon!"

"You're going to drown right here in the Werra if you aren't careful!" I told him.

"You can't drown in the Werra," he told us. "If you fall in, you float. There are lots of salt deposits and salt mines around here. It's so salty you float. Taste it if you don't believe me."

Ruth bent over, scooped up a handful of water and tasted it.

"I don't know if it's salty or not, but it doesn't taste very good," Ruth said making a face.

"Oh, Ruth, I'm so sorry," Fritzi said with a concerned look. "I forgot to tell you to watch out for parasites in the water or you could get tapeworms in your stomach."

Ruth screamed as she spit out water and shook water from her hands.

"He's just teasing you, Ruth. You won't get tapeworms."

By now, Fritzi was back ashore and Ruth slugged him on the shoulder. He took off running up along the bank with Ruth chasing him. After watching their silliness and shaking my head, I started after them.

The month there passed too quickly. We went on bike rides, explored the town, played board games, helped make cookies, and ate big pieces of chocolate cake.

We also learned a little history when we visited a nearby castle, where a famous German clergyman named Martin Luther had hidden for a year. His protests against Catholic Church policies hundreds of years before had gotten him branded a heretic, so he hid there to avoid being burned at the stake. This unpleasant situation had to do with something called the "Diet of Worms," which sounds unpleasant for other reasons.

All too soon, our summer vacation was over, and it was time for a sad and tearful departure for home. Oma was old and we never knew if we would ever see her again. Aunt Rosa was always sorry to see us go too. She would put us on the train and sadly wave goodbye to us as the train left the station.

We were happy, of course, to see Mutti and Vati again when we got back home to Hamburg. But after such wonderful summer trips to my aunt's, it was hard to return to our modest humdrum life at home. Those summer trips were such happy memories, ones I would keep all of my life.

Chapter 6
Good Memories

OCCASIONALLY after school, Mutti, Ruth, and I would join my father at his drinking club. We would sit in a booth along the wall while Vati and his friends stood at the bar drinking, talking, and laughing. Mutti and a friend or two of hers, sometimes Ilse, would knit as they sat and sipped coffee. Periodically Mutti would, from the corner of her eye, glance disapprovingly over at Vati and then back at her knitting.

Ruth and I would do our homework, but we liked to watch the activities at the bar too. If we were good, the friendly bartender would bring us a little glass of "Alster Water." The two big lakes in Hamburg are called the Inner and Outer Alster, but the "Alster Water" in our glasses wasn't water from the lakes. It was a mixture of half beer and half lemon soda with a cherry in it. It was a big treat for us. The bartender would watch us as we tasted it and would laugh at our resulting big grins. With our little drinks, Ruth and I would imitate the men at the bar.

"I remember back in the trenches when I used to cook soup in a pot. Our only roof was the overhanging barbed wire," Ruth would say in her deepest voice.

"I stirred the soup with my bayonet. It still had the blood of the Frenchies on it," I would add.

"Girls! That's enough," Mutti would interrupt as Ruth and I giggled. Mutti would disgustedly look at her friends who were chuckling too.

Most nights were spent at home with Vati reading the paper, Mutti doing some kind of handwork, me doing homework or reading, and Ruth doing homework or drawing. Ruth was getting to be quite talented at artwork. She liked to disturb Vati behind his newspaper to show him what she had drawn. Vati would always tell her how beautiful her drawings were. When Ruth was little, he had praised them even if the drawings were crude. But when older, her drawings were actually very good, and he meant it.

On rare occasions in the summer, we would attend an afternoon concert in the park. Mutti would bustle about beforehand to get us ready.

"Girls, what is taking you so long? Do you want to go to the concert or not? Kätchen, do you have the blanket to sit on?"

"Yes, Mutti."

"Girls, bring your coats. You may need them later." We collected our coats as Vati came out from the bedroom and sat in his chair.

"Vati, why don't you come with us?" asked Ruth.

"I'm sorry, Ruth. I'd go, but I'm too old to be sitting on a blanket on the ground. It would kill my back. Old war wounds, you know."

"Oh, Vati, you weren't wounded in the back. Come with us," Ruth said with a frown.

"That's enough. Let's go. Say goodbye to your father," Mutti interrupted. We all said our goodbyes, and Mutti herded Ruth and me out the door.

Many other people were also arriving when we got to the park entrance. Just inside the city park was an old brick drinking hall with an outdoor terrace on the back facing a large grassy area. The terrace had been cleared of its normal furniture and set up as a bandstand where a band was already playing old German favorites for the people as they filtered in. The grassy area was rapidly filling up with people, spreading their blankets and sitting down to listen.

We found a spot in the grass amongst the others and laid out our blanket. Once settled on the blanket, Mutti squeezed us in her happiness of the moment.

"This reminds me of going to concerts when I was a little girl. Look at all these people. It's a shame Ilse wasn't feeling good, or she would have joined us. Do you see any of your classmates from school?"

Looking around us, I saw a few and we exchanged waves as Ruth ran to say hello to her friend.

The band finished up their song. He then began getting the band ready for the next song. On one side of the bandstand, a person in the costume of an olden day ratcatcher stood waiting to go on stage.

"Oh, look. There's someone dressed as a ratcatcher like in the Pied Piper. They're going to sing the ratcatcher's song," I said excitedly when I noticed him.

Soon the band conductor motioned for the singer to come onstage, and after a brief introduction of the ratcatcher's song, he began to sadly sing.

I became transfixed by the song as I pictured the sad and worn figure of a ratcatcher of olden times pulling his handcart along a dusty road. The song tells of his lonely life traveling from village to village killing rats. He is friendless and scorned by all. When he grows old and dies along the road, his spirit travels up to heaven where Saint Peter welcomes him in, and he finally finds happiness.

My mind finally returned to the concert as the crowd erupted into applause when the song ended. I clapped with everyone else. It was another favorite song of mine.

Chapter 7
Tumultuous Times

ON OUR WAY HOME from the concert that evening, Mutti, Ruth, and I talked as we walked along the lighted street with the others going home from the concert.

"I especially liked the ratcatcher song." I told them.

Thinking about the song, Mutti said, "Such a sad song. The poor ratcatcher lived such a miserable life with no hope of it ever getting better. His only thing, to which he had to look forward, was someday dying and going to heaven. I guess that's why people are religious."

As we passed a few sidewalk cafes, Ruth looked enviously at the diners and said, "Did you see all the food those people were eating? I wish I could eat dinner in a restaurant every night."

"You'd get fat," I said.

Mutti sighed and said, "Yes, it would be nice, but we can't afford it. I remember going sometimes to restaurants as a little girl. My mother and father ran a fine old store, which had been in the family for generations. We lived on the second floor above it and had money then for things like that."

Ruth asked, "What happened to Oma's store?"

"It's a long story and you wouldn't be interested."

"Yes, Mutti, please tell us," Ruth begged.

"Okay, if you want."

"Yes, we do."

After a moment gathering her thoughts, Mutti started, "Back in 1918, near the end of the war, my parents were getting old. When my father became sick, they couldn't run the store any more. With the war going on, no one else in the family could take it over. It broke their hearts, but they were forced to sell their wonderful old store."

"A man came to my father's sick bed and offered a good price for it. My parents sadly agreed and shook hands on it right there in their bedroom," said Mutti with a look of anger as she remembered.

"After that," Mutti continued, "they lived with Aunt Rosa, but my father never really recovered. He died shortly after the war ended."

"If they sold the store for a good price, why isn't Oma rich today?" I asked.

Fewer people were walking near us as Mutti continued, "Well, the man who bought their store paid with cash and a note, which was to be paid off over a number of years. My mother gave me some of the cash for my dowry. I've already told you about that. Much of the money owed on the note was lost during a terrible time of high inflation."

"Inflation? What's that?" Ruth asked.

"I don't know what caused it, but it was an awful time in Germany when prices went crazy for some reason. For about a year, the price of everything seemed to double every day. In no time at all, a loaf of bread cost a hundred thousand marks."

"A hundred thousand marks for a loaf of bread?" I asked incredulously.

"Yes, and it kept getting worse. People's pensions and savings became worthless. People tried to barter or trade things instead of using money. If you received cash, you ran out to buy something quickly before it became worthless. It was awful.

"My poor mother. One day, the man who bought her family's old store came to her door with a sack of money in a wheelbarrow and paid off the note he owed her."

"A wheelbarrow full of money!" Ruth exclaimed.

"Yes, a wheelbarrow with a sack full of bundles and bundles of small bills that no one wanted anymore, enough to pay off his note. It was enough money at the time to only buy a loaf of bread, except no one wanted such small bills, so it could not even do that.

"The man opened the sack and showed her the money. My mother looked sadly at it, sighed, and signed off the note as paid. But she was so heartbroken that she didn't even want to touch the money. She just closed the door.

"With a laugh, the man departed with his wheelbarrow, leaving the sack of money outside her door. The rotten so-and-so thought it was pretty funny. I hope he burns in hell."

"Poor Oma," I said sadly.

"In less than a year, the price of a loaf of bread shot up to 200 billion marks." Our jaws dropped at hearing this.

"My unfortunate mother had very little to show for the family's fine old store." Mutti paused for a moment deep in thought. She sniffled a little and wiped her eyes with her handkerchief as she walked.

"How long ago did this happen?" I asked.

"About ten years ago, a few years after the war," Mutti replied.

After thinking about it a moment, I asked, "Why doesn't a loaf of bread cost a zillion marks today?"

"One day, the government suddenly announced they had changed to a new mark and that all the old ones could be exchanged for the new ones. It took one million million of the old marks to equal one of the new marks."

"A million million million!" Ruth exclaimed.

"No, just a million million," Mutti replied, "Overnight, the price of a loaf of bread changed from 200 billion of the old marks to 20 cents of the new marks. The old money became worthless. Some people used it for wallpaper to show their disgust. Most people just threw it away or burned it. I'm not sure why, but afterward, prices stopped going crazy."

"Gosh," I said as I thought to myself about such awful times.

As we walked on, we saw two teenage boys up ahead on the other side of the street. They were sitting on the steps of their home talking. From around the next corner, a group of four young men in brown shirts appeared and approached. Seeing the two boys, the four brown-shirted men talked excitedly amongst themselves. We watched with surprise when the four men rushed up to the two boys, and began to taunt and bully them. The boys resisted as the men pushed them back and forth, slapped, and hit them.

"Mutti, what's happening?" asked Ruth as Mutti clutched us, and I gasped.

"Here, you boys! Stop that!" Mutti yelled across at the men. One briefly looked up at us, but quickly returned to their antics.

"Stop that I say!" she yelled again. This time, she was totally ignored.

Meanwhile, the boys' parents came rushing out from the residence with umbrellas and canes. They fought with the attackers to get the two boys away from them and then fought their way back into the residence. The attackers continued to taunt them from outside. They knocked over a flower box, threw several rocks through the windows, yelled Jewish slurs, and finally ran off down the street laughing.

Mutti held us close as we stood there, relieved that the young hoodlums were gone.

"Mutti, why did those men do that?" I asked.

"I don't know. Let's keep walking. Hurry up. We should get home." With one of us under each arm, she hurried us along the street.

Looking back over my shoulder, I asked, "Mutti, shouldn't we tell the police what we saw?"

"No, they can't do anything about it. Such things are happening more and more. Some people blame Jews for all our problems. I don't know what this world is coming to."

From then on, we avoided being out on the streets when it started getting dark. I didn't see any more attacks myself, but more and more of the Jewish shops in our area were getting vandalized and marked with anti-Jewish graffiti. It was part of the political turmoil of our times.

In the newspaper, my father read how the communists, holding demonstrations and rallies to organize workers into unions, would get attacked with clubs by the brown-shirted Nazis.

My mother wasn't interested in politics. Her main interest was the day to day struggle to keep the bills paid, and her family fed and clothed. In her view, the attack on teenage boys who had done nothing wrong was part of ugly politics of the time. It was something she wanted nothing to do with and could do nothing about.

Chapter 8
Nazis Take Power

A COUPLE YEARS LATER in 1933 when I was almost fourteen years old, we could no longer avoid politics. The Nazi party, led by a man named Adolf Hitler had come to power in Germany. I was in my last year of grade school, still with Herr Stock.

A local official from the Nazi party visited our school and gave a speech to our four upper classes, which were formed up in ranks in our playground to hear him. He told us that Germany had a new leader, and soon Germany would be great again. Young people would be an important part of it. We would all be expected to participate in Nazi party's youth parades and rallies so we could learn to do our part in the new Germany. It was early April and a dark overcast day, which was probably appropriate for the occasion.

Some parents did not like the Nazis and refused to have their daughters participate in the rallies. These parents soon received threatening visits from Nazi officials such that the parents were forced to relent for fear of being imprisoned.

Aside from participating in the Nazi parades and rallies, there was no mention in school of the Nazis. However, a large picture of Hitler was soon posted in each classroom. Herr Stock neither praised nor criticized the Nazis. His focus, as usual, was on our lessons. All teachers, of course, were required to join the Nazi party. If they didn't, they would lose their jobs and maybe worse.

One of the teachers was Jewish and he was immediately replaced by Herr Wagener, a staunch Nazi supporter and member of the SA. He still wore a coat and tie to school like the other teachers, but he was a proud Nazi and made no secret of it.

About a week after the Nazi official had visited our school, we were lining up again on the playground. This time we were getting ready for our first Nazi parade through the streets to a Nazi rally at a sports field where a local soccer club played. Our school's two classes of eighth grade girls were formed up together beside the seventh and sixth year classes. We could hear the boys on the other side of the playground wall also being formed up. Older girls were passing out armbands to each of us. Marika was next to me, and we helped each other pin them on.

"Wow, Kätchen," Marika said with excitement, "we will be marching in a parade. I've never marched in one before."

"I know. I haven't either. I've seen the strange symbol on these armbands before, but I don't know what it means."

"It's called a swastika. I don't know what it means either," Marika said.

"We're supposed to march like we're in the army. Pretty funny, huh?" Marika said as she started to march in place and then in little squares

"Herr Stock seemed to think we should take it seriously."

"I know. He seemed a little worried about us," Marika replied.

"Oh well, it's just marching in a parade," I said as I started marching around too. "Okay, I'm in the army too." I held my hand up to my forehead in a salute. "How about saluting? Do we salute too?"

"Sure. You salute me, and I'll salute you," Marika said as we marched in little squares saluting each other. A couple other girls joined in.

Our youth leader, an older girl in charge of us, had been busy in the back getting out several flags and assigning them to girls to carry. She was not amused when she returned. "Girls, that's enough of that horseplay. Get back in line."

We quickly did so and weren't as excited about marching as we had been.

Soon each class was given the signal to move out, and we walked in formation to where the parade was forming several blocks away. On the way, our youth leader showed us how to march properly, and we tried to imitate her.

The parade was led by a formation of brown shirted SA men followed by a formation of the brown shirted boys of the Hitler Youth. Next in the parade came a marching band and the first of many student formations from the schools in the area. Like us, they were dressed in their school clothes with Nazi armbands. We got into our position in the parade.

"Remember, girls, no talking while we march. March proudly like I showed you and keep in step with the music," the youth leader instructed us before we started.

The parade soon commenced and was not only new to us marchers but was also new to the curious onlookers. In some places, onlookers clapped enthusiastically in support. Some onlookers seemed to be clapping because they loved marching music and parades in general. But in other places, people did not like what they saw. They openly booed and jeered at the sight of us children marching along wearing our Nazi armbands.

At first, I thought maybe we were not marching well enough for them. But it soon became apparent from the things they were saying that it was the Nazis and their swastikas that they did not like.

In a few places, people showed their contempt for our parade by throwing potatoes at us from the back of a crowd or the windows above. They may have been aiming at the flags being carried, I'm not sure, but some girls in our formation were hit. The girl in front of me, Anka, was hit in the head. She squealed and rubbed her head, but kept marching.

Whenever we saw the potatoes start to fly, we held up an arm to shield our heads. It happened only in a few places, but I soon learned I was not particularly fond of dodging flying potatoes. Marching in parades was not nearly as fun as we thought it would be.

Finally arriving at the sports field, we marched through a large entrance gate, along one end of the field and then along the far side of the field. Upon entering, we could see the long procession of student formations in front of us marching past a viewing stand midfield on the far side.

The marching students were then directed to positions on the playing field in front of the stand. The viewing stand with a podium was elaborately adorned with Nazi banners and flags, and filled with uniformed people. The marching band had taken a position near the stand and continued playing martial tunes to provide a cadence for the marchers.

When we were halfway to the viewing stand, the band began to play, of all things, my favorite old German folk song, the one about the boy only wanting a girl with dark brown hair like his own. Except this time, the band was playing it with forcefulness and a militaristic cadence for marching. All the people on the viewing stand began singing along in a forceful proud way.

Tired and drowsy from the long walk, I had been dully marching along. Hearing my favorite song suddenly got my attention. I didn't like how they were treating it as one of their marching songs. It annoyed me very much for some reason.

"Why are they using that song? It's such a nice old song. What does a hazelnut or a boy kissing a girl have to do with them?" I hissed out of the side of my mouth to Marika.

She didn't say anything in reply for fear of getting into trouble for talking. Someone behind us shushed me, so I didn't say anything else.

After passing the viewing stand, we were marched to our assigned position on the field with the thousands of other school children in front of the viewing stand. Marika beside me looked as uncomfortable as I felt. We stood at attention while a man in uniform came to the podium and began talking forcefully to the assembled mass.

It wasn't long before my attention wandered and his words became a garble of background noise to me. After he finished, another began. The various speakers droned on and on while we stood at attention. I tried to look like I was listening, but I kept thinking about my nice old song and wondering why they were using it.

That night at home, I was telling Mutti about the parade while Vati and Ruth listened.

"During the parade, some people weren't very nice at all. They threw potatoes at us. Anka, right in front of me, got hit in the head."

"Really? Did it hurt?" Ruth asked.

"No, I don't think so. Mutti, do I have to go on these parades anymore?"

Vati interjected, "I'm sorry, Kätchen, but you must. You'll get in trouble if you don't. There are rumors that several people were taken away by Nazi officials because they complained about the parade." In a lower voice, he added, "These officials are fanatics and dangerous."

Mutti asked, "Taken away to where?"

"Nobody knows," he replied. Mutti looked worried at this. Meanwhile, I had decided to ask my teacher anyway.

I stated, "Mutti, I'm going to tell Herr Stock that the crowd threw potatoes at us, and I don't want to march anymore."

With a worried look, Mutti said, "You shouldn't complain about the parades to him. Who knows what might happen. Don't say anything."

"I didn't like it though, not the parade or the rally at the sports field. When we were marching into the field, they played my favorite old folk song and made it sound like a marching song. Why would they want to use it?"

"Do you mean *Dark Brown is the Hazelnut*?" Vati asked.

"Yes, I love singing that song in school. Why do they have to use it?"

Vati responded, "I'm sorry, Kätchen, but you will probably hear them playing it many more times as well."

"But why? What does a boy giving a kiss back to a girl have to do with them?"

"Well, that's the second verse. It's the first verse they like so much. I heard about it down at the club. The color brown is part of the Nazis identity. After the war, they adopted brown shirts for their uniform because they were cheap and plentiful. The brown shirts were war surplus uniforms intended for use by German army units in Africa. Anyway, 'brown' to them means 'Nazi.' When the boy in the first verse says he is 'dark brown', it means to them he is 'brown' as in Nazi."

"But when we say someone is 'dark brown', it means they are dark-haired. It has always meant that!" I objected.

"Yes, that's true, but to them, it now means Nazi. So they sing that song to proudly declare, 'I am a Nazi, and my girl has to be a Nazi too, just like me'. They are really pretty clever or maybe 'devious' is a better word. It's already a favorite old folk song for many Germans and their children. So they plan to sing this popular song at their Nazi youth meetings and tell the youths that they are proudly singing that they are Nazis."

"But it has always meant dark-haired," I protested. To this, Vati could only give me a look of sympathy.

"My favorite song is now a Nazi song?" I asked dejectedly.

"I'm afraid so."

Mutti interjected, "I think it's a shame too, Kätchen, but there's nothing to be done about it. Don't say anything about it to anyone."

In time, I would find that my father was correct. They had created many new awful songs for themselves as well, but I would be vexed and disgusted to learn just how much the Nazis liked and used my favorite old song for their own purposes at their rallies. It had been transformed from an innocent folk song into a political song for Nazi propaganda and recruitment. Soon, I would hate to hear the song and would have to conceal the cringing I felt inside whenever forced to hear or sing it at their rallies.

It was one more reason for me to dislike politics, one more reason not to want to march in political parades. In the classroom next morning before class, I talked with my teacher.

"Herr Stock, Sir. I don't want to march in the parades any more. People were throwing potatoes at us, and I didn't like it."

"Yes, I heard about that, but none of the girls got hurt, I understand," he said with concern.

"Some were hit, but I don't think anyone was hurt."

"Well, I am gratified to hear that. I cannot imagine people throwing potatoes at young girls. These are strange times.

Nevertheless, Kätchen, you must participate in the parades. Participation is not mandatory, per se, but it is expected, so, in effect, it is mandatory. Do you understand?"

I reluctantly nodded my head and replied, "Yes, sir. I still have to march in the parades and have potatoes thrown at me."

"That is correct, except for the part about having potatoes thrown at you," he continued. "I will talk to someone about what happened. But I suspect that the National Socialist party officials are already doing something about it. I doubt there will be any more potato throwing."

With a kind smile, he concluded, "So, Kätchen, it is almost time for class. You had better take your seat."

"Yes, sir."

It was not the answer I had wanted. With a look of disappointment, I turned to go to my desk as other girls began coming into the classroom.

That night I told Mutti and Vati about what I had done, and what Herr Stock had said. Ruth was there listening too. Mutti was at first anxious, but relieved when she heard nothing serious had resulted. She gave me one of her "I told you so" looks.

After a moment of thought, Vati said, "It looks like there's no choice in the matter, just as we suspected. Oh well, a little marching in a parade never hurt anyone. I've done it myself long ago."

"Oh, Vati. Not that story again. You've told us a hundred times about marching off to war through the Brandenburg Gate," I said.

"Well, it was one of the few highlights of my soldiering career," he responded defensively.

With a serious look, he said, "Come closer everyone, so we can talk quietly."

All four of us moved close together, and Vati continued in a low voice, "Getting back to your parades, Kätchen, you should be careful not to let them see that you don't like their parades. These Nazi people are dangerous."

He paused and continued in his low voice, "They just recently took over the city hall. They arrested our elected city officials and replaced them with their own men."

"Arrested them?" Mutti asked.

"Yes, several of the arrested officials dine sometimes at our restaurant. It's a shame. They are highly respected and responsible men. It was an honor to wait on them at the restaurant, not like that stuffed shirt who sends his soup back every day."

"It sounds like we all have to be careful about what we say from now on," Mutti reflected. Pointing her finger at Vati, she added, "And that means you too, at your club with your drunken friends!"

"Yes, yes. I'll try not to embarrass you by getting arrested and shot by a firing squad, my dear."

"Oh, Vati, don't joke about it!" I said.

Remembering himself, he gave me a reassuring hug and said, "I'm sorry, Kätchen. You're right. I shouldn't joke about it. It's a serious matter. We all have to be careful what we say and do."

Looking at Ruth, he said, "Ruth, you understand too, don't you? You remember the brown-shirted men beating up the boys?"

Ruth nodded.

"They are called Nazis, and they are bad people, but you will get in trouble if you say that. We can say that only here among family and you can't tell others what we say here. If someone wants you to join in Nazi activity or talk, don't say anything bad about them, just say you aren't interested. Do you understand what I mean, dear?"

"Yes, I think so," ten year old Ruth said with a worried look.

Giving her a reassuring hug, Vati said, "I'm sorry, Ruth. I don't mean to scare you, but we need to be careful."

Our second Nazi parade, which I already mentioned, took place about two weeks later. The storm troopers were with us again a month later on our third Nazi youth parade. Whenever I saw these brown shirted men, I was reminded of the attack on the two Jewish boys, which we witnessed that night years ago. They walked beside us now and eyed the crowd menacingly.

Things were uneventful in this third parade until we suddenly heard someone in the crowd up ahead of us jeering and booing loudly. Apparently, a drunk had come upon the parade and wanted to voice his disapproval of the Nazis. The nearby brown shirted men were quickly on and violently assaulting him. The nearby people watched in horror and dismay as the man was beaten senseless and bloody.

When the storm troopers finished their work, they stood looking down at the bloody unconscious man lying on the ground. When they looked up at the crowd of nearby onlookers, everyone quickly looked away in fear and pretended to be watching the parade. The brown shirted men picked up the bloody man and carried him off out of sight.

To us down the street a distance, it appeared only as a brief disturbance in the crowd up ahead. When our formation marched past the spot, I looked sidelong and saw one of the storm troopers standing rigidly on the bloody sidewalk looking menacingly around. From the stunned, subdued faces of the crowd, some ugly incident had obviously happened. With a sinking feeling, I continued to march.

By the end of the school year, I had participated, much to my chagrin, in two more of these parades. It was only natural for our marching skills to improve. We stepped in unison well, even when turning corners. Our youth leader had less need for screaming. These parades and rallies were apparently scheduled on days to celebrate the birthdays of high ranking local Nazi officials.

Chapter 9
Middle School

IN JUNE OF 1933, I graduated from the second four years of my eight year grade school. My graduation marked my completion of minimum educational requirements. It was normal for students to attend two more years of middle school, it was not required if a family needed the youth to start working. I had no need to help support my family, so I would attend two years of middle school.

I was happy to continue school. Marika and my other girlfriends were going. Only a few girls in our class chose to not continue. Besides, I thought it might be interesting, for a change, to attend school with boys in the class.

In August, I found myself walking with Marika to our middle school, which was maybe a twenty minute walk away. We asked to be in the same classroom and got our wish. We also were lucky to have been assigned to Herr Klein, who had been a teacher at the school for some time, as opposed to ones recently appointed by the Nazi party to replace teachers considered undesirable. Of the thirty students in our class, seven were girls from my previous grade school class and twelve were boys.

A large picture of Hitler looked down upon us in class, and the day started with a "Heil Hitler" salute to the teacher. We were not required to wear uniforms, so we girls wore dresses or skirts like in grade school, while the boys mostly wore short pants. During the year though, on special days like Hitler's birthday, the boys and girls who were members of Nazi youth organizations would wear their uniforms to school.

The curriculum was just a more advanced treatment of our basic subjects. The math and German language lessons got a little more difficult. History and civic affairs were revamped by the Nazi party to emphasize German nationalism and to glorify the Nazi party and Hitler. Physical fitness and sports were emphasized. Of course, the Nazi parades to a local sports field began again, usually one or two per month.

As we marched along, the mood of the people watching our parades had noticeably changed in six months. Hitler was viewed more favorably by Germans, because he had made progress in reducing unemployment and improving economic conditions. Small crowds of Hitler supporters gathered to watch, cheer, and wave little Nazi flags. Even so, the SA men continued to escort the parades. As a result, we never heard or saw any dissenters among the onlookers or any more ugly incidents.

We girls still marched in separate formations from the boys. As I marched, I looked over at several of my classmates who were smiling and proudly marching. A number of the girls in my class were actively involved in the Hitler youth organization for girls called the "League of German Girls." All other youth organizations such as scouts had been banned. I'm not sure if these girls were active because they really liked politics or because they hoped to be around the boys in uniforms. Several had told me they liked it because of all the sports and camping activities they did.

In the parade, they were wearing their uniforms of dark skirts, white blouses, and black ties. Uniforms of all kinds, such as the Hitler Youth uniform of the boys, became very popular and fashionable at that time.

I participated in the parades and rallies because it was mandatory. I had no interest in their uniforms, politics, or speeches. I suspected these actively involved girls might think it their duty to report me if I were to say something against the Nazis. So I was careful around them like I had promised my father.

Some teachers, as mentioned before, were replacements appointed by Nazi officials. Any slip of the tongue by a student about any forbidden activity or anti-Nazi statements at home might have serious consequences. One couldn't just be cautious around them only though. I had to be cautious around all the teachers and students. I thought I could trust Marika, but it was better just not to say anything, even to her.

Another example was the case of Herr Sauer and his son. Herr Sauer was a nice old man, who had lived on the first floor of our apartment building for many years. His son, after being gassed in the war, had been a bitter, erratic, and discontented young man who had drifted about Germany and gotten involved in Nazi activities. In 1933 after the Nazis had gained power, he came back to stay temporarily with his father in our apartment building. While there, he overhead the couple living next door criticizing the Nazis. He informed on them and denounced them as communists. They were quickly arrested and taken away by the secret police called the Gestapo.

The couple had been long time friends with his father, who was furious at his son. Afterward, they had a terrible argument, in which Herr Sauer called the Nazis a pack of hateful, dangerous bullies. The son said he was going to the Gestapo to denounce his father and stormed out. Distraught over the monster he had spawned, Herr Sauer hung himself the same day in the basement of our apartment building.

Afterward, the son continued to live in his father's apartment. Everyone knew better than to say anything around him. For several months, he kept to himself. Then one afternoon, he left the apartment and never returned, to the great relief of everyone.

Not long afterward, he was found stabbed to death in a seedy section of the city, and no one in our apartment building shed a tear over it.

The distrust of others and need to be careful about what one said made it difficult to make new friends. I had thought classes with boys might prove to be interesting but was greatly disappointed. Most of the boys were caught up in the enthusiasm for uniforms, being soldiers, and doing their part for Nazi Germany. So I had to avoid them. A week after the start of school, one of the boys became curious and approached me during a class break.

"Hello, my name is Reiner. You are Miss Thielke in class, but I believe your first name is Kätchen."

"Yes, that's right."

"I haven't seen you around before. In what neighborhood do you live?"

"I live on Mozart Street. How about you? Where do you live?"

"Farther south by the Eilbek Canal. I think I would have noticed you in our Hitler youth camps. Are you a member of the League of German Girls?"

"No, I am not interested in politics."

"Hmm," he said as he looked at me.

"But you must love Hitler, though, don't you?"

"I don't love or hate him. I just have no interest in that sort of thing, politics, I mean. It must be a flaw in my character. I love to cook and want to start a cooking apprenticeship when done with middle school. How about you?"

"I plan to be a soldier, of course. So you are not in the League of German Girls?"

"No," I replied, as he paused for a moment studying me.

"That's too bad. Well, if you will excuse me, I must get back to my studies," he said with a curt bow and left.

Apparently, he was a "dark brown" boy and not interested in me anymore, because I was not a "dark brown" girl. Later that night, I told my family about our conversation, and my father congratulated me on handling it well. My mother looked worried at hearing it, and Ruth gave me a hug.

The few boys in my class without obvious Nazi ties were friendly and pleasant enough, but they still seemed like shy little boys to me. I was starting to mature already, and they were still little boys. Needless to say, I stuck close to my friend Marika and a few other girls. Thanks to them, the two years of middle school were somewhat enjoyable, given all that was going on.

The two years passed quickly, and then I was at a crossroads in my life. I had to choose whether to go on to secondary school or to pursue a trade. The choice would affect the rest of my life. My grades were good enough for me to attend the least demanding type of secondary school called main school. However, there were costs involved in attending secondary school, which my family probably couldn't afford. Besides, the main jobs available to girls graduating from it seemed to be office jobs, which didn't interest me.

Our Nazi lectures stressed heavily that a German girl's role in the Third Reich was to stay at home, be a good wife and mother, and to have at least four children for the future of the Fatherland. I was surprised the Nazis continued to have secondary school for girls. I suppose girls were still needed to work in offices, and not just stay at home raising their required four children.

No, I had no interest in going on to secondary school. I had already decided on a trade. While growing up, I helped Mutti in the kitchen. She had never liked cooking, while I enjoyed it. Lately, I had been cooking most of our family meals.

Our neighbor, Frau Ickes, knew I liked cooking and would invite me over during the holidays to help her with cakes, candies and holiday breads like Stollen. When I saw yummy looking breads, pastries and desserts in bakeries, I not only wanted to taste, but also to make them.

My interest in cooking made it an easy decision to choose to become a cooking apprentice, which meant I would need to attend a nearly yearlong cooking trade school.

Marika, on the other hand, was interested in becoming a nurse and would be attending the type of secondary school that would lead to it. She had been my best friend for many years, and it was difficult to say goodbye. We hugged tearfully and promised to keep in touch, but with time, we regrettably lost touch.

In those days in our area of Germany, young people were expected to perform a period of service on the land, called a "landyear" prior to beginning secondary school or a trade. In my case, as with many other girls, this would mean working on a farm, although not necessarily a year, more like nine months.

On my last day of middle school, I was given an address and rough directions to a farm northeast of Hamburg, which was within a one day bike ride. I was told to report there in a week to a woman named Frau Euler.

Chapter 10
Meeting Rolf

SO THEN, fresh out of school and just sixteen years old, I strapped an old suitcase to the back of my bike, said goodbye to my family, and began pedaling to my landyear assignment on the farm.

I had a long ride ahead of me, so I tried not to waste time. Fortunately, it was a beautiful June day for my ride. Once out of the city and its traffic, I was in high spirits as I passed through the pretty countryside. I admired the quaint and pretty farms on my way. I couldn't wait to get to the farm where I had been assigned.

A farmer was herding a small herd of dairy cows across the road in one spot, and I had to wait while they crossed. For lunch, I ate some bread and cheese, which Mutti had packed for me.

In the early afternoon, I continued to ride through the countryside, which was all new to me. I was observing the farming activities while I rode along. Horsepower, the kind provided by actual horses, seemed to be the primary power source for the farm equipment and transportation, although I did occasionally see tractors and trucks.

* * *

Unknown to me, a sawdust-covered young man stood in front of the noisy planer machine in a cabinetmaker shop, ahead along my route. He was wearing protective glasses, an apron, and a scarf over his mouth and nose as he fed a board into one end of the planer. After pulling the board out of the other end of the machine, he then put the smoothed board with the other ones he had already done.

He was reaching for the next board when his father came up behind him and tapped him on the shoulder. Rolf looked around and saw his father wanted to tell him something, so he shut off the planer machine. After about ten seconds, its motor wound down enough so they could hear to talk without yelling.

"Rolf, you look like you need a break. I need you to go out to the intersection to make sure the truck delivering wood doesn't miss our road. They have a new driver. When you see their truck, wave to him so he knows to turn. They called to say he was on his way. He should be there in about ten minutes."

"Gladly, I could use a break," Rolf said, taking off his scarf and glasses. On his way to the door, he took off his apron and laid it on a table. He was brushing the fine sawdust from his hair, face, and clothes as he walked out the door.

* * *

I passed through a stretch of tree-lined road with houses on the right and a pasture on the left. Through the roadside trees, I could see black and white dairy cows in the green pasture with many new calves. The cute little calves were romping about playfully near the fence along the road. They were so cute that I wanted to stop but couldn't because of time. Still I couldn't help watching them as I rode past.

Suddenly, I heard a shout and was unexpectedly grabbed and knocked onto the pavement in the road. Everything was confused as I sprawled over the handlebars, and the suitcase was knocked from the bike. Someone from behind was holding me when we tumbled to the pavement. I landed mostly on the other person, but did scrape my elbow a bit in the fall.

As I landed I said, "Oof! What!" Ignoring the rumbling noise in the background, I faced around hotly to see who had tackled me to the ground. I was surprised to see a nice looking brown-haired boy about my age getting up from the ground, looking at me innocently.

"Are you all right?" he asked.

"What do you think you're doing!" I shouted at him hotly.

"You were about to run a stop sign and ride in front of that truck," he said pointing.

I gasped and looked up in astonishment to see the stop sign. Then I swung my gaze around to see a large truck noisily rumbling away from the intersection.

I was, of course, embarrassed that I had yelled at him, only to find out he had saved my life. I turned around and saw the boy straightening up and brushing himself off.

"Oh my goodness. I guess I got distracted watching those calves playing. I could have been killed," I said with embarrassment.

He smiled at me and helped me up. Still confused as to how he had saved me, all I could say was, "How did you happen to be.., I mean…?"

"I was waiting here at the intersection for a lumber truck. I was turned away watching for the truck and only saw you at the last second about to ride in front of the other truck, so I stopped you. Are you sure you are all right?"

"Yes, I think so," I said noticing he had a good deal of sawdust on him, and now it was on me too.

When I started brushing it from my dress, he said, "I'm sorry about that. It's sawdust. I work in my father's cabinet shop."

"It brushes right off, no problem," I said smiling at him.

After glancing at my bike and the suitcase, I added, "I'm all right, I guess, but I'm not sure about my bicycle. The handlebars are twisted."

"They should be easy to straighten out," he said as he picked up my bike and began straightening the handlebars and strapping the suitcase back onto the bike.

"Thank you. I think you saved my life," I said with astonishment.

"I'm glad. Where are you headed?"

"I've come from Hamburg," I said regaining my composure, "I'm on my way to a farm for my landyear. It's still pretty far. I probably should be going so I can get there before dark."

"Not even enough time for a quick break?"

"Thank you, but no. I really need to keep going, …" I paused awkwardly, "I'm sorry, I'm Kätchen. I don't know your name?"

"Rolf," he said smiling.

"Rolf," I said pausing a moment to consider it. "Pleased to meet you, Rolf."

"Pleased to meet you too, Kätchen," he said giving me a little handshake. Next he wheeled the bike back and forth a couple times, looked it over and said, "There, all straightened out. Nothing else seems to be damaged. Good as new."

"Thank you again, Rolf. I really don't know what to say or how to thank you."

"No need. I'm just glad I saw you in time." We stood looking at each other for a moment.

With an embarrassed smile, I said, "I really better get going. I do appreciate what you did."

After hurriedly looking around, I remounted the bike and began peddling across the intersection. Looking back, I waved.

"Goodbye, Kätchen. Good luck on the farm."

"Goodbye, Rolf. Thank you, again."

I rode the rest of the afternoon through the small towns and the picturesque countryside of fields, pastures, lakes, and woods. All the while, I smiled to myself as I thought about the nice looking boy who had saved me.

Later that evening, I was looking at the names on the mailboxes along the road and finally found the correct one. I looked up the dirt driveway at the unattractive poorly maintained farmhouse and felt a great weight of disappointment. Why couldn't I have gotten one of the many pretty ones I had seen on the way? I rechecked the my paperwork and found I was not mistaken. So I sadly headed up the driveway.

"I passed up visiting with a handsome young boy to hurry to this?" I thought to myself.

A grouchy-looking, middle-aged woman was sitting on a chair near the front door of the farmhouse. She saw me coming and stood up. As I approached, she stood with her arms crossed. By the look of her, I thought I might have the wrong place. I pulled my bike to a stop in front of her and got off.

"Hello, I've come from Hamburg to work on a farm for my landyear and am looking for Frau Euler. Is this the right place?"

She eyed me over and said, "So you are the landyear girl from the city. It took you long enough to get here. What's your name?"

"Kätchen, Kätchen Thielke."

"And what do you plan to do?"

"Here?"

"No, after your landyear, silly girl."

"Go to cooking school."

She responded with a grunt and disapproving look, which she probably would have done no matter what I answered.

"I'm Frau Euler. This is my place and I do all the cooking here. I don't need any cooking help. You'll be helping with the work outside. Put your bike behind the house and come inside. Then I'll take you up to the loft where you'll stay."

"Yes, Ma'am," I said as I began wheeling the bike toward the back of the house. I wasn't sure why, but she didn't appear to be very pleased to have my help on her farm.

The farmhouse was a single story half-timber structure with a thatched roof and long flat stones laid like bricks between the timbers. The farmhouse had a high roof line that allowed for the loft, where it seems I was to live. A barn and outbuilding of brick construction stood nearby. The buildings looked neglected and in need of repair, not at all like the well-kept farmhouses I had seen on the way.

I propped my bike against the back wall and carried my suitcase to the back door where Frau Euler met me. She beckoned me in and, carrying an oil lamp, led up to the loft.

The opening at the top of the steep wooden stairs was a large rectangular hole in the floor of the loft. The loft was basically an open attic area for storage. Clutter and boxes were piled everywhere. It smelled of dust and rat droppings.

On one end of the loft was a makeshift wall, some coarse curtain material nailed at the top to a horizontal crossing beam and hanging down nearly to the floor. Her oil lamp was the only light as we clomped across the wooden floor to my "room."

She made an opening in the curtains to reveal a crude bed, a chair and a small table with a wash basin on it. Frau Euler went in and put the lamp on the table. Trying not to show my disappointment, I followed her in and put my suitcase down.

"Here's where you'll stay. We can't afford to be too fancy out here in the country. There's a basin for you to wash in. Be careful with the oil lamp. The outhouse is straight back from the house. You're too late for dinner. Breakfast is at six in the morning."

"Thank you," I said when she passed. She turned and eyed me up and down.

"Good night," she said without emotion.

"Good night," I answered.

She made an opening in the curtains and went out. I could hear her clomp clomping as she left the loft. I sat down on the uncomfortable bed and looked around my new lodgings with disappointment.

"My God, this dreadful place is going to be my home for the next year," I thought.

I was hungry, but I had already eaten all the food I had brought along for the trip. There was nothing I could do other than go to sleep.

Chapter 11
The Farm

AFTER A BREAKFAST of mush the next morning, I was introduced to Herr Schultz. He was a weathered old man, who had worked for Frau Euler for some time.

A couple younger farmhands worked there for him as well as another boy from the city named Joris, who was also there doing his landyear. Frau Euler had instructed Herr Schultz to keep me separate from the male help. She had a low opinion of the morals of city girls and didn't want any hanky-panky on her farm.

As a result, I wasn't around them much and worked mainly for Herr Schultz. The farm raised wheat, potatoes, corn, turnips, and other vegetables. There were animals as well: cows, work horses, sheep, ducks, geese, and chickens. I was kept busy in the fields and large garden.

When I was around the farmhands, they were friendly to me but kind of shy. Being from the country, they didn't seem to know what to say to a sophisticated girl from the city, which is apparently what they thought I was.

When we did run into each other, the landyear boy was polite to me. He was from German upper classes, yet he worked in the fields like the others. Frau Euler did not seem to appreciate her free landyear help. I knew she didn't like me, and I would overhear her talking derisively about the landyear boy.

He stayed in a small room in the barn, which must be cold in the winter. His family was wealthy and owned a large factory in Hamburg. After his landyear, he planned to attend a secondary school called a Gymnasium, which would prepare him for study at a university. Yet, without complaint, he was there performing his landyear like everyone else.

His family always dressed formal for dinner, so every night after cleaning up from his work in the fields, he was dressed immaculately in his suit and tie when he came into the house to eat. It was amazing to me and seemed to gall Frau Euler to no end. Even so, she didn't let him know and would address him with forced respect.

One of the first jobs assigned to me was to feed and sort chickens each morning. Frau Euler sold eggs and had a wooden chicken house with an enclosed pen for her chickens. At night, the chickens were kept inside the chicken house to protect them from foxes and other critters.

Every morning, I was to let the chickens out into the pen where I threw them food. Then I was to separate the laying hens from the non-laying hens by catching each one and putting my finger in its bottom to see if an egg was in there. To catch the chickens, I was given a stiff metal wire that was bent back around at one end to catch on their feet.

The hens with no eggs were put outside the pen to roam free in the yard, while the laying ones were put back in the chicken house so they could lay their eggs in the straw-filled nest boxes.

When I was finished sorting, it was time for Frau Euler to do her inspection and count. Being of the opinion that young girls from the city couldn't be trusted, she counted the number of laying chickens each morning and expected to see the same number of eggs brought to her later.

There were no problems at first, but one day I found two broken eggshells on the ground in the pen. The chickens sometimes laid their eggs out in the pen where they could roam after being sorted. I suspected Frau Euler's two mangy German Shepard-mix dogs were the culprits. Somehow, they were able to climb in and out of the pen.

Later, when I brought the basket of eggs and the eggshells to Frau Euler, I was scolded for having the two broken eggs. I told her the dogs probably did it, but she scolded me anyway. If the dogs did it, then it was my fault for letting them get to the eggs. I must have left the gate of the pen open.

It happened again several more times as the weeks went by, even though I had made sure the gate was closed each morning when I left for the fields. Each time I was scolded for not having the full amount of eggs. She would have docked my pay if I had been getting any.

At night, there wasn't much to do but clean up the kitchen after dinner and then go up to my room. I wasn't allowed to socialize during my year on the land, so I never had a chance to go to a dance in the nearby town or anything like that. I had brought a few books from home, and read them over and over. At other times, I would sit on my bed and stare at the walls. I would think of the nice looking boy who had saved me and wonder if I would ever see him again.

Mutti sent me letters to see how I was doing and tell me news. Nothing much had changed at home. Ruth was on summer break, thankful for her time away from marching with classmates in the Nazi parades and rallies. Luckily, I wasn't required to march in parades or attend rallies during my landyear. For some unlucky ones, landyear was a youth camp of constant Nazi ceremonies, parades, and rallies mixed with times when they were sent out to work on nearby farms.

Being tight with her pennies, Frau Euler also didn't believe in overfeeding her workers. After I had been there a month, I got so hungry that I did steal an egg as often as I dared. I'd slip one into my apron pocket when I was collecting eggs in the afternoon. Then I'd duck behind an outbuilding and quickly suck the egg empty. When you are really hungry, a raw egg tastes pretty good.

When I brought the eggs and the broken shell to Frau Euler, she would scold me, like always, and I would tell her that it was the dogs. Afterward, when the dogs really did get in the pen and eat an egg, I got so mad at them I wanted to beat them with my chicken catcher because it meant less eggs for me.

I had a favorite hen that I pampered because it sometimes laid two eggs at a time. When collecting eggs, I was quick to stick the second one in my apron pocket, and it wasn't missed by Frau Euler.

Even so, I was only able to safely steal two or three eggs a week without risk of being caught. I thought about asking Mutti to send me some food, but decided not to, so they wouldn't be upset or worried. When I asked Frau Euler for more food one morning, she scolded me for being ungrateful and told me to go out to work.

One morning on my way to the field, I met Joris who asked me if I was feeling well. He said I looked like I was losing weight. I thanked him for asking, but told him I was doing fine. He didn't look convinced as I nodded and continued on.

After a month of this, I was out behind a shed sucking down a raw egg when Joris unexpectedly walked around the corner. He was surprised to see me and immediately saw what I was doing.

"Kätchen, raw eggs? You must be hungry. Doesn't she feed you?"

Embarrassed to be discovered, I confessed, "No, I steal her eggs, because I'm hungry."

"Why the old witch! I had no idea. She feeds me normal. I suppose because she thinks my father could stir up trouble for her if she doesn't. So that's why you have been getting thinner."

"You won't tell on me, will you?"

"Of course not. See the rock right there," he said pointing. "I'll put a tin of biscuits under it for you. I have some from home."

"Thank you, Joris. That's very nice of you."

"I'm sorry, Kätchen. I had no idea," he said and then left.

Later in the evening after dinner, I told Frau Euler, I was going out for a walk. I slipped behind the shed and turned over the rock. Sure enough, a tin of biscuits was underneath. I opened it, put several of them in my pocket, placed the tin back under the rock, and kept walking.

I nibbled on them as I walked. They were delicious little buttery cookies, much better than any I had ever tasted before, but I was also hungrier than I had ever been before.

After I went up to my room that night and lay in bed, I heard some discussion happening below, although I couldn't make out what was being said.

The next morning, an amazing change had come over Frau Euler. She was actually nice to me and she gave me a good slice of bread with marmalade for breakfast, much more to eat than normal. I wasn't sure what had happened, but didn't say anything.

On the way out to the field, Joris ran into me and said, "Good morning, Kätchen."

"Good morning, Joris. Thank you again for the biscuits. I tried some last night. They were delicious."

"Excellent. And how did you find breakfast this morning?"

I gasped and started laughing, "It was you! You were the one downstairs with her last night! What did you say to her?"

"You won't have to worry about her anymore. Come on, we'll walk together."

"But she won't like it."

"Don't worry. She won't say a thing."

"What did you say to her, Joris?"

"I told her you were looking thin and hungry, and I was surprised she wasn't feeding and treating you better. She obviously didn't know who your father was."

"What?" I said laughing.

"Yes, I told her your father owns a famous restaurant in Hamburg and is friends with the mayor of the nearby town. I thought she was treating you shabbily, and had advised you to complain to your father and have the local mayor forbid her from selling her produce in town. I told her if you didn't complain, I would. My father also knows the mayor, so she better shape up."

"Oh, Joris. She thinks my father can cause trouble for her?"

"Yes, it was a little white lie, I know, but it doesn't matter, because my threat is real. My father actually does know the local mayor!"

I couldn't help it. Even if we were from different worlds, I gave him a big hug and kiss on the cheek.

Afterward, Frau Euler went out of her way to be nicer to me. The daily egg count was no longer so important. She moved me down into a spare bedroom and seemed to be watching more what she said around me. Knowing that her behavior was better only because she thought my father could make trouble for her, made it a disgusting exhibition to me. Still, I did not take advantage of the new situation, but I took no more guff from her.

I asked Joris why he had complained to Frau Euler about my treatment, but never complained about his own treatment, living out in the barn and all. He told me that he would never complain and give her the satisfaction of thinking she was making him uncomfortable.

Joris gave me new respect for the so-called upper classes. Some of them were pretty good people too, not just stuffy people who send their soup back for no reason.

While Joris was handsome, generous, and very likeable, I could not see him possibly becoming my boyfriend. I admired him and appreciated his friendship very much, but we were from two different worlds, too different to be more than friends.

Instead, I sometimes thought about Rolf, the young man who had saved my life. His world was not so different from mine. He lived somewhere near that intersection if he wasn't already drafted into the military. It had happened to one of the farmhands here about a month after I arrived, and it may have also happened to Rolf by now.

* * *

At a bench in the workshop, Rolf finished the final sanding on the little wooden cow. Now, it only needed painting before he could add it to the set of farm animal toys for his little brother and sister. He had already made a set of toy blocks of different shapes that they would play with for hours. He did it for them, but also to keep his mind busy. He put the cow down and looked out the window.

He was thinking of the young pretty girl on the bike and wondered how she was doing on her farm. Having already completed his own landyear, he now was a cabinetmaker's apprentice to his father. He would like to see her again, but he had no way of knowing where she was. He wondered if she thought about him or if he would ever see her again.

* * *

I worked all summer in the fields and the garden. The farm grew a plant called corn, which I had never seen before. I watched with curiosity as the stalks grew and ears formed. In Germany, it was a grain grown for animal feed. I asked Herr Schultz if people could eat it too and he said no, it was only for animals.

Soon the summer was gone. In the fall, we harvested wheat. Herr Schultz cut the golden wheat with a cutter pulled by a team of horses. Some of the local townspeople came to help bundle it up, bring it in, and thresh it.

Although fall was a busy time on the farm, I wanted to take one Sunday afternoon off to see the beautiful fall colors of the countryside. I also had in mind to revisit a certain place. I got my chance on the third Sunday of September which was a beautiful sunny day, perfect for my bike ride.

It felt wonderful to be out and away from Frau Euler and the work on the farm. The towns were decorated for fall festivals, while the trees and woods were in bright shades of reds, yellows and oranges.

I was smiling as I rode. In a little town square, two serious old men were sitting on a bench eyeing me while I approached. I waved to them and gave them a big smile. It seemed to lift their spirits as they laughed to each other and waved back.

I rode and rode and finally came to the intersection where I had met Rolf. Of course, this was the place that I had often thought of and wanted to revisit. I looked up and down the road in hopes of maybe seeing him again or someone to ask about him. But there was no one to be seen. A couple cars passed. There were some houses down the road a bit, but I didn't think I should knock on doors searching for him. I wasn't sure if he would be interested in seeing me again or even remember me.

I stood before the place in the road where I had fallen to the pavement. I watched the traffic for a time and finally concluded the hoped-for meeting was not going to happen. After one last disappointed look around, I got back on the bike and rode off, feeling pretty low.

I didn't get more than a couple hundred feet before I pulled off the side of the road, deep in thought.

"Don't give up so easily," I told myself. "Are you interested in him or not? There's no harm in knocking on doors to find him, so you can thank him again for saving your life. That's not so unreasonable. If you find him, and he's not interested, at least you tried. Maybe you won't have to go knocking on doors, someone will surely be outside one of the houses to ask."

With an increased level of determination, I turned my bike around and rode back.

On the other side of the intersection were three houses along one side of the road. A little farther down was a house on each side. I rode slowly by the first three houses looking for someone to ask. I didn't see anyone outside. I looked for any clue that one might be the home of a cabinetmaker. There was no such sign, and each house had outbuildings in back, which could a shop. They were nice enough rural houses with stone fences in front and flowers in the yards. But I didn't see anyone outside to ask.

Across the street was the cow pasture where the calves had been romping. No cows were there now and no dairyman to ask either. I looked down the street at the other two houses and thought I should ride by them first before I started knocking on doors. So I started down the road.

Behind me, a little blond girl raced from the front yard of a house and hid on the outside of its stone fence. She popped her head up over the fence, looked quickly toward the house, and popped it down again. She laughed and thought, "He'll never find me here."

As she hid, she turned her head and saw me riding away. She stared a moment in surprise, got wide-eyed, jumped up, and scampered into the road.

I was scanning the houses up in front of me, hoping to see someone outside, when suddenly I heard a shrill voice shout, "Kätchen!"

I pulled to a stop in surprise, unsure if I had really heard my name. I turned to see a little blond girl about four years old in the street. When she saw me stop, her eyes lit up, and she excitedly repeated, "Kätchen! Kätchen! Kätchen!"

Soon a little boy joined her in the street and began to shout my name too, as they excitedly jumped up and down waving their arms.

I was delighted to finally see someone, especially someone calling my name! But the two little children were out in the middle of the road. I turned around and rode back toward them.

Before I got there, a woman came out from the house, saw me, and waved. Then she got the children to the side of the road where they eagerly waited for me. By the time I got to them, I saw Rolf come from the house.

"Rolf!" I called elatedly.

He was there beside the road when I jumped from the bike, and we hugged in a friendly, yet affectionate, way. We were both smiling and excited to see the other.

But not as excited as the little boy and girl who bounced around us jubilantly shouting, "Yeah, we found her! Yeah, we found Kätchen!"

The woman smiled and shook my hand above the din, as Rolf and I laughed at the excited children. Finally, the woman clapped her hand at them to get them to quiet down. They both came and excitedly hugged her.

Rolf laughed, saying, "These two are my little sister Lotti and little brother Gregor. She's four and he's five." He gave them both a hug.

"Thank you, Lotti. Thank you, Gregor. You did great! You found her!" This got them excited again, but their mother again got them calmed down.

"I thought you might be riding back at some point, so they have been watching for you as they play. I told them to watch for a dark haired girl riding by on a bike with a suitcase. If they see you, then to shout your name."

Then laughing, he added, "They have been shouting your name at dozens of people for weeks, girls, boys, blondes, you name it, suitcases or not."

I then bent down and gave them a hug, saying, "Lotti, Gregor. I was hoping to see your big brother again. Now thanks to you, I have. Thank you." They grinned back at me as they clung to their mother's skirt.

"Kätchen, this is my mother."

"Pleased to meet you," I said standing up again.

"You too, Kätchen. Come inside and have some refreshments with us."

"Yes, thanks. I'd like that."

I wheeled the bike farther into the front yard and walked with Rolf and his mother, while the two little ones raced ahead to tell their father.

"I'm so glad my lookout system worked," Rolf said with a chuckle.

"I am too, Rolf. I'm not headed home yet, but came to thank you again for saving me. At the intersection, I looked for you or someone to ask about you. I almost left, but came back in hopes of finding someone to ask. I guess I wanted to see you again, to thank you again. It's not every day that someone saves your life," I told him with a little unintended emotion.

Both he and his mother smiled happily at hearing this.

"I'm so glad you did. Obviously, I was hoping to see you again too. My lookouts have been posted for weeks," he said with a laugh.

When we got inside, his father came to cheerfully greet me. I stayed several hours and had a wonderful visit with them. His mother and father were very kind to me and warmly wished me well when I left.

I growled and gave the kids a bear hug goodbye, which got them going again. Rolf and I exchanged addresses, and he promised to write, even though he wasn't very good at it. He gave me an affectionate hug goodbye.

Needless to say, I felt wonderful on my ride back to Frau Euler's farm. Even thoughts of her could not dampen my happiness. Maybe I was being silly, but I envisioned him as the "dark-haired" boy for this "dark-haired" girl, in the old sense of the term.

On the way, I passed through a small town in the midst of a fall harvest festival. I stopped and watched as boys and girls performed their traditional harvest dances in their colorful costumes. The festive mood of the place was right in line with my high spirits.

Chapter 12
Old Comrades

GUSTAV WAS STANDING at the bar with his friends, beer steins in hand and talking as usual. When someone came in the front door behind him, his friends looked up and commented that they had never seen these two newcomers before. He turned around, he thought the one in front looked awful familiar.

"Gustav, you old drunk, I expected I'd find you in a bar," said the familiar voice of the first one.

"Kurt. You old troublemaker. Is it really you?" Gustav exclaimed with delight, as he hugged Kurt vigorously and then held him at arm's length looking him over.

"You're looking good, Kurt. Good and fat! What are you doing here?"

"I heard not long ago from a friend of a friend of a friend that my old comrade Gustav was working at that stuffy restaurant where you work. So I thought I would come look you up. I went there, and they told me I would probably find you here. And they were right."

"I'm so glad you did, Kurt," Gustav said beaming.

"Gustav. I brought a friend with me too." Only then did Gustav notice the person standing next to Kurt.

"Isak! I can't believe it!" Gustav said with astonishment. He let loose of Kurt and hugged Isak with equal vigor.

"Gustav, it's good to see you again. You're one to talk about Kurt. You're on the heavy side now too," Isak said jokingly.

"Well, it's no wonder I look heavy compared to those times. Hell, they half-starved us in the trenches. I'm sure you remember," Gustav retorted.

"Yes, I certainly do," Isak said smiling. Gustav hugged Isak again in his happiness to see him, and then looked him over.

"Isak, I'm so glad to see you made it! You were badly wounded when Kurt and I last saw you. We thought you might pull through if they got you to a field hospital soon enough. It looks like they did."

"Yes, they did. I'm doing fine," Isak said.

Gustav now slapped Kurt on the shoulder again and turned to his friends at the bar, who had been watching.

"Gentlemen, I'd like you to meet Kurt and Isak, my old comrades-in-arms from the trenches. Yes, we were true comrades-in-arms, in every sense of the term."

His friends came forward, introducing themselves and shaking hands.

"Unfortunately though, Isak cost Germany the war."

His bar friends looked at Gustav in surprise at this.

"Yes, if it hadn't been for Isak here getting hit, I'd have fought on against the Frenchies, and then Germany would have won," Gustav announced.

They all moaned and laughed at his silly bravado, as he explained.

"Kurt and I surrendered when Isak got hit. The last time I saw Isak, he was lying on the ground bleeding and an American medic was attending to him."

"You forget, Gustav, we were surrounded and had nowhere to go anyway," Kurt said in Isak's defense.

"Oh,..well,.. I guess I forgot that part," Gustav said laughing.

And so it went for several hours at the bar. As they laughed and drank, the memories of his days in the war and the trenches came flooding back to Gustav. He had told about his time in the trenches many, many times before in the bar, but seeing his actual old comrades from the trenches again and hearing their recollections, brought it back to him in vivid detail. They could laugh and joke about those times now, even though it had been very unpleasant at the time.

Gustav remembered even back to the very beginning, the day it all started in 1914. It was a beautiful warm summer day, much like other summer days that year in Hamburg.

* * *

Dressed in an elegant waiter uniform, Gustav was uncorking a bottle of wine for the two gentlemen seated at the table. They were on the outdoor terrace dining area overlooking the tree-lined avenue in front of the restaurant. Street cars and horse-drawn carriages moved along the street. A few automobiles sputtered by from time to time. Well-dressed couples strolled by on the sidewalk.

Gustav poured a sample of the wine into a glass on the table for one of the gentlemen to approve before serving. The gentleman took the glass, examined the wine, breathed in its bouquet, and was about to bring the glass to his lips when an uproar could be heard down the avenue. People were shouting and celebrating. Automobile horns were honking.

"What on earth?" the gentleman said lowering the wine glass without tasting it.

In a few moments, a honking automobile arrived in front of the restaurant. The people inside were waving, honking, and shouting.

"We've declared war! God bless the Kaiser! We've declared war on Russia!" they shouted gleefully and honked their horn. People along the sidewalk began cheering.

The two gentlemen at the table stood up abruptly from their chairs.

"Hurry, Klaus! Commodity prices will be going through the roof. We must get there quickly, before it is too late!" one shouted anxiously to the other.

"But, gentlemen, what about your wine?" Gustav protested. They paid no attention to him as they rushed out of the restaurant and ran down the street.

A man with a newspaper appeared and the people on the street huddled around him to read it. People continued to celebrate and church bells began to ring out. Meanwhile Gustav looked frowning at the wine bottle still in his hand.

"My boss will probably make me pay for this," he thought.

"Why are they celebrating?" he pondered, looking up and out at the people. "What does the Austrian archduke have to do with any of them, or with me, for that matter?"

When World War I began in early August of 1914, Gustav had been twenty seven years old. He had a successful career as a waiter in a small prosperous restaurant in Hamburg, Germany. Gustav was not a particularly adventurous young man. Being a waiter was sufficient adventure for him. When war was declared, he was not the type to rush out to volunteer for military service.

Seven years earlier in 1907, he had mustered for peacetime military service with his twenty-year-old age group, as required. He had been found fit for duty, but he had drawn what he considered a lucky lottery number, one which did not require him to serve two to three years of active military service.

Instead, he became part of an untrained reserve, which could still be called up in wartime if necessary. Without having this previous peacetime military service, Gustav was not part of the massive mobilization of German troops at the start of the war.

When Russia's ally France declared war on Germany, the German high command was ready with a plan to invade France and capture the French capital as they had done in the war of 1870.

But with the help of the British, the French were able to halt the German advance just ten miles from Paris. The opposing sides found themselves afterward facing each other from well-fortified trenches separated by a no-man's land of devastation and barbed wire. For months, both sides repeatedly attempted massive offensives to capture and break through the other's defenses.

Gustav had continued to work at the restaurant, where business was good with all the war activity. But knowing he would be called up for military service if needed, he unhappily read in the newspapers how hundreds of thousands of German soldiers had been lost in the fighting along the western front.

It was no surprise to Gustav when he received an official looking letter the next spring. The dreaded, yet expected, notice to report for military service had arrived. Like all German men, he would report for military service, even if he was not particularly keen for such wartime adventure.

At the age of twenty eight, Gustav was not a fine physical specimen, but he was still fit for duty. He was subjected to a short period of military training, in which he exercised, learned to march, learned to shoot his rifle, learned to kill with his bayonet, and most importantly, learned to follow orders no matter what. Soon he was deemed ready for the front.

The departure for the front from his training camp near Berlin was celebrated with a parade through the heart of Berlin, past the Royal Palace, along the tree-lined avenue called "Unter Den Linden," and out through the Brandenburg Gate. As they marched, the crowd cheered and waved little flags.

A marching band accompanied them and played a favorite German marching song called *Wenn Wir Marschieren* (*When We Are Marching*), which was very appropriate for the event. The parading soldiers were in high spirits and sang as they marched.

"When we are marching,
Out through our German gate we go,
Dark brown-haired maiden,
You stay at home,
And so then, wave, my maiden, wave, wave, wave,
As we march beneath the linden trees,
Where a little finch, finch, finch,
Calls out to you, maiden, wave.
Where a little finch, finch, finch,
Calls out to you, maiden, wave."

So went the first verse. The song's upbeat tempo and the cheering crowd seemed to energize them and make them step even more smartly.

When an excited, flag-waving girl ran out to their ranks to kiss him and several others on the cheek, Gustav thought, "So far, this soldiering stuff is not so bad."

But things were quite different a week later, when Gustav was part of a formation of fresh troops arriving on the Western Front. There was no marching band any more as they marched in loose formation along a supply road past a supply train of horse drawn wagons.

It was August of 1915, one full year after the start of the war. They were seeing some destruction and evidence of war, so they knew they were probably just behind the front lines. The mangled woods on both sides of the road concealed them to some degree from the open areas. They could see and hear something up in the air in front of them off to the west.

Turning to the soldier walking beside him, Gustav said, "Ernst, look at that. It's a flying machine. They sometimes fly over the restaurant in Hamburg. They have a port for them in Hamburg where they take off and land.

"I've heard of them, but have never seen one before, Gustav. Is it ours or theirs?"

"I don't know."

"Well, if it's theirs, and we can see it, then it can see us too. I don't like it."

They passed a line of trenches and several bunkers for gun emplacements along the road. Gustav looked up ahead and saw the leading wagon of the supply train was being unloaded at what looked like a supply bunker.

"We must be getting close to the front," Gustav said.

Ernst continued to watch the circling airplane up ahead in the distance. To the sergeant at the head of their formation, Ernst yelled, "Sergeant, are we almost to the front?"

The sergeant turned and glaring back, growled, "Hold your tongue, maggot! I'll tell you when we're there."

Suddenly they heard some booming in the distance ahead. Ernst looked into the distance toward the sounds with concern. Within seconds, whistling sounds were heard and then the exploding artillery shells began landing all around them. The sergeant yelled at them to take cover.

One wagon nearby behind them exploded, raining debris down around them. The horses pulling the wagons reared and screamed in fear as the drivers tried to control them. The newly reporting troops weren't sure what to do. Some cowered down, others hid by the wagons.

Many like Gustav and Ernst hit the ground. As they lay facing each other on the ground, Ernst cursed, "Damnation! I knew that flying machine was trouble. He's a spotter for their artillery."

Shells continued to land all around them and they heard the German artillery begin booming in response. The sergeant hollered at the troops, "Everybody up and follow me! If you are still wondering, maggot, we're here. Now let's go!" He started running forward along the road with his unit of soldiers trailing close behind.

Some wagon drivers were trying to turn around and get out of there, but they were having trouble controlling the horses. Gustav's unit ran by a team of horses that reared up in fear at all the noise and excitement. When a shell exploded beside them, the horses were suddenly blown into the air toward the passing soldiers.

Gustav and Ernst were hurled to the ground by the blast, and the horses landed hard on them and another unlucky soldier. Fortunately, the horses were not large ones, but still, Gustav was knocked senseless and breathless by their impact.

The next thing Gustav remembered was the sergeant and the other soldiers all around him dragging the dead animals and harness gear from him.

Once free of debris, the others helped Gustav to his feet. Although not seriously injured, he was too sore to walk. The soldiers hoisted him up and hurried with him and other injured soldiers off the road and into the nearest trench.

Ernst suffered a broken leg, but the third unlucky soldier later died of his head wounds. It did not seem to Gustav like a very promising start for his adventure as a soldier.

Gustav recovered after about a week of light duty, which gave him a chance to get used to his new surroundings of trenches, obstacles, barbed wire, and underground shelters. The trenches along the Western Front stretched 500 miles from the English Channel in Belgium south through France to the Swiss Alps. Paris was about 55 miles away from his location on the front, as close to Paris as any German soldier could be.

He cursed his luck. Being in the closest position to Paris on the front, his position would surely be the launching point for offensives to capture the French capitol. After his terrible first day, he feared the worst. He would be one of the many mowed down or blown to bits in one of those offensives. It was not an easy thing to accept. Not being a religious man, Gustav decided that he would carry out his orders, do his share of the fighting for his comrades, and hope for the best.

However, to Gustav's great relief, his position was *not* a location of major offensives during 1915, 1916, and 1917. Both sides at his location conducted frequent shellings and raids testing the defenses of the other, but he was not part of the massive offensives and counter offensives that killed nearly two million soldiers along the Western Front in those years.

Before the Americans joined the fighting early in 1918, both warring sides had been exhausted after years of bloody stalemate. The Americans joining the fighting breathed new life into the Allied forces opposing the Germans. The Allies stopped a massive German spring offensive, and by the fall of 1918, pushed the Germans back to a fortified line of defense called the Hindenburg Line.

Gustav had, somehow, survived three years of fighting in the trenches without being killed or severely wounded. He and his two friends, Isak and Kurt, were the only ones left from their original twenty two man unit.

Instead of leaves gently falling from trees that fall, there were no trees left, and the things falling were artillery shells, as Gustav and the others in their position in this defensive line were facing a relentless assault by tanks and troops. The enemy steadily advanced, despite heavy losses, through the German's elaborate systems of defensive trenches. After several days of fierce fighting, the enemy tanks and troops had broken through their third and last layer of defense. When retreat was sounded, the surviving German soldiers ran from the trenches to the rear.

Gustav, Isak, and Kurt were among them, running for their lives. The enemy troops were close behind as the three comrades ran into a destroyed town to seek cover. The streets in front of the shattered buildings were littered with the debris of battle and abandoned equipment. They ducked for cover into the doorway of one of the few remaining intact buildings. Bullets struck nearby while other German soldiers ran past in the street.

Taking a moment to catch their breath as the battle raged outside, they knew they couldn't stay, so they rushed through the damaged rooms to the back where they found a large hole blown in the outside wall. Peering out, they saw backyards outlined by stone walls facing a wide back alley. On the other side of the alley were the stone walls of the backyards of other heavily damaged buildings.

In the lead, Isak looked quickly up and down the alley and told the others, "It looks clear. Let's run for it across the alley to those buildings on the other side."

Gustav and Kurt nodded. Isak sprinted out across the backyard with Gustav and Kurt behind him. Shots rang out down the alley, and bullets struck nearby. Just as Isak got to the alley, he was hit and fell to the ground. Not yet to the open area of the alley, Gustav and Kurt stopped and took cover behind a stone wall.

Hunched down behind the wall, they looked out and saw Isak lying about ten feet out in the open area of the alley struggling in pain to crawl back to the cover of the stone wall.

"Cover me!" Gustav shouted to Kurt, as he rushed out and pulled Isak back from the alley to the cover of the stone wall. Bullets pinged around him and Kurt fired as rapidly as he could.

With Isak back beside them, both Gustav and Kurt were breathing hard as they looked at each other, relieved they were still alive. They looked at Isak who grimaced with pain. While the noise of battle continued, they noticed no more bullets pinged around them.

"Come out and surrender!" they heard from nearby down the street.

Gustav popped his head above the wall quickly to look and he saw several enemy troops positioned in doorways pointing their rifles at them, but not firing. He popped back down.

"There's a bunch of them down the alley. Isak needs a doctor and we've got nowhere to go. They're giving us a chance to surrender. I suggest we do it," Gustav told Kurt, breathing heavily and pointing.

"After three years of this, I'm ready," Kurt said nodding.

Gustav and Kurt raised their rifles above the level of the wall and nervously started to rise up.

"Don't shoot! Don't shoot!" Gustav yelled as they continued to rise with their rifles in their outstretched arms above their heads.

They saw four soldiers, two Americans and two Australians, emerge from their cover with their rifles trained on them. As ordered, they dropped their rifles and put their hands on their heads. While Gustav and Kurt were being frisked and disarmed, one of the American soldiers quickly checked out Isak's wounds and ran off.

When Gustav and Kurt were told to march, they hesitated, looking back at Isak. One of the Australians pushed them forward and gruffly said, "Don't mind 'im, Fritz. You just march!"

Gustav and Kurt began walking down the alley with their hands on their heads with the three soldiers guarding them. Ahead of them at the end of the alley, a growing stream of American and Australian men and equipment flowed rapidly along the street in pursuit of the retreating Germans. On the far side of the street, they saw other German prisoners with their hands on their heads.

An American medic and two soldiers with a stretcher ran past them in the alley toward Isak. Gustav looked back for a moment as he walked and saw they were attending to him.

Someone up ahead yelled something and two of their guards hustled off leaving Gustav and Kurt with an Australian who prodded them to keep moving using the bayonet on his rifle. As he walked toward the street, Gustav watched the stream of enemy men and equipment rush past on it. This time, it seemed to him that they would not be easily stopped.

Gustav and Kurt were confined in a make-shift prison camp with a thousand other prisoners. Conditions were not great, but they were fed and sheltered to some degree. Germany surrendered about a month after their capture, and soon afterward, Gustav and Kurt were released and went home. They lost touch after the war and never heard whether their friend Isak had survived his wounds.

The war and its defeat greatly affected all Germans. The shame felt over the surrender terms as well as the economic hardship created by them brought years of political and economic turmoil to Germany.

* * *

Later in the evening, Gustav, Kurt, and Isak were still at the club where they sat at one of the booths talking by themselves.

"I read about it in the papers last month," Gustav said in a low voice. "I can't believe that law would apply to you, Isak, someone who fought and almost died for Germany in the war. I thought they would have some exemptions or something. So now, you are no longer a German citizen and you have no rights?"

"It's true, Gustav. They passed the law last month. Having fought for Germany in the last war doesn't matter. The only thing that matters to them is I'm Jewish," Isak replied in a low voice.

"And what about the other part of the law, Isak? Is your wife Jewish?" Kurt asked.

"Fortunately I married within the faith as we are supposed to do. If I had married a non-Jew, the marriage would be invalid and I would be sent to prison if I continued to live with her."

"Isak. These Nazis are unbridled maniacs," Gustav said in a harsh whisper. "Who knows what they will do next. Isak, what are you going to do?"

"I agree with you, Gustav. If they can do this, no telling what else they might do. The Nazis seem to be getting stronger and stronger. I don't see any chance of them losing power. I have no choice but to leave Germany with my family while we can."

"Where will you go, Isak?" Kurt asked.

"I have relations in the Netherlands. I'll take my family there."

"Isak, how can we help you? Do you need some money to help you get to the Netherlands? I don't have much, but I could send you some," Kurt offered.

"Yes, I could send you some too," Gustav added.

"No thanks, my old friends. You need your money. Just knowing my old comrades-in-arms are still with me is enough. I really mean it," Isak said with sincerity and misty eyes.

"It warms my heart to know you are still my friends and don't believe any of this political nonsense. I'm still a German at heart. I was there with you in the trenches. You know that. I still remember you two risking your lives to drag me back to cover from that alley, and all the other times too. I knew I could count on you then and can still."

As he spoke, the three comrades had placed their arms together on the table in a bond of solidarity and mutual affection. They sat for a moment looking at one another without speaking. They had fought together under terrible conditions and had lived to tell about it. Their shared suffering and comradery had bonded them together for life.

Some loud voices at the bar behind them interrupted their momentary silence. Looking around, they sat back smiling. They next hoisted their glasses to one another and drank down their beers.

"Kurt, we'd better get going, before someone overhears us," Isak said as he rose.

"Yes, I guess we should," Kurt said getting up.

"Good seeing you again, Gustav," they both said.

"Yes, you too, comrades, very much so," Gustav said as he waved to the others at the bar and headed for the door with his two comrades.

Once outside, Gustav pleaded, "Are you sure you won't come back to my place for a little dinner or some sleep? Please?"

"Thank you, Gustav, but we have to get going," Kurt said. So Gustav embraced them both one last time and they left.

Gustav was much more thoughtful than normal when he got back to the apartment. Mutti started to give him a hard time about being late, but noticed something was wrong. Gustav said he was sorry about being late and he wasn't hungry.

He went to his chair in the living room and sat down deep in thought. Mutti and Ruth thought they had better leave him alone for a while. After about a half hour, he stood up and went to bed without saying anything.

Chapter 13
The Dairy

WHEN I GOT HOME that night after my visit with Rolf, I wrote a letter right away to thank him and his family for their hospitality. I told him how much I enjoyed the visit and wished that I could do it again soon. The possible rain and cold of our fall weather might prevent it though. If we had a lot of storms in the upcoming weeks, then we would have to settle for writing. Hopefully, he would remember his promise to write and not forget me.

I also wanted him to know that I made it home all right. I told him about seeing the colorful harvest festival with the traditional dancing in the little town on the way home. All in all, I told him, it was a wonderful afternoon.

I posted the letter in Frau Euler's mailbox first thing the next morning. To my delight, I received a letter from him five days later. He too had enjoyed my visit and proposed that we meet the second Sunday after my visit in the little town where I had seen the festival. He knew the place and thought it was close enough to half way that it would be a good place for meeting. He would meet me at the town square there, weather permitting. I was very excited. I sent him a letter back right away to let him know I liked the idea and would be there, weather permitting.

I began to watch the weather closely and agonized when I saw bad weather moving in a few days after sending Rolf my reply. Fortunately, the bad weather did not last long. The day before our planned meeting, I looked to the partly cloudy skies constantly to see if they might turn better or worse.

The next morning, I was gratified to see good weather. After completing my chores that morning, I told Frau

Euler I wanted to go on another bike ride, and she reluctantly consented. She had noted my happiness and interest in the weather, and suspected I was meeting someone.

I met Rolf there in the afternoon. The town was still celebrating. They still had vendors selling arts and crafts, and a small band playing in the square. We walked about looking at the various booths, bought a bag of hard candy for Lotti and Gregor, and sat on a bench having coffee and a pastry for lunch. We talked, listened to the music, and watched the people. Afterward, we strolled about the town a little. By the time we had to go, we were holding hands. We didn't think the weather would allow us to meet too many more Sundays this fall, so we wanted to do it again next Sunday, weather permitting. We kissed goodbye when we left.

Weather did permit us to meet again in the little town that next Sunday too. The town's harvest celebration was still happening, and probably would continue on weekends until the weather turned bad. Rolf brought with him a few of his mother's books for me to read. One was a German translation of *Pride and Prejudice,* which I enjoyed very much. Thank goodness, they weren't something like *Faust.* I hate that kind of stuff.

When we browsed through the arts and craft booths, I saw an inexpensive little set of small carved wooden birds. I bought them for Lotti and Gregor. It was my gift to them for being such good lookouts.

This time, when we sat on the bench listening to the music, Rolf put his arm around me, and I snuggled up against him. We wanted to meet again next weekend too. There was a lake and woods nearby where we could have a picnic. His mother would pack a lunch for us. We kissed again when we said goodbye, and I rode back to the farm very happy.

Unfortunately, the next weekend was stormy, and we couldn't meet. The weather on the following weeks continued to be rainy and cold. Even on clear days in late October, it was getting cool, probably too cool for long bike rides, so we had to give it up.

We exchanged weekly letters for the rest of the fall. Still, it was a great improvement over before, when I could only think about the handsome boy who saved me and wonder if I would ever see him again. I wrote my family back in Hamburg to tell them about finding Rolf again and our visits. They were very happy for me.

I also told Joris about Rolf and thanked him again. If he had not straightened out Frau Euler, she would never have given me time off for my bike rides. It pleased him to see me so happy and have some responsibility for it. He jokingly said that it was unfortunate that the weather did not permit Rolf to come visit the farm so he could meet him and give his approval or not.

Once harvest time on Frau Euler's farm was over, the only remaining work was to prepare the farm for the winter. Afterward, my labor on the farm was no longer needed, so I was transferred to a nearby dairy farm.

On the early November day when I said my goodbyes, the weather was overcast, and the driveway was wet and muddy from rain over the last two days. Out by the barn, I shook hands with Herr Schultz and thanked him for everything.

I next said goodbye to Joris. Life at the farm had been much better after his intervention. He would also be leaving soon, possibly to work in the nearby town to help with city functions during the winter. I guessed he would be staying at the mayor's house. He laughed and said yes.

I asked him if it would be okay for me to visit him back in Hamburg so I could bring him a cake or something, some kind of small thank you. I told him I wanted to meet his parents, so I could tell them what a wonderful son they had raised. He replied that it really wasn't necessary, but he gave me his address and said he would be happy to have me stop by. We shook hands, and I hugged him goodbye.

Relieved to be leaving, I looked around one last time at the place where I had spent the last five months. Frau Euler watched from the porch as I got on my bike. We looked at each other for a moment without saying anything. So I headed down the muddy driveway. On my way out to the road, I broke out into a smile, glad to be leaving.

My new assignment, the dairy farm, was only two kilometers away. As I rode up into its muddy driveway, I looked it over. Several old large brick barns with thatched roofs were surrounded by mud and puddles from the recent rains. No cows or people were to be seen. Behind the barns were a brick farmhouse and another brick building. I rode up to what looked like the back door of the farmhouse.

I was met by Frau Meyer who with her husband owned and ran the dairy. She was another stern-looking, middle-aged woman, so apparently, my luck had not changed. She led me in the back door and looked me over. The bottoms of my legs and coat as well as my shoes were muddy from the bike ride.

"You'll be staying in a room upstairs. Look at you. You're a mess from your ride," she said pointing. "Get the washcloth off the wall there, put some water on it from the sink, and wipe off your coat and legs. Your shoes are pretty dirty. Better take them off and clean them too."

I put down my suitcase and began to wash off while she looked on.

A week later, I was tossing feed to the chickens in the yard and thinking about my stay so far on the dairy. Even though Frau Meyer was also a stern woman, she was much better to me than Frau Euler. I didn't mind the work, my room was good, and I got enough to eat without having to steal chicken eggs.

My job was to help Frau Meyer with her work, such as cooking, cleaning, feeding, and other chores. I was her only landyear worker. She watched me closely at first, but when she saw I was a reliable and steady worker, she became less stern and more friendly.

I saw very little of Herr Meyer who was nice enough to me when I did see him, but he was usually off taking care of things. I ate by myself in the kitchen and began washing dishes and pans as soon as I was finished eating.

My room was a small bedroom upstairs with a bed, chair, table with a washbasin, small dresser, and small window. Early in the morning, Frau Meyer would stand at the bottom of the stairs and holler up, "Yoohoo, Kätchen, time to get up."

"Yes, Ma'am," I'd holler back. Then I'd get up, quickly pull on my clothes, wash my face in the washbasin, and hurry downstairs to warm up next to the stove in the kitchen. The second floor had no heat, and on the coldest days that winter, my washbasin had a layer of ice in it.

Sometimes when the dairy hands were busy with other things, I rode along with Herr Meyer to help take our milk to the milk processing and bottling plant in town. Our stake-bed truck would be loaded with shiny milk cans full of milk.

He'd back the truck up to a loading dock at the plant, and we'd begin transferring milk cans from the truck to the dock. The double doors of the building would open, and several young men wearing white aprons and caps would come out to carry the cans inside where they were emptied.

The boys on the loading dock were always friendly and wanting to help me. Being sixteen and a half years old and almost a woman, I was liking when they paid attention to me.

Looking around one morning, Herr Meyer said to one young man, "You're shorthanded this morning. Where is Horst?"

"Drafted," he replied with a frown as if he expected it soon too.

At night, I would sit at the table in my room and write letters home and to Rolf. I told him about my life at the dairy. The weather was still too cold and unpredictable to plan a meeting. Occasionally, we would get several days of nice sunny weather, but there was no way to arrange a meeting on such short notice.

Other than letter writing, there wasn't much to do. Frau Meyer had a few books that I borrowed and read. I wasn't allowed to socialize by going to dances, but I felt no need for it anyway.

The quarters where the dairy hands stayed had a kitchen and table where they ate their meals prepared by Frau Meyer. The dairy hands got the same thing every day for lunch and dinner, which was milk soup and fried potatoes.

One day, she was busy frying potatoes in a large skillet and had a large pot of milk soup cooking next to it. She suddenly noticed the soup burning, swore under her breath, and switched over to stirring the soup. I had finished with my work in the house and came out.

"Do you need any help, Frau Meyer?" I asked coming in with a pitcher of water,

"Yes, thanks, would you turn the potatoes while I stir the soup?"

"Yes, Ma'am."

As I turned the fried potatoes, I watched as Frau Meyer tasted the soup, considered the taste, and added cinnamon.

"You're adding cinnamon to the soup?" I asked.

"Yes, sometimes I add it to give it a little more flavor."

Voices and footsteps were heard outside where the dairy hands were cleaning up. Four strapping young men then came bursting through the door, eager to see if the food was ready.

"Go ahead. Sit down if you have clean hands. The food is ready," she told them. The four rushed over to take seats around the square table. Frau Meyer ladled out the soup into bowls, which I took to the men, who immediately started to spoon it down. The dairy hands worked long hard hours on the dairy. I saw them mainly at their meal times. They were ravenous when they came in. I think they noticed I was there, but they paid far greater attention to their food than to me.

Using a pot holder, Frau Meyer carried the large skillet of fried potatoes over to the table. She put it down on a trivet in the center of the table. All four immediately started eating potatoes from the section of the pan directly in front of them. I watched in wonder at their amazing appetites.

Invisible lines apparently defined their portion of potatoes in the pan, and these line were not to be crossed. The dairy hands especially loved the pieces of potatoes that were more burnt and crispy. So occasionally, one would try to get a nice burnt piece from another's portion and usually got a fork stabbed at his hand for trying.

One day, Frau Meyer needed to go into town for some business, and I was to make the meal for the dairy hands. I prepared the potatoes and soup just like I had seen Frau Meyer do it. Everything was piping hot and ready when I heard the dairy hands outside cleaning up.

When they burst through the door, I told them, "You can sit down. The food is ready."

I carried the pan of fried potatoes over to the table. They quickly sat down and started digging into the fried potatoes like normal. I ladled out the soup into bowls and took them to the table.

As they started spooning down the soup, one burst out, "Dammit Kätchen! Can't you cook either!" They all stopped eating and glared at me.

"What? What's the matter?" I said in surprise.

"It's bad enough that we have to put up with burnt soup from Frau Meyer. Do you have to burn the soup too!"

"What are you mean? I didn't burn the soup," I said in my defense.

"Then why in hell did you put cinnamon in it?"

"I saw Frau Meyer add it and thought I was supposed to."

"The soup burns whenever she forgets to stir it, then she adds cinnamon to it to hide the burnt taste."

"I didn't know. Look." I went to the stove and tilted the soup pot to show them it wasn't burnt on the bottom.

"See."

"Well, okay, just don't add cinnamon to the soup anymore!"

"I won't," I said.

"My mother makes milk soup. She adds more butter, salt and sugar," said one of them.

"I can add a little more next time if you want," I offered.

"Yes, thank you." The dairy hands all nodded and immediately dove back into their meal. I was left to look on at them in amazement as they gulped down their meal.

When I went back to the stove, I saw the cinnamon container on the shelf. I reached up and brought it down. Looking at it in amusement, I started to chuckle. I tried to stop but began laughing even more. Soon, the four dairy hands were laughing too.

The dairy did not deliver all their milk to the processing plant. Several times a month, Frau Meyer set aside some milk for making butter, cheese, and a fresh cheese called quark, which is something like a cross between sour cream and cottage cheese. She made them for their own use and for the trading of goods with their neighbors. I sampled the cheese and quark, and thought they were very tasty, much better than what we could afford back in Hamburg.

I didn't think I would learn to make such things in my upcoming cooking school. Not wanting to miss the opportunity here, I told Frau Meyers I would like to learn and to help her make them. With the added help, she decided to set aside more milk and make more than normal. The butter and cheese products were a more profitable use of the raw milk than selling it to the milk processor.

She showed me how it was done, and I was soon proficient at making butter, cheese and quark. This time, I made sure of no mistakes with the ingredients. We made such large quantities that she took samples into town to the restaurants and markets and soon she had orders for more.

We started making quantities of them regularly each week. I slipped some samples into meals for the dairy hands too. Frau Meyer was so pleased with the extra money from the sales that she considered going into the cheese business for real.

In December, the weather got colder. Periodic ice and snow were normal, making any thoughts of a long bike ride to meet Rolf out of the question. Unfortunately, it made any thoughts of going home for Christmas out of the question too.

Frau Meyer and her husband took me into town the week before Christmas to see their town's Christmas market and have a taste of their "famous" mulled wine. German like their wines too, as well as their beers. I tried it, but it didn't appeal to me. I much preferred my "Alster Water."

In January, one of the dairy hands, Herman, was drafted, and we had to say goodbye to him. I gave him a hug and wished him well. Afterward, it saddened me to see his empty chair at the table. To prevent any arguments, I separated the fried potatoes myself into three equal portions before putting the pan on the table for them.

Chapter 14
Bike Ride Home

AFTER A WINTER of work on the dairy, spring finally arrived. It was the beginning of April in 1936, and my "year on the land" was over. On a pretty morning, I was shaking hands with the dairy hands outside the milking barn. Herr Meyer had given them a short break to say goodbye to me. They said they were sorry to see me go because I had cooked "pretty good" after that first day. We had lost only one of these innocent, decent young men to military service while I was there. I imagined it was only a matter of time.

A few minutes later in front of the farm house, I was saying goodbye to Herr and Frau Meyer. I had my suitcase strapped to my bike. She gave me a small bundle of food for the trip back to Hamburg. Inside she had put several cheese samples to show my family back in Hamburg what I had made here.

When I arrived five months earlier, Frau Meyer had seemed stern, but now she gave me a hug goodbye. About halfway through my stay at the dairy, Frau Meyer had told me to "du" her rather than "Sie" her, which meant she wanted me to think of her like friend or family rather than an authority figure or boss.

I think she appreciated my help and would miss me. I would miss her and her husband too. I got on my bike and, with a wave goodbye, headed down the driveway.

As I rode my bike on the trip home, I saw the sunny sky, the pretty countryside, and the early spring flowers, but I probably didn't appreciate them like I should have. I was too eager to get down the road and finally see Rolf again.

When I came to the intersection near his house, I slowed only a little as I looked again at the spot in the road where he had tackled me. I remembered looking up at him as he asked me if I was all right.

As I thought about it, I heard a familiar shrill voice shout, "Kätchen!"

Soon, little Lotti and Gregor were again in the road jumping up and down shouting, "Kätchen! Kätchen! Kätchen!"

The lookout system had worked again. I hurried ahead and got off my bike quickly to give them a big hug.

Next, I was greeting and hugging Rolf's mother as they continued to excitedly bounce around us waving their arms.

Rolf then appeared, and we hugged. He hadn't changed much in the six months since I last saw him, still boyish. A hello kiss would have to wait until later if we could get a moment of privacy.

But we never did. Despite his mother's efforts to distract Lotti and Gregor, they were always with us, excitedly listening and talking. Still, I had a nice visit with Rolf and his family, even if it lacked intimacy. It was also a short visit, by necessity, so I could make it to Hamburg before dark.

I let them sample my cheese, which they said was delicious. They, in turn, gave me a bag of chestnuts to take to my family. Many chestnut trees grew nearby along the roads, and they still had a supply of chestnuts from Christmas.

After many heartfelt hugs and smiling waves, my happy, short visit was over, and I headed down the road. I rode in high spirits the rest of the way, going over every minute of my visit with Rolf. I vividly remembered his happiness at seeing me, hearing a shrill voice call my name, the jubilant jumping kids, and his nice parents. I even began to imagine being married to a cabinetmaker and living near his parents where we would raise a family. Silly me, I was getting carried away.

I told myself I had to think of something else, so I reflected on the nine plus months I had been on my own. I would be living with my family again while attending cooking school. After completing school, I might be out on my own again. After the experience of the last year, I knew I was capable of it. But who knows, maybe I wouldn't need to be all by myself.

Still in high spirits, I arrived back home in the late evening. Tired and sore from my long bike ride, I was relieved to be back.

"Hello, I'm home," I happily announced when I walked in the apartment with my suitcase in hand.

Mutti jumped up from her chair and rushed over to give me a hug. Vati and Ruth were close behind. As we hugged, I thought how glad I was to be home again.

"Oh, Kätchen," Mutti said, "it's so good to see you again. Look at you! You've grown up so much. You're a young woman now! I think you're taller too."

"Maybe a little taller," I replied.

"Good to have you back, Kätchen," Vati said as he hugged me. "You have grown, but I hope you're still my little girl."

"Wait a minute, Vati! I thought I was your little girl!" Ruth said in jest.

"Yes, you are too. I have two little girls, you know," he said giving us each a hug.

"Hi, Sis," Ruth said when I hugged her, "I'm glad you're back, even though I have to share my bed again."

"Hi, Ruth. You're as pretty as ever." After looking her over, I added, "You've grown a lot too. It's going to be crowded in that bed."

"It'll be fine," she said.

After sitting on the bicycle seat all day, I was glad to sit on the soft seat of the sofa. Mutti rushed to get me some food as I began to tell them about my year on the land and about Rolf.

I sent Rolf a letter the day after I arrived back, telling him I had made it safely. Six days later I received a letter from him, saying that he suspected he would soon be called up for military service like so many other of the young men in his town. He wanted to see me again before it should happen, so he proposed visiting me on an upcoming weekend. He would take a train in from a nearby town, and did I have a place where he could stay?

I was, of course, all for it and quickly wrote back telling him so. Mutti thought that setting up a place to sleep in our storage area would be better than Rolf sleeping on the sofa. On the floor above were storage rooms for each of the building tenants. Not enough room was probably available in our storage room, so we would make up a bed in the area outside of it. We soon were busy cleaning up the area, borrowing a mattress from a neighbor, and getting it ready for our guest.

On Friday evening of the designated weekend, I met him at the train station by myself and finally got my hello kiss. When I brought him back to the apartment, all of my family were there to meet him. Vati happily came forward to shake his hand.

"Good to meet you, Rolf. So you are soon to be a military man. Well, as one military man to another, welcome. Maybe I should take you down to the club to meet my friends, so you can hear all sorts of stories about being in the army."

"Oh, Vati!" said Ruth with a look.

"That is probably about the last thing he needs, Gustav," said Mutti derisively, "but I suppose if there is time, he might be interested in seeing one of our drinking clubs, even if he has to put up with your friends there."

This caused us all to laugh, possibly at Vati's expense. Meanwhile Rolf smiled as he shook his hand and said, "Thank you, sir, I'd like that. It's good to meet you."

To me, Vati then said, "Kätchen, I admire your taste in young men. I like him already."

Mutti then hugged Rolf, saying, "Welcome, Rolf. I'm happy to meet you. I'm sure you want to spend time with Kätchen and not Gustav's friends, but it might be interesting for a short time."

Then Ruth came forward, smiling and gave him a bashful hug.

Stepping back, Rolf said, "Your sister is a pretty little thing like my little sister Lotti, only older. Hopefully, she doesn't still bounce around, excitedly screaming like Lotti."

"No, I gave that up last week," replied Ruth, and they laughed.

Mutti had trays of foods for snacking laid out, and we snacked, drank, and talked for several hours before taking Rolf up to see his sleeping quarters, which proved to be quite comfortable for him that night.

After breakfast the next morning, he and I were off by ourselves for a day of sightseeing in Hamburg. We rode buses and trolleys around the city, stopping to see the various sites, all the while, holding hands, and occasionally sneaking a kiss. We were back in the late afternoon, so we could join my family at my father's club. There Rolf had to join Vati and his friends at the bar in their beer drinking, talking, and singing. After a time though, Mutti got up and brought Rolf and my father back to spend time with us women at a table.

"Rolf has a pretty good voice," my father said when they came to our table.

Rolf then spend some time with us and got to sample our "Alster Water," which he said was tasty. Ilse was there with us too. My father's friends soon came over to take them back to the bar, but Mutti shooed them away.

Rolf told us about cabinetmaking with his father. My father shook his head in admiration, saying that he wished he knew how to do such honest work with his hands instead of catering to the foibles of the wealthy people at his restaurant. I then told him about Joris and how not all the rich were like his arrogant customers, some were good people. Vati was happy to hear it and agreed that it must be true. "Even so," he told us, "the arrogant, selfish ones seem to congregate at my restaurant."

After our late evening at the club, we came home and without too much delay, went to bed. The next morning, Rolf, Ruth, and I rode bikes to see Hamburg's airport, about thirty minutes ride to the north. Rolf had an interest in aviation and hoped to be assigned to the Luftwaffe (the German air force) when drafted. He looked with great interest at the planes nearby on the tarmac and could tell us the names of each type. We spent an hour or two there looking at planes and watching them taking off and landing.

Next we rode south and west to the Harvestehude area of Hamburg. The restaurant, in which my cooking school was held, was located there. Unfortunately, my school started the very next morning, so I wouldn't be able to see Rolf off at the train station. We found the restaurant without trouble and stopped to look at it. I was eager to start, but didn't know much about it yet. I would find out in the morning.

After our stop at the restaurant, we rode along Outer Alster Lake on the way home. After arriving home, there was still time before dinner, so Rolf and I went out for a walk along the Osterbek Canal by ourselves. It would be the last time we would be together alone, so we got in our goodbye kisses then.

We had dinner at home, and afterward talked about our visit to the airport. Vati, of course, told Rolf all about his flying machine experiences in the war. He had cursed them many times for the artillery barrages that they directed down on them. Mutti had to finally interrupt and suggest Ruth show Rolf some of her artwork, which Vati agreed was a good idea. She brought them out, and Rolf was very complimentary of them. After many pleasant hours, we went to our beds.

In the morning, we had a quick breakfast together, and then I had to be off to school. Mutti and Ruth saw Rolf off later that morning at the train station. Several days later, I got a letter from him telling me that he made it back safely and thanking my family for their wonderful hospitality.

Only a week later, I received a letter from Rolf saying that he had received a notice to report for military service within two days. Thank goodness, he had come to visit us when he did. If not, with only two days to report, he would have been unable to visit us here like he did.

He passed his physical and, after expressing his interest in flying, was assigned to the Luftwaffe. Soon afterward, he was loaded in the back of a truck with twenty other new "volunteers" for transport to basic training.

Chapter 15
Cooking School

WHEN I RETURNED from my land year in early April of 1936, I was fortunate to get a place in the cooking school starting later that month. A vacancy had recently become available. The restaurant, which sponsored and ran the school, was located on the other side of Outer Alster Lake from us. It was less than fifteen minutes away on my bike.

I could not miss the first day of school or I might lose my place. So I had to say goodbye to Rolf at breakfast instead of the train station. I thought about him on the ride to school though if that counts.

As I had been instructed, I arrived early on the first morning in a presentable dress. Soon after arrival, I was given a white full-length wrap, which tied at the waist, to wear over my dress during school.

Most of the nine girls in my class were much like me, girls from working class families in Hamburg who had just completed their landyear and were living at home while attending the school. They also had chosen cooking for a trade and were attending the school as part of their cooking apprenticeship.

Our schooling consisted of initial training on the basics of cooking followed by on-the-job training in the kitchen of the restaurant. After a brief introduction, we were soon learning how to measure, weigh, slice, dice, sharpen, and clean. We progressed into making breads, salads, soups, sauces, sides, and desserts for the meals they served.

The foods and dishes we prepared were for use in the restaurant. The cost for us students to attend the school was minimal since we were expected to work a number of hours each day for the restaurant at little or no pay in return for the schooling.

The culmination of our yearlong schooling was the preparation of the many entrees, such as roulade, schnitzel, and several different wursts served at the restaurant. An order would come in from a customer in the restaurant, and an instructor would show us how to prepare it. We would prepare it the next time as he supervised us as we prepared it.

During lunch break at cooking school, we girls would sit in our white wraps on the steps outside in back and eat our lunches. We would talk and tell one another about ourselves. I became friends with Greta and Krista, two of my classmates.

One day after talking about her boyfriends, Greta asked, "So, Kätchen, how about you? How is Rolf doing?"

"He's doing fine. He's been in basic training about a month. He must be in pretty good shape now. They run, march, and exercise all day. He sent me a picture." I pulled the picture out of my pocket and handed it to her.

"He normally is smiling and cheerful, not like this picture," I said.

"Yes, I know. I've seen a lot of them. They're all like that. Still, he's very handsome, just like the boys at the base. You really should go with us one Saturday to the dance there. You'll have fun."

"I don't know. I like dancing well enough. We used to do folk dancing sometimes in our music classes at school, but I doubt if the soldiers do those kinds of dances."

"Haven't you ever done the foxtrot or a waltz?" Krista asked with surprise.

I shook my head.

"Well, it doesn't matter," Greta said. "We'll show you how before we go. It's easy. We can practice out here during lunchbreak! Oh, and there's also one called the Paso Doble where you kind of hop around a lot."

Seeing my worried look, she added, "No need to worry. You'll catch on quick. All you really do is imitate what everyone else is doing."

"Oh, I don't know about going. I have Rolf and don't need lots of boyfriends."

"Have you ever had any other boyfriends, Kätchen?"

"No, not really."

Slapping her leg, Greta declared, "It's time you met some more boys. How do you know if Rolf is the right one if you haven't met any others!"

"So many men, so little time," Krista said with a laugh, "That's Greta's motto."

"You're not *helping*, Krista," Greta said with a look. Then returning to me, "Ignore her, Kätchen. The dances at the base here are on Saturdays and don't cost anything to get in. Why don't you come with us?"

"No. I'd better not. Thanks, maybe some other time."

"Oooh. Come with us. You'll have a good time," she kept coaxing.

"No, not this time. Thanks though," I said, thinking of Rolf.

Later in the summer, I finally gave in to Greta and went with her and Krista to the Saturday night dance at the base. Several military bases were in our area. One of them, an Army base, was not too far away and could be reached by bus or walking. So we met on Saturday night and decided to walk to the dance.

The dance for enlisted men and was held in a large auditorium draped with many Nazi banners. The men in their uniforms heavily outnumbered the girls. The entrance was crowded with soldiers there to eye the girls as they walked in.

We walked up to the cloak room just outside the entrance to check our coats. While Greta and Krista finished checking their coats, I observed for a moment the clamor at the crowded entrance.

When Greta came up, I said, "Wow. Is it always like this?"

"Yes, but don't worry. It seems a little intimidating at first, but you get used to it," Greta replied, taking my arm and pulling me forward.

"Why do I feel like a piece of meat?" I asked.

"Oh come on, Kätchen. It's not that bad. Let's just have fun," Greta said as she and Krista pulled me forward.

When we reached the entrance, we were snatched up by young men who took us to the dance floor. When one dance was over, another soldier would break in, and I'd be dancing again. The band played mostly the waltzes and foxtrots, which Greta and Krista had shown me how to do.

The soldiers behaved themselves in general, although some had been drinking and wanted me to have a drink with them, which I tried to graciously decline. Some told me about themselves and asked questions about me. The young men were handsome enough in their uniforms, but I guess I wasn't eager to meet someone new.

After some time, Greta, Krista, and I took a break and met at the refreshment counter as a number of soldiers hovered nearby. Krista told how one of her dance partners was an army cook and they had talked about making apple strudel.

After our laugh, Greta asked me, "And how about you, Kätchen? Are you having a good time?"

"Yes, but my feet are getting tired," I replied, "Me and my shoes aren't used to all this dancing. And they've been stepped on a few times too. I think I will take a few of these cookies for Mutti and Ruth, and head home while I'm still able to walk."

"Noo, don't leave yet. It's still early. And you can't walk home alone," Greta pleaded.

"Don't worry. I'll be fine walking home. You both stay and have a good time. I'll see you at school on Monday," I said as I picked out several different cookies, wrapped them in a napkin, and put them in my pocket.

I said goodbye and made my way to the entrance, as Greta looked on with disappointment.

Chapter 16
Someone in Need

WHEN I WALKED home from the dance, it was nearly ten o'clock, and the sun was setting. The scattering of people on the street were mostly on their way to the dance and not coming from it. The street lights were beginning to come on along the darkening street in front of me. I thought about my time at the crazy dance. While I had enjoyed the dancing and the attention of all the soldiers, it was a little much for me on the first time there.

My times with Rolf had been much more enjoyable. We were still writing regularly. He didn't think he would be able to get any time off any time soon, so my prospects of seeing him again in the near future were not good.

As I was walking and thinking, I noticed some movement up ahead in some bushes along the sidewalk. As I got nearer, I thought I heard some weak crying, then sniffling and a sneeze. Pausing and straining to hear more, I heard the crying again. It sounded like someone needing help, so I went over to investigate. On the other side of the bushes I found a little girl, maybe about seven or eight years old, in a hooded coat. She was sitting on the ground with her head in her hands crying weakly.

"Oh, my goodness. Little girl! What are you doing out here? Where are your parents?" I said in surprise.

Kneeling down in front of her, I cleared her hair and hands from her face to get a better look at her. She looked pale and thin.

"Help me. Please help me," she pleaded with a pitiful look.

I picked her up off the ground, stood her up and knelt in front of her.

"Of course, I'll help you, you poor thing. Do you live around here? Can I take you home?"

"I live that way," she said pointing, "but there's nobody home."

"What? What do you mean? Your parents are out looking for you?"

"No, they were arrested."

After my initial surprise and gasp, I asked, "The police arrested your parents and left you there?"

"My mama and papa hid me this morning when the police came and took them away. The policemen looked for me, but didn't find me. I hid all day and came out tonight to look for help."

As I tried to fathom what she had said, a thought dawned on me. This dark-haired little waif might be Jewish. The Nazis' hatred and harsh treatment of the Jews seemed to be getting worse. This might be some new example. I stood up, looked around us, saw no one nearby in the street, and knelt down in front of her again.

"Little girl, are you Jewish?"

"Yes."

Her Jewish parents had been arrested for some reason. The authorities would probably expect me to take her to a police station. I might get in trouble if I help her.

It took me a moment to totally grasp the seriousness of the situation as I looked at the little girl. But I felt sorry for the poor thing and wanted to help her. Then I thought of Frau Zöllmer at the sewing shop. She was Jewish and would know how to help her. If I could get this girl back to our apartment, Frau Zöllmer could come to get her and then get her to her relations.

"What's your name, dear?"

"Anna."

"Anna, I'm Kätchen. I'm not Jewish, but I know a Jewish lady who I think can help you. If you come with me, I'll take you to her. I won't take you to the police. Okay?"

"Okay, but what about Max?" she said.

"Max? Anna, who's Max?" I said with surprise, looking around for a little boy, but not seeing one.

"He lives next door. He's four years old. My mama said his mama and papa might be in trouble too, so I should watch out for him. They must have hid him too because I saw him on the floor in his house crying. I knocked on his door. He didn't answer, but I know he's inside."

I was taken aback and disturbed by the growing magnitude and risk of my offer to help. I sighed and paused for a moment to think. Finally I said, "Okay, Anna. We'll try to help Max too. Show me where he lives. Let's hurry."

We started off in the direction Anna had pointed. Her hand in mine was cold. She sniffled several times, then coughed and sneezed.

"You've got a bad cold. We have to get you out of this night air as soon as we can," I said stopping to button her coat and make sure the hood of her coat was snuggly on her head.

"Oh, you're probably hungry, too. I have a few cookies," I said as we started to walk briskly again.

I pulled a cookie out of my pocket and gave it to Anna. She thanked me and began to munch on it eagerly.

After several minutes, we came to a dark intersection. Anna stopped and pointed down the cross street at the two-story houses along it.

"That's Max's house, the one with the pot in front," she said. "My house is the one after it."

I took another look up and down the streets, and all looked quiet.

"Okay, let's go."

We walked briskly down the street and stopped on the sidewalk in front of Max's house. I looked around again quickly, then we went up the steps and past the pot to the front door. The doorstep and the house inside were unlit. I tried the front door, which was locked.

I knocked on the door quietly. I looked in the front windows and knocked again. I looked quickly under the doormat and on the door frame above the door for a key. I knocked again.

"Max! It's Anna. Open the door. Let us in," Anna said in a loud whisper.

Suddenly we heard the door unlock. I turned the knob and opened the door. We saw a sad cute little blonde-haired, blue-eyed boy who brightened up at seeing Anna.

"Anna," he said a little too loudly. Both Anna and I shushed him as we quickly got inside with him, closed the door, and locked it. Anna and Max hugged, and I got on my knees in front of Max.

"Max, I'm Kätchen. Anna asked me to come and help you. Are your mama and papa here?"

"No, Mama told me hide and be quiet. When I came out they were gone. I'm hungry," he said with his lower lip sticking out.

I took the another cookie out of my pocket and handed it to him. He took it and began eating.

"Is anyone else here?" I asked.

"No."

We then heard a car pull to a stop out in the street. I looked up with concern and quickly moved them back into a hallway away from the front room. I bolted upright when I heard a car door slam.

"Quick. We have to get out of here. Where is the back door?"

"I know where it is," Anna said, motioning me to follow her. I picked up Max and followed Anna through several rooms to a back door. I saw a small coat hanging near the door and grabbed it as I went by.

Anna waited while I peered out through the window of the back door. Not seeing anyone, I opened the door and poked my head out.

"Be very quiet. We must hurry. Let's go," I told them.

The back door and alley were unlit. I went out the door carrying Max and his coat with Anna close behind holding my hand. After quietly closing the door, we tiptoed down the back steps and into a concrete alley behind the houses.

Walking hurriedly along the alley, I listened intently to see if we were being followed. The night was quiet, and I didn't hear any sounds in the alley behind us. When we got to the street from the alley, I looked up and down the street quickly, seeing no traffic.

After walking a distance down the street, I stopped briefly to put Max's coat on him. With looks like a little Aryan poster child, he would not be suspected of being Jewish, but Anna might be if inspected. So we needed to avoid the police and keep her hood on. Anna needed it on anyway. She was coughing, and I noticed her nose was runny. As I nervously looked about, I searched in my pockets and found the napkin. I wiped her nose quickly and put the napkin back in my pocket. I gave them the last two cookies, and then we were off again. We crossed an intersection and heard a car coming up from behind us.

"Try to walk normal. Don't look back," I whispered to Anna.

I was anxious as the car passed by us. When it continued on, I sighed with relief, and we kept walking. A second car passed us. We crossed an intersection and continued to walk briskly. A third car passed us and pulled to a stop in front of us.

I saw it was a police car and hesitated for a split second, wanting to run. I glanced around. Two policemen in uniforms were getting out of the car. There was no other way. My only hope was to continue walking and try to bluff my way past them. I could feel Anna grip my hand tightly.

"Anna, try to stay calm. I'm not going to turn you in," I whispered sidelong to her. She gave my hand a squeeze.

The two policemen were out of their car and walking toward us. Anna's face was hidden by the hood of her coat as she walked beside me. If they examined Anna and suspected she was Jewish, they would take us in for questioning. Max looked up, saw the men, and buried his head in my shoulder. I put on my best frown.

The first policeman said, "Good evening, Fräulein. You are out late tonight."

"Yes, my little brother and sister were at a friend's house and got sick. I had to leave a very nice party to bring them home. I'm not in a very good mood. I have to get them home and out of this night air. Please let us pass," I said, moving to go by them.

One of the policemen stepped in front of me to block my way. He shined a light in my face, examining me and Max, and said, "We're looking for some missing Jewish children. We just want to have a look. It will only take a moment."

With as much bravado as I could muster, I said, "Officer, I really don't have time for any of your inspections. I told you already, my brother and sister are very sick and cold. I need to get them home." Anna coughed. "There, you see. I have to be going." I started to move by him, but again he stepped in front of me.

My heart stopped when he moved toward Anna and said, "I'm sorry, Fräulein, but it will only take a …"

Before he could finish, Anna, still concealed under her hood, suddenly sneezed twice and sprayed a mucous mess onto the pant legs and shoes of the policeman, who stopped and looked disgustedly at it.

As the policeman looked down, Max turned and coughed spittle into his face. The policeman was wiping the spittle from his cheek and staring down at his pants as I said, "I'm terribly sorry, officer, but now you see how sick they are. We really must be going. Goodbye and I'm sorry again about your uniform."

I moved past him and this time he did not try to stop us, but instead he continued to stare in disbelief at the foul mess on his neatly pressed uniform pants and highly polished shoes.

My heart pounded as we briskly walked away down the street without looking back. We could hear the first policeman getting angry with the second one who was jesting about his slimy pants and shoes. In a few moments, we heard the car start up again, turn around, and pull away. I could hardly believe we had escaped arrest.

We encountered two young men on the sidewalk who passed without paying much attention to us. Next, a woman passed by looking at us with curiosity. A car drove by. After a few more minutes of walking in silence, we reached the side street I wanted.

"We'll take this street here. It will be safer with less traffic and people," I said anxiously, nodding toward it.

I looked up and down on the street one more time, and all seemed quiet. We turned onto the side street, and I began to relax a little. I was still shaky from our close call and thanking heaven for the fortunate timing of Anna's sneezes. Then I became more curious about it.

"Anna, did you sneeze on the policeman on purpose or was it an accident?" I asked.

"I thought you needed a little help," she replied.

I laughed in amazement and surprise.

"You are such a smart little girl. How old are you?"

"Eight."

"I helped too," Max added.

"You both were a big help. I'm proud of you. It's not much farther now. We'll be there soon," I said as we continued along.

Chapter 17
Fear of Arrest

WHEN WE ENTERED the apartment, Mutti was sitting in a chair knitting. She looked up in astonishment at seeing me come in with two children and quickly shut the door. Before she could say anything, I put my finger to my lips and shushed her.

"Kätchen! What's going on? Who are these children?" Mutti asked in an excited whisper, getting up in alarm.

Without answering, I brought the children to the sofa, laying Max down on one end and Anna on the other end. I put pillows under their heads and a blanket over both of them. Mutti helped, but was apprehensively looking at me for an explanation.

"They are Jewish children whose parents have been arrested by the police. I found them and thought Frau Zöllmer could help them. They need to stay here tonight, and we can get her early tomorrow," I told her in a low voice.

Mutti was astounded at the news and staggered a few steps backward.

"They needed help. What could I do? How could I refuse to help them?"

Recovering her senses, Mutti looked at the two children.

"Yes, of course. I can see that now. They must be hungry and thirsty. I'll get them some food and water. We have to be careful no one in the apartment building knows," she said a low voice.

She turned to go to the kitchen and stopped for a few moments thinking.

"Yes, Johanna will know what to do. Your father is sound asleep in the bedroom, and Ruth is at a friend's house. If Johanna can come early enough tomorrow, they won't need to know about it either," she said in a low voice.

Just prior to dawn the next morning, Mutti had brought Frau Zöllmer to the apartment, and we were talking quietly while we prepared the children. Frau Zöllmer was near the sofa putting Anna's coat on her. I propped up a sleeping Max on the sofa and put his coat on him. Mutti looked on as Frau Zöllmer talked to Anna.

"Anna, the sun isn't up yet, so it's still dark outside. It will take about twenty minutes to walk to my apartment. I'll carry Max. Can you walk that far?"

"Yes."

"And you have to be very quiet in the building here when we're leaving. Okay?"

Anna nodded, then turned and gave me a hug. She did the same to Mutti. Mutti and I hugged Frau Zöllmer.

"Thank you, Johanna," said Mutti.

"No, I thank you, Margarete, and you, Kätchen. It was very lucky for Anna and Max that she found Kätchen."

"Be careful, Johanna," said Mutti with a pat on Frau Zöllmer's shoulder.

"We will. Goodbye," she said picking up the still sleeping Max.

We said goodbye to her and waved goodbye to Anna, who waved back to us as they slipped quietly out the door and down the hallway. We watched as they turned and disappeared into the stairwell.

After we closed the door, Mutti gave me a hug and a concerned look. Yes, we were concerned that the children would safely get back to their relatives. But, we were also concerned for our own safety. If Frau Zöllmer was caught and interrogated, we might still be in trouble. We sat down in the living room exhausted and thought about getting some sleep.

We heard from Frau Zöllmer later that she and the two children made it back to her house without problem. Max had awakened about half way there and did not know Frau Zöllmer who was carrying him. He had started to make a loud fuss at being carried by a stranger, but when he saw Anna, he quit fussing and went back to sleep.

Frau Zöllmer was able to locate Anna's aunt and uncle who were taking care of her and trying to find out what happened to her mother and father. They, in turn, found Max's relations who were taking care of him. We didn't tell anyone else what happened.

We had no idea why Anna's parents had been arrested. It was probably not just because they were Jewish. Frau Zöllmer was Jewish and she had not been arrested. The parents must have said or done something that was reported, and they were arrested.

The whole affair has left me feeling less than brave. I was initially afraid to help, afraid when I did help, and afraid now after helping.

A couple nights later, we all were sitting like normal in the living room after dinner. Vati was looking at a magazine, and I was reading a book. Mutti and Ruth were crocheting. All of us looked up when we heard loud noises and voices outside in the hallway. Mutti and I were startled by the sound. Mutti's shaking hands interrupted her crocheting. We looked nervously at each other and at the door. Both Vati and Ruth noticed.

"Mutti, Kätchen, what's the matter?" Ruth asked with a laugh.

"Yes, why do you both look so scared?" Vati chimed in.

"Oh, no reason. We were just startled by the noise," said Mutti as we tried to compose ourselves.

"It's just Hugo coming in late," Vati said.

"Yes, I know," Mutti replied.

Unconvinced, Vati and Ruth looked at us curiously. Soon the noises subsided and we returned to our activities, although Mutti and I still felt and probably looked a little shaken.

For the next week, Mutti and I worried the police or whoever might find out and burst in the door of our apartment to arrest us. After a week, we began to think we were safe and could relax. It was a relief for us, although it was still upsetting to think we were worried about such a thing.

* * *

Rolf, meanwhile, was lying on a stretcher with his head heavily bandaged with red showing through the bandages. The bandages around his neck partially covered his mouth. He slowly opened his eyes and looked up at the various people around him. Looking down, he saw his arm was heavily bandaged and in a sling. A splint was being applied to his leg.

"Manfred, aren't you finished yet? How long does it take? I could have bandaged ten elephants in the time it's taking you," Rolf said.

"Quiet down, Rolf. Am I going to have to use some of this gauze to shut you up?" said his partner in his first aid training, looking up from his work applying the splint.

"You just wait until it's your turn, Manfred."

Rolf had begun training to be a member of a bomber crew. All the crew members were trained in basic first aid procedures, such things as: dressing wounds, stopping bleeding, applying tourniquets, applying splints, injecting morphine, etc.

As a machine gunner, he trained to become familiar with the machine guns on the bombers. Soon he would be assigned to a specific bomber and aircrew, and they would begin training at an aircraft plant where the bombers were being built.

Once there, he would be trained on the various systems of the plane, how to operate them and how to make emergency repairs to battle damage. There seemed to be little chance Rolf would get any time off to visit his family or me.

* * *

Life went on for me at the cooking school. The instructors and supervisors in the restaurant liked me since I was a good worker and enthusiastic to learn all I could. My classmates continued to get along together very well. Occasionally, one of the girls brought a camera, and we would pose for group pictures on the steps out back during our lunch break.

Several weeks after the first dance at the base, I let Greta talk me into going to another dance. I felt bad for leaving early from my first time, so there I was, dancing again with one soldier after another. This time, I was enjoying it more. I thought my foxtrot and waltz were not bad. I stayed the whole time and danced with many young men.

These young men were, in general, well-behaved despite their possible thoughts that Hamburg girls might be somewhat less than chaste. By that statement, I mean Hamburg has been a favorite liberty port of sailors and soldiers for many years. The city's famous red light district called the Reeperbahn was very popular. The pretty girls there and in other night spots of the city did not help the reputation of Hamburg girls. A popular army song is called *Hamburg Ist Ein Schönes Städtchen* (*Hamburg is a Great Little City*). One of the lines in the song says that in Hamburg there are lots of pretty girls, but not any virgins.

Of course, if the hands of a soldier did start to roam where they shouldn't, I let them know I didn't like it, and they'd stop.

While dancing, a soldier would sometimes give a girl a picture of themselves when they wanted you to remember them. It would be impolite not to accept them. I received several pictures that night at the dance. I would look at the picture, tell the young soldier how handsome he looked, thank him, and put it in my pocket. Like Rolf's picture, these pictures were also serious poses of them in uniform. One group of girls at the dance seemed to be competing with one another as to who could collect the most pictures during the night. Not very nice of them, I thought.

Walking home after the dance, Greta, Krista, and I were laughing and telling stories about the night.

"I don't think it was a very respectful of him to ask! You know what I mean? Am I a real blonde?" said Greta indignantly.

"Sounds pretty forward of him to me," Krista said.

Just then we were approaching the bushes where I had discovered Anna. My thoughts became distracted as I glanced sidelong at the passing bushes. Then I heard Greta again.

"As if I would have to dye my hair blonde because I'm so desperate to get a date with him," Greta said derisively.

"So, what did you tell him?" Krista asked with great interest.

"I smacked him across the face and told him, 'You'll never find out!' Then I walked away," Greta said triumphantly. Krista and I gasped, and we all three giggled and laughed as we walked on.

Next morning, I showed Mutti the pictures that the soldiers had given me at the dance. Ruth had come in from another room to look too.

Going over the pictures one by one, I said, "This is Herman. He's in a panzer division and is a gunner on his tank. He was a very good dancer. This is Reiner. He's in the infantry and is from Eisenach, which isn't very far from Oma and Aunt Rosa. His eyes were so blue. And this is Otto. He's from Bremen and wanted to be in the navy, but got put in the army. He was a little bit grabby like a sailor, but not bad."

"My, what handsome young men. Oh, how serious they look," Mutti said.

"It's the way these military pictures are supposed to look."

"This one here is not bad looking. Should I send his picture to Rolf?" teased Ruth.

"You do and I'll beat you!" I said teasing back.

With a giggle, Ruth picked up another one.

With a laugh and pointing, Ruth said, "This one looks like he has to go to the bathroom real bad."

"Oh, go away," I said.

"Well, he does," she said, giggling and rushing off to get away from me before I could punch her.

Ruth was thirteen years old at the time. She and I were good friends, the way sisters should be. Later that summer, I felt bad I hadn't done more with her since returning home. I had been too preoccupied with cooking school and should have been a better big sister to her. I tried to think of a good outing for us and thought of Hamburg's famous zoo. For some reason, Mutti and Vati had never taken us there.

One day after school, I told Mutti what I was thinking and asked if she might want to go along too.

"Hagenbeck Zoo? No! I don't like that place."

"What? Why wouldn't you like seeing all the strange animals from around the world?"

"I went there one time before the war and don't want to go back. I was in my early twenties here visiting your Uncle Fritz and his wife. They took me there."

"So what happened? Why didn't you like it?" I asked in amazement.

"At first, I was enjoying myself, seeing all the interesting animals like the lions, monkeys, bears, and elephants. They keep them in big enclosures with moats between you and the animals, not in cages like other zoos. I was having a good time, but then we went to see the African village."

"African village? What's that?"

"It was a real life African village with black natives they had brought here from Africa. They were there in an enclosure to be viewed like the other exotic things from Africa."

"Really?" I said surprised.

"Yes, they were dressed in their native costumes and jewelry, and milling around in their village, I guess doing what they normally do. I had seen a few stereoscope images of Africa before, but to see real life African natives in their village was a very unusual and curious thing for us to see."

"Go on," I said.

"Well. then they all got up to put on their show of their native dancing," she continued looking uncomfortable.

"They started beating those awful drums. The dancers wore such hideous scary masks and headgear as they did their rhythmic dances with their spears and painted shields.

When they danced up close to the low fence separating us from them, they were scary, making threatening gestures at us. I got so frightened I had to leave. I've never been back. I'm sorry to say I think of it whenever I see a black person, which isn't very often."

"My gosh," I said, "so that's why you've never taken us to the zoo?"

"Yes, I know I was being silly, but I couldn't help it."

"It sounds like a pretty awful thing in the first place, having humans displayed at a zoo. Those were different times. They don't do it anymore. They only have animals there now."

"I still don't want to go, but you and Ruth should go. If I don't go, you can ride bikes there instead of taking buses and trams."

"Maybe Vati would want to go," I mused.

"I doubt it. It doesn't involve beer and war stories. You can ask him, but I don't want to go."

"Well, if Vati doesn't want to go, we'll take our bikes.

"Good."

"Wow, I'm still amazed to hear what they used to do there," I said.

"I certainly could have done without it."

When I asked her later, Ruth was excited about the idea and tried to talk Vati into going too, but he declined, saying something about a bad back from the war.

On Saturday, the weather was gorgeous when we woke up, so after breakfast, we set out on our bikes. Located on the northwest side of Hamburg, it would take less than a half hour of pedaling to get to the zoo.

Ruth had brought her drawing materials with her. As we went from enclosure to enclosure, she would sometimes stop to make a drawing of an animal. The ones that posed well were better for her. Her drawings of a tiger lying down and flamingos standing on one leg in a pond were very good. She especially liked the pattern and coloring on the giraffes.

As she drew, we talked about her school, my school, and lots of other things. I felt like I was finally being a good big sister and found I liked my little sister very much. We shared a big soft warm pretzel for lunch and had a wonderful day. In the evening back at home, her drawings were a big hit with Mutti and Vati.

After having such a nice time, I regretted not having done more with Ruth when we were going up. I promised myself I would do better from now on.

Remembering my desire to thank Joris in some way, I got in touch with him and set up a time to visit him and his family at his house. I baked a Black Forest Cake at our cooking school for the occasion. I took it along as a small token of my thanks. I also took Mutti along with me, so my visit wouldn't have the appearance of me scheming to land a rich husband. I only wanted to thank him for what he had done.

We had a wonderful visit. Joris was happy to see me again, and we had a great time telling about nasty old Frau Euler. His father was there to greet us, but could only briefly stay before having to leave on some pressing matter at the factory.

His mother was very cordial to us and beamed with happiness at her son when I told how he had helped me. She was teary and fairly glowed with pride at hearing what a fine son she had reared.

They seemed to me like very good people, and I could see how he had turned out so well. He was now attending secondary school before going to the university. It would be several years before he would be able to take a position in the family business. His two older brothers were already in the university.

Joris' family and their family business appeared to have a bright future. Their business was prospering with many new orders for the pumps and valves they manufactured.

I would find out much later, to my great sadness, that this fine family and their honest family business would suffer greatly in the war, like so many others. Factory production would suffer from shortages of raw materials. The Nazis would make them use forced labor to keep up production for the war effort. Bombing raids would destroy much of the factory. And saddest of all, Joris and his oldest brother were both killed in the war.

Chapter 18
Cousin Willie

IN EARLY DECEMBER of 1936, my cousin Willie came to visit us for a week. He had grown up in South Africa and had come to Germany several years before to learn a trade. My Uncle Karl was an engineer at a Junkers Aircraft Plant in Dessau and had gotten Willie a job there.

Willie, now in his early twenties, lived with Uncle Karl and his family. He came to Hamburg periodically for a taste of the big city. We offered to set up a bed for him in our storage area, but he was content to sleep on our sofa.

We looked forward to his visits, not only because he was a congenial young man, but also because he had the habit of bringing us delicious sausages from central Germany, a style of sausage not readily available in our area. On his second night, we all crowded around our kitchen table to enjoy a meal of fried sausage.

As serving bowls were passed and food put on plates, my father asked, "So, Willie, how are things at the Junkers plant?"

"Very busy. We have lots of orders for aircraft and are adding a shift soon to keep up with them."

"Hmm. What an unbelievable turnaround from just a few years ago. There's very little unemployment these days. I'm not sure how, but Hitler has made Germany prosperous again," Vati reluctantly admitted.

"All I know is we are busy," Willie said.

"Girls," Mutti said, "isn't it wonderful your cousin Willie has come to visit and brought us these delicious pork sausages?"

We both enthusiastically agreed and thanked him.

"I'm glad you like them. It's the least I could do for you letting me stay here for a few days," Willie said.

"What do you have planned while you're here?" Vati asked.

"I thought I would visit the Hamburg Dom, your wonderful city's winter fair, to do a little Christmas shopping and have a little fun."

"Without getting into too much trouble, I hope," Vati said with a wry smile. Willie looked a little embarrassed at this and everyone laughed.

For many, many years in olden times, a raucous winter fair was held in front of the Hamburg Dom (Hamburg's ancient catholic cathedral). When the cathedral itself was physically torn down a hundred years ago, the raucous winter fair lived on. Still called the Hamburg Dom, the fair was moved to a different place across town near the city's famous red light district, where it was easy to find a little trouble.

"Well, please stay as long as you like, Willie," Mutti said.

"Thank you, Aunt Margarete. And how have you all been? Has anything exciting been happening here?"

"No. Nothing exciting. Vati goes to work, I sew, and the girls go to school," Mutti said.

"Kätchen has a boyfriend," Ruth said. Mutti glared at Ruth, and all eyes turned toward me.

"A boy I met in the country on my landyear. He's in the Luftwaffe now and we exchange letters."

Willie nodded his approval and paused to examine me more closely. "Kätchen, I haven't seen you in a while. You're not a little girl anymore. I'm surprised you don't have all sorts of boyfriends," he said.

"Oh, go on," I said with embarrassment.

"Kätchen did the cooking tonight too. She's a real cook even though she hasn't finished her cooking school yet," Mutti said trying to change the subject.

"You did well," Willie said.

"I didn't do anything fancy to the sausages. I just fried them in oil and made a simple onion sauce for them," I replied.

"I like the sauce very much. You've obviously been paying attention. How do you like your school?" Willie asked.

"Very much, and I haven't burned the restaurant down yet."

"Oh, she's being modest. She learns to cook and bake all sorts of things at her school. And she does well too," Mutti said.

At this, Willie paused for a moment in thought and then mused, "You know what. I just realized that Kätchen is just the girl my Great Aunt Minna is looking for."

"Who?" I said.

"My father in South Africa mentioned in a letter that my Great Aunt Minna wants help in her restaurant in America. She immigrated there from South Africa several years ago. She is running a restaurant and wants to bring over girls from the family to work in it."

"My goodness. Where in America?" Mutti asked in surprise.

"I don't know. He didn't say. I did not know her very well when I was growing up. I suspect she is just looking for cheap labor."

"What's 'immigrated' mean?" Ruth asked.

"It means you go there to work and stay, not just visit and come back," Willie explained.

"Can anyone immigrate? Even me?" Ruth asked.

"Ruth, you're too young to go, so you don't need to worry about it," Mutti said.

"I'm almost fourteen."

"That's too young."

"How does it work? I mean, her bringing someone over to work?" I asked out of curiosity.

"Aunt Minna would be your American sponsor and is responsible for you there. You both fill out paperwork somehow to request for you to immigrate."

"How do you get there?"

"I don't know for sure, but I suspect she pays your way over by ship and you pay her back from your wages while working in her restaurant," he said.

"There may be something said for leaving Germany in these times. Things are a bit unsettling here now. I agree that Ruth is too young, but Kätchen, maybe you should think about it," said Vati thoughtfully.

"Is the government allowing people to leave Germany?" Mutti asked with interest.

"Well," Vati inserted, "we all know Hitler would gladly let all the Jews leave. I'm not so sure about others."

"Yes, I hear others, not just Jews, are being allowed to immigrate. But you will need a passport to leave the country. You apply for one and some official decides whether to give you one. A person like me or Uncle Karl, male and working in an aircraft plant, would not be allowed to immigrate. For that matter, we probably could not even get a passport for a weekend to Paris. But I would think you, Kätchen, should be able to."

"Are you interested, Kätchen?" Mutti asked.

"No. This is the first time I have even heard or thought of such a thing. I was just asking out of curiosity," I said.

"Kätchen, if you're interested, I'll ask my father to have Aunt Minna write you," Willie said.

"No, I'm not interested in going to America," I said.

"But it doesn't hurt to ask about it, Kätchen," Mutti urged.

"I'd go, but the beer there is so inferior," Vati joked. "But seriously, Kätchen, there's no harm in finding out more," he added.

"Okay, I'll write my father," Willie said.

I didn't protest and gave Willie a weak smile. Then I looked over at Mutti who was looking at me.

In my next letter to Rolf, I told him about Cousin Willie's visit, but I didn't mention Aunt Minna. I had only been curious about it and saw no reason to bother him with it unnecessarily. Several weeks later, Mutti asked me what Rolf said about it.

"I didn't mention it to him in my letter," I told her.

"You should tell Rolf about it and hear what he thinks."

"Mutti, you seem to be interested in me going?"

"No, I just think that Rolf deserves to know about it too."

So the next time I wrote him, I told him about Aunt Minna needing help in America and Willie sending her a letter to find out more. My mother and father thought I should find out more about it. But, I told Rolf, I could never accept an offer to work in America. How could I? If I moved so far away, we would never see each other again. I told him I wanted to be here when he completed his military service in a year.

Chapter 19
Safety in America

ROLF PULLED the letter from his jacket pocket. He leaned against the outside of a wooden building on base. It was a cool clear January afternoon with a dusting of snow on the ground.

He examined Kätchen's writing on the envelope, smiled, and opened it. He started to read, but several aircraft zoomed by at low altitude. He turned around at the noise and shielded his eyes from the glare of the sun while momentarily watching the planes. Returning his attention to the letter, he began to read again. He looked more and more troubled as he read. When he finished, he was deep in thought.

Looking up from the letter, he stared out across the base. He watched two formations of thirty men from the training school march by. He looked away at a convoy of supply trucks roar down a street. In another direction, he saw the construction activity where a new hangar and bunker were being built. He heard more planes and looked up to see another formation of planes zoom by. Watching and taking it all in, Rolf was deep in thought with the letter still in his hand.

In the afternoon, he sat in a briefing room with a hundred other airmen attending a required political briefing. Nazi flags and pictures of the Fuhrer were prominently displayed around the room. The air group's political officer stood behind the podium.

He was a member of the SchutzStaffel (Elite Guard), known as the SS. It was the Nazi Party's elite paramilitary organization of men fiercely loyal to Hitler and dedicated to protecting him. The Gestapo was also a branch of the SS. The SS men like this one assigned as political officers to regular military units were there to provide political training and ensure absolute loyalty to Hitler was maintained.

He stood behind the podium in his black uniform dramatically gesturing while railing on about how Germany would avenge the humiliation it suffered in the war, win much needed room for its people, and rule the world for a thousand years. He waved Hitler's book, *Mein Kampf*, repeatedly as if that made it all true.

Rolf had heard this sort of thing for several years. Their words appealed to the German people's proud roots and love of strength and power. He had always considered these strong words to be bombast and propaganda aimed at increasing the Nazi party's popular support and power base within Germany.

Now with a sinking feeling, he began to realize they actually meant and believed it. A war would be unavoidable in order to achieve such goals. Hitler said reassuring words to other countries of his desire for peace, but he saw proof on a daily basis of preparations for war.

That night, after much thought, he wrote a letter to Kätchen. Rolf wished he could get some days off to see her and fully explain himself, but he could not. He would have to write and be careful in what he said. He could not say too much, because their political officers, like the one that afternoon, read their letters. Still he had to let Kätchen know what he suspected and thought.

* * *

A couple weeks after sending my letter to Rolf about Aunt Minna, I walked in the door of the apartment. I was tired after a full day at cooking school. Mutti had been sitting in a chair in the living room knitting, but she bounced up when I entered. She had been waiting eagerly for me to get home for some time.

"Kätchen, you got a letter from Aunt Minna today and one from Rolf too. They're on the table," she said, eagerly pointing. I took off my coat and put it on the chair.

"Oh," I said, walking over to the table. I had hopes that someday Rolf and I might be together. How could I go to America and still hope to someday be with Rolf?

So, with mixed emotions, I picked up the letters as Mutti watched. I first examined Aunt Minna's envelope.

"Oh, my goodness. Aunt Minna's address is in California."

"I noticed it too," Mutti said excitedly.

"Hmm. California. That's a sunny, warm place like Italy or Spain, isn't it?"

"I think so," said Mutti enthusiastically. "Johanna told me that America is the land of opportunity. If you work hard, you can live well there, even buy a house and an automobile. Can you imagine?"

"But it's so far away," I said putting down the letter.

"Well, aren't you going to open it?" Mutti asked with surprise and disappointment.

"No, I'll read Rolf's letter first."

With a sigh, Mutti sat back down on the chair.

I opened his letter with a smile and began to eagerly read. As I read, my smile disappeared, and I became more and more upset.

Mutti saw this and asked, "Kätchen, what's the matter? Did something happen to Rolf?"

"No, but he thinks I should go to America," I said, with tears welling up. "He says he's sure there will be another war in Europe soon. He thinks I should go to America because it would be safer there. He wants me to write to him from America."

Mutti was beside me now with a concerned look.

"How could he think so little of me?" I blurted out, as I began to cry and rushed into the bedroom. I threw myself on the bed and covered my face as I cried. Mutti followed me into the bedroom and tried to comfort me.

"Kätchen, I think he's only worried about you. He wants you to be safe. I agree with him."

"What?"

"Yes, you've seen what's going on here. It's getting worse. The Nazis have too much power. They scare me, and they scare your father too. It's no good here anymore," she said in a low voice.

She paused stroking my hair and added, "Rolf may be right. There could be a war soon and who knows what might happen. It would be good if Ruth could go too, but she is too young. You should think about it."

"And what about the rest of you? Why should I go and leave you here if a war is coming?" I said looking up.

"Don't worry about Vati and me," Mutti said. "We've already survived a lot and can survive some more. We can send Ruth later in a year or two. I think you should read Aunt Minna's letter and see what she says. And don't be too hard on Rolf. He's already saved your life once. I think he is trying to save you a second time."

Somehow, her words did not make me feel any better. I began to sob while I continued to hug Mutti.

Chapter 20
Interview

AFTER RECOVERING a little, I read Aunt Minna's letter. In it, she said she needed a cook, so the fact that I was soon finishing cooking school was perfect. She would buy and send to me the $125 ticket for my boat passage. I would pay her back $25 per month working at her restaurant. Afterward, she would pay me $25 per month to continue to work there.

With my pain and disappointment from Rolf's letter still fresh, I wrote Aunt Minna a letter accepting her offer. I told her I would apply for my German passport. I didn't know how the immigration visa application was done, but I gave her my information for her use should she need to start the application on her end.

I took the letter to the post office and numbly handed it to the postal clerk. The clerk weighed the letter and told me how much international postage would cost. I paid him. He put stamps on the letter and walked a few steps to place it in an overseas bin. I watched him as he did.

When he returned to the window, he saw me still staring vacantly at the overseas bin. He cleared his throat, and only then, did I notice he was back in front of me. With some embarrassment, I turned and left.

I got the passport application forms from the passport office. The forms were not hard to fill out, probably because I had not lived a very long or complicated life yet. Mutti helped me. There were many copies and a messy carbon paper we put between the copies. We sat at the kitchen table reading and filling them out.

When completed, I took the forms back to the passport office. Many people were sitting and waiting in the crowded waiting room. I got into the long line in front of a clerk behind a counter. After a long wait, it was finally my turn.

"Good morning, my name is Kätchen Thielke. I have filled out the forms to apply for a passport," I said, handing the forms to him.

He looked them over without saying anything and seemed satisfied they were fully filled out. After referring to an appointment book, he handed me a piece of paper on which he had written the appointment date and time.

"Three weeks from today?" I asked after reading it.

"Yes, Fräulein. That is the earliest appointment I have," he said.

"I see. Thank you."

I turned to leave as he put my forms in a tray.

In February of 1937, I completed cooking school and had to say goodbye to Greta, Krista, and my other classmates. After our graduation class picture in the kitchen we started to hug one another goodbye. We had been together for nearly a year. Like most of the other girls, I was not eighteen years old yet.

Greta surprised us with news that she was getting married to the boy who had asked her if she was a real blonde. Apparently, they had gotten together again, and she discovered his family had money.

After graduation, I found a job as an apprentice cook in the kitchen of a hotel restaurant. As the new apprentice, I was the peeler, slicer and dicer of raw ingredients for use in the cooking as well as the stirrer of things cooking in pots.

Still I watched and learned from the cooks, and assisted them when I could. I tried to stay busy to keep from thinking about Rolf. Even so, periodically I caught myself thinking about him while I vacantly stirred a sauce. Still heartbroken by Rolf's letter, I had not written him back.

After three weeks had passed, I went back to the passport office to my scheduled appointment. This time I was led into a windowless interview room where two men waited. The first stiff-looking man, wearing a suit and a Nazi armband, was seated behind a desk, reading a set of completed forms in front of him. The second man, also wearing a suit and Nazi armband, sat in a chair beside the desk with a clipboard on his lap. Several filing cabinets stood along one wall of the room, and an empty chair stood in front of the desk. The men remained seated when I, a little nervous, entered.

"You are Fräulein Thielke?" the man behind the desk asked.

"Yes."

In an expressionless tone and with his eyes fixed on me, the man behind the desk said, "Good morning. I am Herr Keller. This is my assistant Herr Schröder. Please sit down." He motioned me to the empty chair. I sat down in the chair and tried to not look nervous.

"You are Kätchen Thielke from 52B Mozart Street in the Barmbek district of Hamburg?" Herr Keller continued.

"Yes, Herr Keller."

"Fräulein Thielke, on your passport application, you indicated you will be applying to immigrate to the United States. Why do you want to leave Germany?"

"My aunt in America needs help in her restaurant and has asked me to come there to help her," I responded.

"And what is her name?"

"Minna Siebold," I replied. I then noticed Herr Schröder writing this down on his clipboard.

"Are you Jewish?"

"No, Herr Keller."

"Are you a member of the National Socialist German Workers' Party?"

"No, Herr Keller. I'm a young girl. I don't know anything about politics."

"Surely you have participated in school in the parades and rallies of the National Socialist German Workers' Party."

"Yes, Herr Keller," I said as he eyed me suspiciously.

"And still you were not inspired to join the Party's youth organization, the League of German Girls?"

"I'm sorry, but politics don't interest me."

"Hmmm," he said with a frown.

"You do know, at least, Fräulein Thielke, who is the head of the National Socialist German Workers' Party, do you not?"

"Yes, Herr Keller. His name is Herr Hitler."

"And what do you know about Herr Hitler?"

"Nothing."

"Nothing!" he exclaimed in disbelief.

"I know nothing about him just like I know nothing about whoever he replaced and whoever was replaced before him."

"Surely you must know something about Herr Hitler!" he demanded.

After considering for a moment, I said, "He has an odd mustache."

This caused Herr Keller to clench his teeth severely. Fortunately, he was not a pipe smoker or he would have bitten off the stem. I noticed Herr Schröder bending down to pick up the pencil he had dropped.

Herr Keller stared at me intensely. Seeing the innocent expression, which I was trying to maintain, he began to believe I was telling the truth and had no brains at all.

He frowned again, exchanged exasperated glances with Herr Schroeder, and looked down at the information on my forms.

"You recently completed cooking school, I see?"

"Yes, Herr Keller."

"Who was your youth leader while you attended middle school?"

"Youth leader Klara Hoffman," I responded.

Every other month, we girls in cooking school participated in the larger Nazi parades wearing our armbands. Klara Hoffman was a proud and active Nazi in charge of forming up the girls from various trade schools in our area. I didn't think she would have anything bad to say about me, but I didn't really know her.

"And what will youth leader Hoffman tell us about you?"

"That I have been present at all events and have performed all my duties satisfactorily, I hope."

"And still you have no interest in our League of German Girls?"

"No, Herr Keller, I'm a young girl who likes cooking and dancing. The job in America seems like a good opportunity for me. That is all," I said with conviction.

After hearing this, Herr Keller looked me over for a long moment without expression.

"Thank you, Fräulein Thielke. I think that will be enough for today," he said finally. "If we have further questions, we will call you back. This office will be in touch with you. You may go now. Good day."

"Thank you. Good day, Herr Keller, Herr Schröder," I said when I got up, nodded to them, turned, and left the interview room.

Chapter 21
Preparations Complete

I BREATHED a great sigh of relief when I got outside on the street. Fortunately, Herr Keller had asked me what I knew about Herr Hitler and not what I thought about him. I don't know if I would have been as convincing responding "nothing" to that question.

He also had not asked me how I felt about the Nazi Party itself or of Jews. I was planning to say I was not interested in those things, but I wasn't sure if it would have raised their suspicions about me. So now I had to wait to hear from them.

I suspected they might investigate me, question my neighbors, teachers and classmates. I had not told anyone about Anna and Max. As far as I knew, none of the neighbors were aware of it either. But I didn't know for certain.

A number of the residents of our apartment building, who we didn't know, seemed to be nosy busybody types who are always snooping and thought it their duty to inform on others for anti-Nazi sentiment or activity. Such mean-spirited people were, in effect, the eyes and ears of the Gestapo and made the job of the secret police much easier. Good or bad, I would find out my fate when they called me back for my next appointment to the passport office.

My days were spent at work in the restaurant. It was easy to stay busy in the kitchen, which helped to make my days of waiting pass more quickly. Sometimes at work my mind would drift off thinking of Rolf. Then I would catch myself and get back to work before getting in trouble or ruining something I was preparing.

After the interview, I had no idea if they would give me a passport. It didn't seem to bother me. I still hadn't written to Rolf, and he had not written again to me. I supposed that he thought it might be easier for me to go if we weren't writing. Or he had possibly found someone else. I didn't know.

Two weeks later, I received a letter from the passport office telling me to come back in. It didn't say whether I was approved. I feared they had somehow found out about Anna and Max, and wanted to question me further. For all I knew, I might be handcuffed and taken off to a prison camp then and there. I went back to the passport office not knowing what to expect.

After waiting in line, the man in front of me finished, and I stepped forward. I uneasily handed him the letter and said, "My name is Kätchen Thielke. I have a letter telling me to come in concerning my passport application."

He took the letter, got a file from a cabinet behind him and turned back to me. I swallowed hard not knowing what to expect.

"Yes, Fräulein Thielke. Your passport has been approved. If you will wait a few minutes over there, we will call your name and take your picture."

Tears welled up in my eyes and I wasn't sure if it was from happiness I was not being arrested or from sadness that I could now leave the country and Rolf. After a momentary struggle, I collected myself and managed to get out some words, "Wonderful. Thank you."

The clerk was not sure what to make of my reaction, as he pointed to some chairs in the waiting area. "Wait over there please. We will call your name."

"Thank you," I replied and went to sit down.

They called my name after a wait, and I had to struggle again to compose myself for the picture. I received the passport in the mail two weeks later. The picture was awful as I expected it would be, but now I had my passport.

I had already received immigration paperwork from Aunt Minna. With my passport and immigration paperwork in hand, I went to the American Consulate in Hamburg to finish getting approval to immigrate. There were interviews, a medical exam, and some shots, but in a matter of weeks, I had an immigration visa stamp in my passport. All I needed now was the ticket to get there, so I sent Aunt Minna a letter to tell her I had been approved.

I could remember only a little of the English we learned in school. Since I now seemed to actually be going, I tried to work on my English skills at night in the apartment from a book checked out from the library.

I didn't know yet how much time I had before leaving, but I had resigned myself to go to America and try to make the most of it. I thought of Rolf, but we still had not written.

"What would be the point?" I said to myself.

One night in the apartment after dinner, Mutti and I talked as she washed dishes and I dried.

"Mutti, when I get to America, I can save up some money and send for you all."

"You just keep in touch and get your own life started there in America. You'll have enough of your own worries. In a couple years when Ruth graduates from school, we can look then into sending her over."

"Hopefully, the war will hold off until we can bring her to America too. I just hate the thought of leaving you and Vati here," I said, and we both hugged tearfully.

"I'll miss you," I continued. "Please take care of yourself and if things get bad here, go to live with Aunt Rosa in the country."

"We'll see. Just keep in touch. We will miss you too," she said.

A month later in May 1937, I received a letter from Aunt Minna with a ticket for the voyage to America, which seemed to be the final nail in the coffin. I didn't see any way out of going.

The ticket was for third-class passage on the steamship *Vancouver* leaving from Hamburg in six weeks. Soon I would be traveling to the other side of the world on the steamship *Vancouver.* At work, I found myself absentmindedly making V patterns in the sauces I stirred.

* * *

A month later at the crew barracks near the aircraft plant, Rolf sat on his bunk reading one of Kätchen's old letters. In his letter to her back in January, he had recommended she go to America. With a war coming, she would be safer there. He hadn't heard from her since. It was Kätchen's turn to write, and after five months, she still hadn't done so. He guessed she was upset that he had not wanted her to stay in Germany with him.

At first, he had been undecided whether to write to her again. He had chosen to wait to hear from her and now had waited too long. He couldn't imagine that writing now would do any good. There was no way Kätchen would forgive him at this point. He had asked about getting leave to see her and was told no. It was just as well, since she probably didn't want to see him anyway.

Rolf had no idea if Kätchen was going to America or if she was already there. In any case, she apparently wanted nothing more to do with him. She was the girl of his dreams, and he had lost her. He was mad that circumstances had deprived them of a life together. But most of all, he was unhappy and depressed at the thought of Kätchen hating him.

The guys had noticed and tried to cheer him up. Their advice had been to forget Kätchen, get drunk, and latch up with another girl. He hadn't taken their advice.

His only consolation now was that Kätchen would be safe in America. She would forget him and find happiness there. He willingly would sacrifice his own happiness for her safety. He would not have to live with his unhappiness for long anyway, since he probably would be killed in the war. The important thing was that she would be safe. He did not regret recommending for her to go to America.

Looking up sadly from the letter, Rolf watched the mail orderly walking along the bunks distributing mail, tossing letters on the various bunks. He stopped at Rolf's bunk, turning a letter over several times, examining it.

"Lucky you, Rolf," he said tossing it at Rolf's feet on the bunk.

Chapter 22
Saying Goodbye

ANNA WAS SITTING on her bed in her bedroom, quietly playing with a small doll. It was nighttime, and a lamp on a bed stand illuminated the room. She had stayed with her aunt and uncle for some time now since being found and helped by the nice people. The whole time, she had been kept inside in hiding, in case the police were still looking for her. She missed going outside and playing, but most of all she missed her parents. Her aunt and uncle had heard nothing from or about them.

Anna heard the bedroom door open. It was probably her aunt coming to tell her it was time to go to sleep, as she usually did about this time of the evening. She turned to look and saw two people in the dimly lit doorway.

"Mama! Papa!" she screamed as she leapt from the bed and into their arms.

"Anna, oh, Anna," was all her mother and father could manage to say as the three of them huddled together in the doorway, crying.

* * *

Over the months, Mutti had inquired periodically with her friend Johanna about Anna and Max. Her news about them was always the same. The children were doing well, and no news had been heard of the parents.

During Mutti's most recent trip to her sewing shop, Frau Zöllmer happily told Mutti the good news. Both Anna's parents and Max's parents were released and together again with their children. After their arrest, the children's parents had been tried and convicted in a closed court of inciting political unrest. The fathers were lawyers who had made the mistake of asking the whereabouts of a Jewish man who had been arrested.

After serving a ten month sentence in a prison camp named Dachau in southern Germany, they had been released, given passports and told to leave the country immediately. Now back together with their children, they would shortly be leaving Germany.

Frau Zöllmer told Mutti that the parents had been allowed no letters or visitors in prison. It was only after their release when they learned their children were safe with relatives. When they were told a non-Jewish girl had found and gotten them to safety, they were overcome with emotion and gratitude. They wanted very much to thank us in person, but thought it would endanger us, so they asked Frau Zöllmer to thank us for them.

Mutti and I were gratified to hear of their release and to have been able to help. She told her friend Johanna to please pass that on to the parents.

The weeks passed and the day of departure neared. Several days before my departure, I went to say goodbye to Frau Zöllmer at her sewing shop. Many times before, I had walked there to get materials for my mother. Arriving at her shop, I looked with disgust at the outside of it.

On the window of her shop was a big sign reading "Germans! Fight back! Do not buy from Jews!" Star of David symbols and the word "Jew" were scrawled many times on the outside walls. On some days, the brown shirted thugs stood out front to discourage people from going in. They weren't there this time. With a frown, I went inside.

Anticipating the anti-Jewish harassment and actions by the Nazi government would only get worse, Frau Zöllmer was also planning to leave. Her husband had contacted a cousin in Chicago in America to see if he would sponsor their family.

Frau Zöllmer had been a friend and business associate of my mother for many years. I knew her to be a good person and a good German. It was awful the way she and others were being treated. I wished her the best in her efforts to get away and said a sad goodbye. We hugged a last time, and I left.

On my way back home, I was passing under a row of linden trees along the street. I recognized it as the same spot where so many years before I had waved to the friendly little finch that was chirping to me. I had probably passed below these linden trees many times since. But it was only now when I was passing for the last time that I thought again of the little finch.

In the years since then, so much had changed in Germany. And in a matter of days, I would be leaving for good. Looking up in the tree, I searched its branches for one of the little finches. I was hoping again to see one and wave to it like I had done as a little girl. Only this time, it would be a wave of goodbye. But sadly I didn't see or hear one.

Even so, I waved a tearful goodbye to the little finch wherever it was. I suppose I was also thinking of Rolf as I did so.

Chapter 23
The Visitor

THE AFTERNOON before I was due to leave, Mutti and I were making final preparations. Ruth was trying to be supportive as she stood with us. Two of my outfits were spread out on the sofa, and I was trying to decide which one to wear in the morning. With my time of departure only hours away in the morning, I had sadly accepted my fate. I was leaving and would never see Rolf again.

"I like the brown outfit," Mutti said. "It's warmer and you may need it tomorrow. It'll be cool down on the docks and on the water."

"I guess you are right," I replied still sad and numb at the thought of leaving. "It's all the same to me. I hope I haven't forgotten anything,"

When we heard a knock on the door, we all looked up and at one another.

"I wonder who that is?" Mutti asked.

"I don't know, but I'll get it," I said, being the closest to the door. I opened it and gasped when I saw Rolf in his military uniform standing in the doorway.

"Rolf!" I said in surprise and delight.

"Kätchen," he said with a smile. Then we simultaneously rushed forward, embraced, and kissed. I was so happy to see him. I couldn't help but cry. We continued to hug as Mutti and Ruth looked on. A couple of curious ladies down the hallway had come out and started clapping. With a little embarrassment, we waved to them. Turning around, we saw Mutti and Ruth, both teary eyed and smiling, watching us too.

Mutti motioned for us to come in, and we both came in smiling, embarrassed, and happy. After Mutti and Ruth gave

Rolf teary hugs, Mutti quickly moved the outfits aside from the sofa and motioned for Rolf and me to sit down.

"Rolf, can I get you something to drink or eat?" Mutti asked. "You must have traveled a long way."

"No thanks. I'm sorry, but I can't stay long," he replied.

At seeing my disappointment, he explained to me, "I could only get away for a short time. I arrived here on a train only half an hour ago and I have to leave on a train three hours from now."

"Three hours!" I exclaimed. "You can't stay any longer?"

"I'm sorry, Kätchen. I came knowing I would only have a few hours. It was all the time I could get. But I wanted to see you before you sailed tomorrow."

"But how did you know I was sailing tomorrow? We haven't written in such a long time," I asked puzzled.

"Your mother wrote me a letter to let me know." With surprise, I looked at Mutti and she explained.

"We thought Rolf would want to know and would write you a letter. You've been so unhappy since you haven't been writing. Ruth suggested it."

Again surprised, I looked at Ruth. I stood up and went to her. She rose to meet me, and we hugged tearfully.

"You were so sad, Kätchen," Ruth said.

"Thank you, Ruth," I said, and I kissed her on the cheek. I don't think I could have felt any closer to her than I did at that moment. After another quick hug, I returned to the sofa with Rolf.

Mutti gleefully added, "But Rolf came in person instead. What a nice surprise. And doesn't he look handsome in his uniform."

Rolf smiled and looked down at himself. "Quite a change from a sawdust-covered cabinetmaker's apron, like before."

"Goodness, Rolf," Mutti said abruptly, rising from her chair, "you shouldn't be sitting here talking with all of us. You're here to see Kätchen and don't have much time to do it."

"Kätchen, you're all ready for your trip tomorrow," she continued. "Why don't you and Rolf go out together by yourself and get something to eat? Then Kätchen can see you off at the train."

"Yes, thank you, Mutti. I'd like that," I said.

"That's very thoughtful. Thank you," Rolf added.

"Okay, it's settled then. Oh, it's too bad Vati won't get a chance to see you again, Rolf. But you two need to get going," Mutti said as we all stood.

We all exchanged hurried hugs and goodbyes at the door before Rolf and I walked briskly away.

The streets were busy in the early evening as we walked arm in arm along Mozart Street. I was so happy to finally be with him again even if it was only for a few hours. We passed several cafes and drinking places. There would be many on the way to the train station, so we were in no rush to find a place to eat.

"Rolf, I'm not going to America tomorrow. If I do, I'll never see you again."

He pulled me aside, away from the passing crowd on the sidewalk, and said with firmness in a low voice, "Kätchen, there's a war coming. And you'll be much safer there. I couldn't tell you any details in the letter, but I see the preparations for war first hand every day. We aren't going to see each other anyway until it's over. If I'm not killed in the war..."

"Oh Rolf, don't say that! Besides, maybe there won't be a war."

"No, there will be a war. It's only a matter of when. The coming war is all they talk about in our training. Everything we do is in preparation for it. Germany will avenge the humiliation it suffered in the last war, win much-needed room for its people, and rule the world for a thousand years. They really believe all that stuff.

"Germany is building up a powerful air force, army, and probably navy too. Who knows what will happen? Hitler wants to take over Europe. The Englanders and French will try to stop him. Kätchen, there is definitely going to be a war here in Europe. America probably won't be in it, and I'll much feel better knowing you are safe there."

We then stepped back out onto the sidewalk and he continued in a gentler voice, "If I survive it, I'll contact you in America and we'll get together then. I don't know whether here or there, but somewhere. I don't know when either. It may be years. But someday, if I survive, we will finally be together."

"I'll wait for you, Rolf. And if you can't make it to America, I'll come back here."

"Then maybe we can marry and have a few kids," he said.

At this, we stopped walking and kissed. We were in the middle of the sidewalk with people passing by, looking at us in amusement. After our kiss, we began walking again arm in arm even more closely.

Seeing a promising looking café, we stepped inside. We sat across from each other holding hands, talking while we waited for our food. We talked about our regrets at not writing and caught up on things that had happened in the last six months. He told me again how he will feel much better with me safe in America.

"I hate the thought of my own family being here, but at least they are out in the rural countryside," he said.

"I told Mutti that they should all go to Aunt Rosa's in the country if things get bad," I said sadly.

"That's good advice. If they can't for some reason, then they might try going to my parents."

"I'll tell them.

"Ruth would be better off in America too," Rolf suggested.

"We are hoping to send her there in a year."

While at the table, I borrowed a pencil from the waitress and wrote down Aunt Minna's address on a napkin for him.

I don't remember what we ate. I don't think we ate much. I do remember the waitress flirting with Rolf. He did look very handsome in his uniform. After leaving the restaurant, we walked toward the train station stopping at a bench in a park on the way where we spent a few last romantic moments before leaving.

"I love you, Kätchen," he said during a tearful embrace.

"I love you too, Rolf," I replied and we kissed.

Later at the train station, he said sadly, "Kätchen, if I am killed, you have to be brave and go on without me. You'll have your whole life ahead of you. Just remember me and that I loved you very much."

Our parting at the train station was the parting of the young girl and her guy, which has happened a million times before. We hugged tightly one last time on the platform. Tears were rolling down my face. The train began to move. We kissed one last time before Rolf ran and jumped onto the doorway of the moving train.

I pulled out a handkerchief to dab my tears and had it in my hand as I waved goodbye to Rolf. He stood in the door of the train and waved back as the train moved away. It was a miserable moment for us just like it was for the million couples before us.

Somehow, I managed to find my way back to the apartment from the train station. They all were waiting for me when I arrived back home. They stood up when I opened the door, and Mutti came forward. Without taking off my coat, we sadly hugged without saying anything.

As Ruth watched, Vati came over and putting his arms around me, said, "It's too bad I missed Rolf. But you got to see him. That's the important thing."

Chapter 24
Departure

THE NEXT MORNING on the Hamburg docks, the weather was overcast with rain expected later in the day. Both the pier and the cargo ship were busy with activity. A boom up forward on the ship were busy with the last minute loading of cargo pallets from the pier into the forward hold of the ship. Sailors on the pier were getting mooring lines ready to be taken in. The ship's boilers had already been lit off in preparation for getting underway and their smoke was coming from the stack of the ship. Everything was proceeding in readiness for the ship's departure that July morning of 1937.

A long canvas with the ship's name *Vancouver* was hung on a gangway located forward on the ship. The first class passengers were already starting to come aboard there. Porters carried their trunks and bags. A ship's officer greeted them cordially when they stepped onto the ship.

Farther back, the ship's accommodation ladder was rigged to provide a portable flight of steps from the pier up to the main deck of the ship. Two trucks loaded with fresh food supplies were nearby on the pier. A working party was busy carrying boxes from the trucks up the ladder and onto the ship. The small crowd of third class passengers waiting on the pier would be boarding the ship on this ladder when the loading of supplies was completed.

With my old suitcase beside me, I stood with Mutti, Vati, and Ruth in the crowd of people on the pier. The ticket agent at the bottom of the ladder had informed us that boarding would begin soon. My ticket and passport with visa stamp had taken months to get. I held them in my hand as we waited for boarding to start. But, now at the last minute, I wasn't sure I could do it. I was feeling pretty nervous as Mutti watched me with a concerned look. Although sad at my leaving, my parents and sister were trying to look upbeat.

Shortly after the loading of stores was completed, the ticket agent at the bottom of the ladder announced it was time for third class boarding. At this, my legs suddenly got weak and wobbly.

"I know I told Rolf I would go, but I can't do it!" I said, frantically turning to Mutti.

"Yes, you can, dear," Mutti reassured me. "Do it for him and us. We will all feel much better knowing you're safer there if war should come like he says. We'll see about sending Ruth later too if we can."

"You should go, Kätchen. It may be a big help for us later to have you there. Think of it that way," added Vati.

"Don't worry, Kätchen," Ruth said. "I'll watch out for Mutti and Vati."

She was only fourteen years old and I could not help but smile through my tears at this as I hugged Ruth.

"I know you will, Ruth. Take care of yourself too. Goodbye."

"Goodbye, Kätchen."

After tearful hugs with Vati and Mutti, I struggled to say, "I'll miss you all so much."

"We'll miss you too," said Mutti with emotion. "Write to tell us how you are doing, what America is like, and if you need anything."

"I will. Goodbye." With that, I picked up my suitcase and walked to the short line at the bottom of the ship's ladder. The small crowd of passengers was being quickly checked in and walking up the ladder onto the ship. Mutti, Vati, and Ruth stood where I had left them, holding one another.

In the few minutes while waiting in line, I looked back at them several times and tried to show a brave face, even though I wasn't. Soon I was next. I set down my suitcase and handed the ticket agent my ticket and passport.

He checked them carefully, said everything was in order, and pointing to the ladder, welcomed me aboard.

I thanked him, picked up my suitcase, and stepped onto the ladder. It was a little shaky but not too bad. As I walked up, I turned, waved again to my family, and they waved back. I looked up and saw a number of sailors eyeing me and the other passengers coming aboard. At the top of the ladder an agent pointed me toward a hatch, which I entered.

Back on the pier, they watched as I disappeared into the hatch. Mutti choked back a cry as she felt the reality of my leaving. She buried her face in my father's shoulder as he patted her on the back.

"Oh, Gustav. Kätchen is really leaving us. We may never see her again."

"Don't worry, Mutti. She's grown up now and she should be leaving to start her own life. America is the best place for her now. She can always come back later if things look better here. Rolf may be wrong about war coming. Who knows."

"For now, we still have Ruth, at least for a little while until she grows up too," he said, putting an arm around Ruth's shoulders. Ruth and Mutti smiled at this.

Mutti daubed her handkerchief at her eyes and glanced forward on the pier. The loading of cargo forward was apparently complete. Several sailors were taking down the *Vancouver* sign from the gangway.

After putting my suitcase on my assigned berth in third class berthing, I returned outside onto the main deck, where I stood by the railing and waved again to my family below on the pier. I noticed another girl about my age in the nearby crowd on deck. She smiled at me. I smiled back but then returned my attention to my family.

I might never see them again and didn't want to take my eyes off them in our last moments together. The sight of them there standing together on the pier waving bravely to me would have to last me for a long time.

The sailors had rigged the accommodation ladder to be hoisted back onboard and were starting to raise it up off the pier. I had a sudden urge to run down it and get off while I still could. I must have been panting hard and looking faint.

"Are you all right, Fräulein?" the man beside me asked, clutching my arm.

I looked around at him, recovered a little bit, and said, "Yes, I think so. Thank you."

I took a few more breaths and looked again at my family on the pier. They must have seen me panicking and tried to give me reassuring looks and waves.

With the ladder back onboard, an officer high on the ship's structure forward was now rapidly calling out orders with a megaphone. The mooring lines were singled up. With a feeling of finality, I saw the sailors remove the gangway and lay it on the pier. More orders were shouted and the men on the pier began throwing the mooring lines off the fittings while the sailors onboard began hauling them in. The ship sounded a long deep blast from its horn.

When the ship began moving away from the pier, Mutti, Vati, and Ruth held one another closely as they waved and called goodbye. And I tearfully waved and said my last goodbyes to them. Steadily they grew smaller, and at last, they were out of sight. I felt an overwhelming sadness as I stood at the ship's railing numbly staring at the distant pier.

It was painful to be leaving them behind in their modest situation with the threat of war looming. I could only hope I could earn enough money in America in a few years so I could bring them over too. At the time, I had no idea how miserable their situation would become.

I wandered forward forlornly and stood by the railing watching the inbound ships pass by as we sailed outbound in the shipping channel of the Elbe River. Staring out, I thought back on the fond memories of my family and growing up in the place I was leaving.

Slowly, I became aware of activity around me. The crew was busy stowing gear and securing the ship for sea. Two sailors passed by and tipped their hats. I smiled back at them.

The girl, who had smiled at me earlier, came up with another girl who was also our age. They had noticed how sad I was and wanted to cheer me up. We walked along the main deck to the front of the ship where it was very windy. Although sad, I couldn't help smile and laugh a little at their antics and laughter as we huddled together in the wind, holding our skirts, and watching the ships pass by.

Back at the apartment in Hamburg that night, Ruth lay in bed. She had just said good night to Mutti and climbed in bed in her nightclothes. She had slept with me in the same bed for most of her life. Even though it was nice to have her own bed again, it felt empty to her. It was the middle of summer and a warm humid night. She didn't need the blanket. She and I had become close, and she would miss her big sister. She had caught Mutti crying earlier and had sat with her for a time.

As she lay there, Ruth pondered, "What if Rolf is right and there is another war soon?"

On the way back from the docks, she had asked Vati what happened to the people at home during the last war. He could not recollect hearing of any German cities being seriously attacked in the last war. The main suffering at home during the war was the separation from loved ones off fighting and then the devastating news that they had been killed or maimed. The war had taken a terrible toll.

As Ruth lay in bed, she heard the rain falling outside on the leaves of the trees. A cool breeze blew into her bedroom through the partially open window and she drifted off to sleep.

After thinking about Ruth's question further, Vati really couldn't say what the next war would be like here in Hamburg. The machines of war, like airplanes and tanks, their engines, and their weapons, were advancing so rapidly it would be hard to predict.

He had seen the death and destruction of war firsthand in the trenches of the last one, and was still amazed that he himself had not been blown to bits like so many others. Although he was not a praying man, he hoped and prayed that he would not see it again here with his family, should there be another war.

Chapter 25
The Vancouver

ON THE SHIP, we three girls became fast friends and were always together. We all were immigrating to America. The first girl named Magda was from Hungary and spoke broken German. She was a nice looking girl, a little shorter than me with dark hair and eyes. Magda was traveling by herself to America after saying goodbye to her family in Hungary. The second girl named Hanni was from Berlin and traveling with her mother and father.

After a brief stop the next day in Antwerp, Belgium, our ship headed westward for the English Channel on the first leg of its voyage across the Atlantic. We had heard that the thing to do on a sea voyage was to sit in deck chairs and get sun. Still being in northern latitudes, it was a little too cool for swimsuits, so we sat for hours on end on the lounge chairs in our dresses and talked about anything and everything.

The ship's crew, of course, had taken notice of a group of young girls onboard. They always seemed to be passing by where we were on deck and were always very friendly. We didn't flirt with them, but tried to be friendly.

On the second afternoon out, we were sitting in our lounge chairs. A sailor carrying a grease gun and some rags stopped to get acquainted. He had barely said hello and what a fine day it was, when we all heard a voice from above firmly say, "Back to work, sailor!" We all looked up with surprise to see one of the ship's senior officers above glaring down at us. The sailor quickly doffed his hat to us and departed, while the officer above continued to glare down at us.

We learned he was Senior Officer Schneider, the second in command aboard, the one responsible to the captain for the ship's operations and getting its daily work done. Apparently, he thought our presence onboard was distracting his sailors from their work. He may have even ordered his crew to stay away from us.

But we were doing nothing wrong, so we continued to do what you are supposed to do on a sea voyage, sun on deck in lounge chairs. We tried improving and practicing our English at times but not nearly as much as we should have.

It wasn't too long before sitting on deck in lounge chairs got old. There wasn't much else to do onboard, so we started exploring the ship. We were walking along a passageway on the upper decks when we came to a door with a "First Class Only" sign. The door was opened suddenly by a haughty well-dressed man, who was surprised to see us and looked down at us with distaste. In response, I threw my head back with my own haughty expression, and strode off. The others followed my example, and behind us, we heard him say, "Well!"

One of the senior engineers named Paul offered us the use of his stateroom during the day while he was down below in the engineering spaces standing watches and working. I'm not sure if he was feeling sorry for us, or if it was an attempt by Herr Schneider to keep us secluded and away from the crew. Either way, it was nice to have a private place to go during the day.

Hanni's mother was not thrilled about us girls being in a crewman's stateroom, but she consented if, in fact, the crewman was never there at the same time we were. The stateroom was small but had a small table with benches. A picture of Hitler in a dramatic pose stared down at us from the wall above the table.

Sometimes we would hear a knock on the door, and Hanni's mother would poke her head in to say hello, make sure we were safe, and see that no crewman was there with us. She would usually chat with us for a few minutes, feel reassured, and then leave.

Hanni, Magda, and I spent a lot of time during the day in the stateroom talking, reading, and playing cards.

"What will it be like living in California?" asked Hanni one day.

"I don't know. I'll be cooking in my Aunt's restaurant," I said.

"But surely you'll get time off?" Hanni asked.

"I suppose so," I said with a shrug.

"I'm going to the beach every day and see the movie stars there," Magda broke in. "They say in California, there are palm trees everywhere and it is always sunny."

Just then, there was a knock on the door and Paul, a middle-aged man in blue coveralls, poked his head in. "Sorry girls, but I've been up all night fixing a pump and I need to get some sleep. I need the stateroom."

As we quickly gathered up our things, Hanni asked, "Paul, we were just talking about California. You've been there. What will it be like when we get to San Francisco?"

Paul thought for a moment and said, "Well, let's see. This time of the year, it might be cool and foggy."

We all filed out past Paul with surprised looks.

The weather was good on our passage across the Atlantic toward the Panama Canal. We saw no land for weeks or at least it seemed like weeks. As the ocean swells rolled by, the horizon of sea and sky was an unbroken line in all directions.

Once we reached the tropical heat of the Caribbean, we were dismayed to find it was too hot to sun in our swimsuits on deck in the lounge chairs. Worse yet, our berthing spaces below became unbearably hot during the day. We needed to cool off in the ship's pool, whether we were a distraction to ship's work or not.

Being a cargo ship and not a cruise liner, the ship's pool was a temporary swimming pool installed on the main deck alongside one of the cargo hatches. It consisted of a waterproof canvas inside a twelve foot square wooden frame, which was about six feet in height. A ladder attached to one side enabled swimmers to climb up and get into it.

Certain hours of the day were the designated swimming hours for the first class passengers and other hours were designated for the third class passengers. We quickly noticed the first class passengers rarely used the pool. It was certainly not a very elegant looking pool. Maybe their staterooms were airy and well ventilated, and they didn't need the pool for cooling off.

We watched for days as the pool went unused during the hottest hours of the afternoon when it was designated for first class. On one particularly hot afternoon, Magda, Hanni, and I were sweltering in the heat and decided to risk it. We put on our swimsuits, grabbed our towels, and climbed up the ladders to the main deck. Seeing no one in the pool, we climbed in and started to paddle around.

Suddenly we heard, "What are you girls doing in the pool? This is the time for first class passengers to use the pool, not third class." It was Herr Schneider again. He had come out from the pilot house onto the bridge wing, seen us in the pool, checked his watch, and then hollered down at us.

We all looked up, and Hanni said, "We're sorry, Sir. We were just trying to cool off. No one else was using it." We all started to paddle toward the ladder to get out.

Meanwhile the ship's captain inside the pilot house had heard the exchange and had also come out onto the bridge wing. Herr Schneider continued, "Third class passengers are not allowed to use the pool during first class passenger hours."

In a calm voice, the Captain said, "Senior Officer Schneider, it's a hot day, and there's no harm in letting them swim if no first class passengers are using the pool."

Then down to us girls climbing out of the pool, "Go ahead and swim, girls. But you have to leave if any first class passengers come."

I waved and called back, "We will. Thank you, Captain." With a smile, the Captain returned into the pilot house, leaving Herr Schneider on the bridge wing furious and glaring down at us.

The embarrassment of having his orders publicly overridden by the Captain had totally infuriated him. We began paddling around in the pool again, but we felt more than a little uncomfortable when we would look up and see him glaring down at us.

Afterward, we tried our best to keep our distance from Senior Officer Schneider, but it seemed everywhere we went, we would look up and there he would be staring down at us.

During the ship's brief port visit to the island of Curacao in the Dutch West Indies, we girls went ashore with Hanni's parents and walked through the outdoor markets. We marveled at the strange Caribbean goods there for sale, but all I bought was a postcard, which I wrote out and mailed there.

It was a very hot and humid day when we started our passage through the Panama Canal. We stood along the ship's railing and watched the locomotives on rails pulling our ship through the locks. I chanced to look up, and there was Herr Schneider staring down at us.

But the real highlight of the trip was finally reaching the entrance to San Francisco Bay. The bridge across the entrance had recently been finished, and we were all out on deck looking up as we steamed beneath it into the bay. After nearly a month in transit, we were finally here.

Fortunately, the weather was clear and sunny, not one of the possible cool and foggy days. We could see the rolling hills of the city to the south, the many buildings, and the piers along the waterfront where we speculated the ship would be docking. Excited to soon be arriving, we had our things packed in preparation for leaving the ship. But soon, we saw a small ferry coming out to the ship, and the sailors began lowering the accommodation ladder over the side apparently to bring someone onboard. The ferry pulled up alongside the ladder and a man looking something like a policemen came onboard.

An agent from the immigration office, he collected all the immigrant passengers and our baggage on the main deck. It was basically all the third class passengers. Documents and passports were checked, and announcements made. We were told we would be boarding the ferry with the agent and not going on with the ship to the piers. Soon we were ready to debark and began filing down the ladder to the ferry.

Standing on the bottom platform of the ladder, I had my suitcase in one hand and was waiting for the person ahead of me to step onto the ferry. I looked up and sure enough, Herr Schneider was there above glaring down at me to the very last. This time, I glared right back, stuck my tongue out at him, and promptly stepped onto the ferry.

He was at first surprised, then reddened, and stormed off when a subdued laughter broke out among the crewmen who had seen me do it. I looked up a moment later from inside the ferry and didn't see him anymore.

Soon we were all on board, and the ferry shoved off from the ship. With all the trunks and luggage, it was fairly crowded onboard. Fogbanks or clouds hung on the hills back toward the ocean, but it was sunny and a little windy inside the bay on the water. The ferry pitched and cut through the choppy water.

I sat with Magda, Hanni, and Hanni's parents. We girls had not understood the announcements made earlier onboard the ship, so Hanni asked her parents about what was happening.

"Don't worry, girls," Hanni's mother tried to reassure us. "It won't be much longer. They are taking us to the island there, Angel Island."

She pointed to a large island to the north, which looked like a big hill jutting out of the water. "They will process us there before releasing us to our sponsors."

"How long does processing take?" asked Magda.

"I don't know. We hope only a few hours," Hanni's mother said with a little shrug. This news made us feel a little better.

"Just think," I thought to myself, "in a few hours I'll finally meet my Aunt Minna. I hope she is a sweet lady with spectacles like my Aunt Rosa."

We craned our necks and watched as the big hill jutting out of the water got closer and grew larger. Soon we could make out a pier and buildings on one side of the island.

Chapter 26
Angel Island

THE FERRY pulled up alongside the wooden pier extending out into the water in front of the buildings. With my suitcase in hand, I stood on the pier and looked around.

The island was mostly a dry and grassy hill with some trees along the lower elevations including some exotic-looking large trees of a kind I had never seen before. I learned later they were Eucalyptus trees. In front of the pier was a large white two-story stucco building with a tile roof. It looked well maintained with painted shutters on the windows, neatly trimmed lawn and shrubs, and a row of bushy palm trees. Magda was beside me with her suitcase.

"Look, Magda. Palm trees," I said nudging her and pointing. She smiled.

Other buildings of similar stucco style were close by on a hill to the left and also behind the main building. It was a very inviting, somewhat tropical scene, which gave me a very good first impression of my new country.

Several agents on the pier were directing the offloading of the people and luggage from the ferry. We were told to walk with our suitcases from the pier to the main building. Trunks and large suitcases, which couldn't be carried, were put into a storage building on the pier.

I looked back and saw another ferry pull up to the pier. Inside were what looked to be people from the Far East.

As we stepped off the wide wooden pier and onto the walkway to the building ahead, we girls looked at one another and smiled. It was our first step on American soil. Soon we would be on our way to meet our families and sponsors.

As we approached, we saw three entrances in the front of the building with labels of European, Japanese, and Chinese. We stood in line in front of our entrance as people ahead of us entered slowly to be processed.

While waiting, the immigrants from the ferry behind us came up and were directed to the Japanese entrance, which was the one nearest ours. The Japanese women were dressed in beautiful long silk dresses of a style very unusual to us. Their dark hair was elaborately styled on top of their heads with long jeweled pins to hold it in place. The men wore more western style suits. They talked to one another in their native language. We watched them with curiosity and marveled at their clothing, appearance, and language.

I noticed a young Japanese girl about my age in the line. She was patiently waiting and also noticed me. She blinked at me in a friendly way as if to say hello. I smiled and gave her a little wave. She smiled and gave a little wave back. Our line started to move forward, so I picked up my suitcase and entered the doorway.

Once inside, men and women were separated into different processing lines. The initial check and review of our paperwork didn't take long, and then there was an interview with questions about our plans in America.

Our hopes for being quickly released to our sponsors were dashed immediately when we learned we would next be given a medical exam and kept for at least one night of quarantine.

We were taken in small groups across the street to the hospital for the exams.

As we walked along the short path from the road uphill to their hospital's entrance, I looked around at the buildings. Steel mesh screens covered every window. The second large building behind and uphill of the main building had a steel mesh-enclosed stairway to its entrance. On the ends of the buildings were fenced-in enclosures where bored-looking men from the Far East stood about staring blankly out. When leaving the main building, we had passed through locked gates and security fences. It was beginning to feel like a prison.

I had already passed a medical exam back in Germany in order to get my immigration visa. Still, I was relieved when the doctor here also assessed me to be healthy, not wanting my release delayed by some unforeseen medical issue.

On the way back to the main building, I saw the Japanese girl who had waved to me. Her group of Japanese women were on their way to the hospital, and she gave me a cheerful smile as she passed.

Back at the main building, we made our way to the second floor landing where a woman guard sat in a chair. The landing had a locked door on each side and an open doorway toward the back. From the unpleasant odors I smelled, I guessed it was the communal bathroom.

The guard unlocked the door on one side, and we entered a small recreation room with a table and chairs, then a large bunk room filled with rows of three high bunk beds attached to large steel stanchions. Each bed was a steel pipe outer frame with a wire mesh screen stretched across it. On the steel mesh screen was a rudimentary mattress and pillow. About a third of the bunks were occupied by people lying in them or standing by them, talking and staying close to their possessions.

We picked our bunks and were issued bed linen and a blanket to us. If we needed to go to the bathroom, the guard on the landing would let us out to use the communal bathroom and let us back in. A guard will escort us down to the dining room during meal hours. The agent, who had taken our group around, then left. When I heard the outer door being locked again behind her, I turned to Magda.

"Well, Magda, this bunk room settles it. We are in prison! Are you going to go down to eat later? I'm not. I don't care how hungry I am. If I eat something, then I'll have to go to the toilet in that awful smelling bathroom. I got a whiff of it on the way in."

"They are going to let us leave tomorrow, aren't they?" Magda asked.

"I hope so," I said.

With no ladders or other furniture in the room, I climbed up the metal frames of the bunks to look at the mattress on my top bed. I sighed at the sight of it, but thought it was better than sleeping on the steel mesh. I was putting the linen on it when we heard the outside door unlock again.

Hanni and her mother came in with the next group, and I was happy to see them. They picked bunks near ours. I finished making up my bunk and Magda helped me hoist my suitcase up onto it.

Sitting on the bed with my suitcase, I looked around at the stark, uninviting room. In some places, the belongings of the immigrants were strewn about, and clothes were hung on lines strung between pillars. I could hear various languages, mostly ones that sounded eastern European. I saw a few families with little children.

I looked at Magda and couldn't believe how cheerful and contented she looked. She smiled at me, and I couldn't help but smile too.

"It's not so bad. We'll be out of here soon," she said.

"At least we're all together still," I said.

"Except for my father," Hanni corrected me. "He must be somewhere here in a men's bunk room."

"Probably," I said climbing down. I walked over to the open window and looked out through the wire mesh grate at the nearby building behind ours. So far, my life on American soil was not what I expected.

An escort came later to take us down to dinner. Although I wasn't eating, we all were required to leave and go down to the dining room. While the others ate, I refrained from doing so. I mostly sat observing all the different people. After returning from dinner, there was nothing to do. We played cards for a short time, then retired early to our crude beds.

Late that night, I was awakened by the sounds of pathetic crying. I lay awake and listened. The muffled crying and wailing in a Far East language were coming from the building behind us. I could hear it through the open window. I leaned over the side of the bunk.

"Magda, are you awake?"

"Yes, I can't sleep."

"Do you hear the crying?" I asked.

"Yes, it sounds like it's coming from the other building," Magda said.

"It sounds like the Far East people. Maybe they didn't pass their medical exams," I said.

"It's the Chinese. Their rules are different." said a nearby Polish woman, speaking German. "They may be here weeks, months, even years. The Chinese women weep a lot at night. One of the guards told me about it."

Magda gasped, "How terrible! One night in this place is bad enough. I can't imagine a month or a-"

Someone in the dark shushed us to be quiet and mumbled sharp sounding words in some Slavic language, so we quit talking.

I lay back in my top bunk and stared up at the dark ceiling. The muffled crying from the other building continued, but after a time I managed to fall back asleep.

Chapter 27
Aunt Minna

AFTER A LESS THAN restful night in quarantine, Magda, Hanni, her mother, and I were packed and ready to go early in the morning. We were escorted down to breakfast, where I just had a few sips of coffee.

At about nine in the morning, an agent came into the bunkroom with a clipboard and read a list of names. All of our names were called. Everyone called had to line up there in the bunkroom while a medical person walked by us doing one last cursory check of our health. We all passed and were approved to go.

Two hours later, I was locked arm-in-arm with Hanni and Magda, sitting in a crowded ferry bouncing across the bay to the landing on one of the piers in San Francisco. Hanni's mother and father sat next to us. We were all smiles and huddling closely one last time before having to say goodbye. After being constantly together since the first day of the voyage, we promised to write one another and get together periodically if we could.

We saw a small crowd of people waiting along the piers when our ferry approached. Several people on aboard recognized and excitedly waved to relatives in the crowd. Once tied up to the landing, we debarked with our luggage and were ushered from the landing, up some stairs and into an entrance to the immigration offices there on the pier.

We were led into a reception room where sponsors were waiting behind a wooden balustrade. At the front of our line, an agent checked our passports and paperwork, and then called the name of the sponsor. The sponsor was identified, brought forward, and their paperwork was also checked. If everything was satisfactory, a gate in the balustrade was opened, and the new immigrant was released to the sponsor. They hugged, cried, and laughed. But soon, they were gathering up their luggage and disappearing out of the building.

I looked at the crowd of sponsors there, I had no idea what Aunt Minna looked like. When it was my turn, the agent looked over my paperwork, seemed satisfied and called out my Aunt's name. A heavy-set, cross-looking woman wearing a lot of makeup emerged from the crowd.

Her paperwork was checked, proved to be satisfactory, and I was released to her. As we started to walked off, I looked back over my shoulder and waved goodbye to Magda and Hanni, who waved back.

With me hurriedly following, Aunt Minna hustled through the small crowd and out the building. Once outside, she stopped, turned around, and fixed her gaze on me as I caught up with her.

"Hello, Aunt Minna, how do you do?" I said in introduction.

"Oh, never mind that. I've had a devil of a time. Let's get going. We can talk on the way."

And with that introduction and greeting, she briskly ushered me from the pier and out to the street where automobiles were parked. I was carrying my suitcase, but managed to keep up with her. She wasn't in a very good mood.

"God in Heaven! You're a lot of trouble. Why didn't somebody tell me they would hold you there on that island overnight? I drove up here from San Carlos yesterday thinking I would pick you up when your ship docked. I found out they had taken you off to that island and wouldn't release you to me until today. Well, I gave them a piece of my mind. I'll tell you."

"I'm sorry, Aunt Minna, but I didn't know either."

"Something about some sickness reported on board, so everyone had to go through quarantine. A fine kettle of fish for me!" she continued to grouse. "I had to drive two hours back to San Carlos, get up this morning, and drive two hours up here again. That's a lot of gas, and wear and tear on my old car. And then there's the cost of food along the way. You'll have to repay me out of your wages."

"Yes, Ma'am," I replied.

* * *

Meanwhile, back in Hamburg in Gustav's favorite drinking place, several of his friends crowded around him at the bar looking at a postcard he held in his hand.

"Where is this place again, Gustav?" one of his friends asked.

"Curacao in the Dutch West Indies. Kätchen's ship made a port call there on her trip to America."

"It looks similar to our cities, not Mediterranean or tropical," one said.

"I thought the same thing," Gustav agreed. "It must be one of their main streets there that the Dutch tried to make look like a Dutch city. She said it was very hot there. It must be close to the equator."

"It's really pretty funny, isn't it, Gustav? You don't ever venture more than a mile or two from home, and your daughter travels half way around the world," his friend mused.

"How true, Bruno. If it hadn't been for the war, I probably would have never made it outside of Hamburg itself," Gustav laughed.

"Ah yes, it was like a paid vacation for you, a chance to travel and see the world. How lucky you were to see lovely France."

Choking on his beer at this, Gustav replied with spirit, "Sure, sure, the only lucky thing about that vacation was that I made it back! No, no. I'm content here in Hamburg and plan to stay. I've no need to see any more of the world. Thank you."

Looking again at the postcard, Gustav continued, "Not like my Kätchen. We received this in the post yesterday, and it took a long time getting here. I think she might already be there in America. She may already be working at her aunt's restaurant, serving the inferior beer they drink over there."

Another one of Gustav's friends, Herman, mused, "It's a shame we're exporting our German girls out of Germany. It should be just all the Jews. Why would she want to leave?"

Not liking the tone of the question, Gustav shot back, "Believe me, she was sad enough to leave. She has a boyfriend here in the Luftwaffe and everything. She's just adventurous and wants to make the most of an unexpected opportunity."

Herman continued, "We have plenty of opportunities right here, especially since the economy is so good. Seems like a long way to go for an opportunity."

Gustav bristled at this and started for Herman, but was restrained by his friends, "Now see here, Herman. Don't you be suggesting anything unpatriotic about anyone in my family! I've done my share of bayonet work in the war and she's done nothing wrong!"

Bruno stepped in to calm things down, "Calm down, Gustav. I don't think Herman meant anything by it. Did you, Herman?"

"Nah. Buy me a beer, Gustav and we'll forget about it," he said with a smirk.

As Gustav's rage subsided, he continued to stare at Herman without saying anything.

Putting the postcard back in his pocket, he finally said, "You're always looking for some excuse for me to buy you beer. Well, buy your own damn beer, Herman. I've had enough for today."

He drained the remaining beer in his stein, turned, and left as the others watched in dismay. On his way home, Gustav was fuming and swore he would never go back again.

Less than a week later, his friend Bruno found him and asked him if he would come back. His friends at the bar had been unhappy with Herman and had chastised him for his behavior.

Herman had not taken it well. After a day or two of sullen drinking, he had announced he didn't feel welcome anymore and was going to find another place to drink. Herman was expecting to get apologies and regrets, but instead, Bruno promptly went to the door, opened it, and with a sweep of his arm, beckoned him to do so. At seeing this, Herman banged his beer stein down on the bar, stomped out, and never returned.

So Gustav rejoined his friends at the bar, and the episode provided them with yet another story they could tell over and over again.

* * *

Back in the streets of San Francisco, Aunt Minna and I hustled along the sidewalk. I was thinking about what she had said about sickness on the ship. I didn't recall any. I began to suspect Herr Schneider might have been behind it. Maybe as a last swipe at us girls, he had reported some sickness onboard to cause us to spend a night in quarantine and spoil our arrival. Or maybe I was giving the unpleasant man too much credit.

My thoughts were suddenly interrupted when Aunt Minna abruptly veered off the sidewalk to the driver's side of a black four door sedan parked along the street.

"Here's the car. Throw your suitcase in the back seat and climb in the front."

I was a little surprised by this. Back home I had seen other people like chauffeurs open car doors, but I had never opened a car door or ridden in a car myself. These door handles were different than the ones back on the truck at the dairy farm. I fumbled with the door handle for a moment and managed to get it unlatched. I opened the door carefully and put the suitcase on the seat. It took two slams of the door to get it to close and latch.

"Good grief. What's taking you so long?" Aunt Minna asked impatiently.

I next worked the handle on the front door and opened it. I climbed in and pulled it closed. It took another two tries to get it fully closed. I then adjusted myself in the seat and looked all around inside. By now, Aunt Minna was revving the engine and looking over at me.

"Land Sakes. Haven't you ever been in an automobile before?" she asked.

"No, I've been in a dairy truck, but this is my first time in an automobile. It's very nice," I replied.

With an incredulous look at me, she jammed the car into gear and revved the engine again. With her head out the window and her arms waving at the traffic, she pulled out in front of a large truck whose driver slammed on his brakes to avoid hitting her. For some reason, he and other drivers were honking their horns a great deal, but Aunt Minna ignored it.

She made a few more determined maneuvers, which resulted in more horns. Soon we seemed to be finished with our turns, and things were somewhat calmer. We drove along a wide busy street with street cars, buses, and more cars than I had ever seen before. And they all seemed to be honking at Aunt Minna as she swerved through the traffic. We pulled to a stop at a red light, and she looked over at me.

"Well, you have good looks and a good figure. That's good. There's a lot of construction going on in San Carlos down below the restaurant, and the men stop by at lunch. Your job is to be friendly to them. It keeps them coming back, and you get good tips out of it. Now mind you, you only get half of your tip money."

The light turned green, and she took off.

I didn't know what tips were and was surprised to hear that I wasn't just the cook.

"Aunt Minna …"

"Ma," she interrupted, "everyone calls me Ma. You may as well too."

"Okay, Ma, then. I thought you needed a cook?"

"Sugar, I got a small place. You'll be doing cooking and everything else too, just like me. I'll be behind the bar mostly though. You'll have to bartend too sometimes. I got a part-time Mexican kid named Pepe who does some cleaning, but you'll have to do clean up too."

"Where will I stay?" I asked.

"I set up a room for you in the back of the place."

"Ma, I just wanted to say that I do appreciate you bringing me here and sponsoring me. I'll try to be a good worker for you."

I saw for the first time just a hint of kindness in her face when she replied, "I think you'll like it here. It should work out well for both of us. You know about the $125 price of your ticket. There also was about a $100 of other expenses too."

"Oh?" I said with a little surprise, not being aware of any other expenses to be repaid.

She continued, "Let's see, I pay you $25 per month to work for me, so it'll take you nine months to pay me back. You should be practically running the place by then. Afterward, I'll continue to pay you $25 per month."

"I guess that will work," I said, although it was longer than I was expecting. If I didn't like working for my aunt, I would find another job when my nine month obligation to her was completed. I thought of my family back in Germany. There would be little I could do for them for some time.

"So, Kätchen, tell me something about yourself."

I told her about my family and growing up in Hamburg, while she listened with interest and drove.

Two hours later, we pulled up in front of Aunt Minna's restaurant. It was a simple looking single-story stucco building not much bigger than a house.

Very few other structures were nearby, just open, rolling, grass-covered green hills with a few lines of the large Eucalyptus trees nearby and farther back on the hills a dense clump of some kind of large coastal evergreen tree.

Across the length of the front of the building was a tile-roofed overhang with archways supported by spiraling pillars. A concrete area in front with an awning-covered walkway extended to the sidewalk.

No sign saying something like "Minna's Restaurant" was on the building. The only sign was a wooden sandwich board-like sign standing in front by the curb.

The little place was located about halfway down the San Francisco peninsula and situated on the bay side of the coastal mountains in the hills above the town of San Carlos. The restaurant faced eastward with a panoramic view of the south bay and the growing towns along it. It was a warm clear sunny afternoon, the kind of California weather we had heard about.

Several main highways and a railway could be seen running north and south between the towns along the bay. Clumps and lines of large Eucalyptus trees dotted the scene below. Large areas of orchards filled some places between the towns. A scattering of stucco and tile-roofed houses down the hill were the outskirts of San Carlos.

When we arrived in front of the restaurant, I stepped out of the car and stood admiring the very scenic vista, trying to take it all in for the first time. Aunt Minna saw me and said, "We do have a nice view here. Get your suitcase and I'll show you to your room. If you're hungry, I'll get you a sandwich."

"I have to admit, I'm pretty hungry. I haven't eaten in over a day. The island where we spent the night was like a prison. I didn't eat or drink anything, so I could avoid using their bathrooms. A sandwich sounds really good to me. Thank you."

"Okay, follow me."

Chapter 28
The Restaurant

AUNT MINNA put me to work soon afterward and seemed determined to get her full measure of work for the $25 per month she was paying me. The wooden sign in front of the restaurant said "Dutch Lunch, Daily Dinner Specials, Buffalo Beer on tap and by the bottle, Liquor, Wine, Coca Cola."

I soon learned how to prepare a "Dutch Lunch", the main item served at lunch. It was a very simple meal consisting of a plate of meat and cheese slices, a plate of tomato and onion slices, a plate of bread slices, and small dishes of mustard and mayonnaise.

It provided the fixings to make several sandwiches. Of course, a big glass of cold Buffalo beer was needed to wash it down. It was a popular meal and easy to learn to prepare.

Aunt Minna was also beginning to serve another item for lunch called a hamburger sandwich, which was a round ground beef patty cooked on the grill and served on a sliced round bun with mustard and diced raw onions on it. I tasted one and liked it. I had never heard of or tasted a hamburger before, even though I was a Hamburger from Hamburg myself.

It wasn't long before I gave up trying to call my aunt "Ma", which sounded so unnatural to me. I began calling her "Aunt Minna" again, and she didn't seem to mind. She didn't speak much German anymore and wanted me to learn better English, so she spoke only English with me.

Aunt Minna would show me how to make a dish, and I would watch and take a few notes if needed. Although my English wasn't very good yet, I soon was able to prepare all the evening daily dinner specials such as roast beef with mashed potatoes. There were soups to be made from the previous day's leftovers as well as desserts. I was surprised at how different American food was from German food, and that Americans didn't eat sausage. My favorite dinner special was meatloaf, the one most like sausage.

I met the hard-working twelve year old Mexican boy named Pepe who came in part-time to clean. I would look up from my work, see him coming out of the bathroom with a bucket and mop, and say hello.

"Hello, Señorita. I have finished cleaning the bathroom. It is muy clean. You could eat off the floor. Now I will sweep in here," he would say grinning.

I would smile even though I didn't yet understand everything he said.

After a week or so of mostly cooking in the kitchen, Aunt Minna wanted me to start learning to wait on tables and interact with customers, in order to learn that part of the work as well as to improve my English. As you can imagine, I was a little nervous.

"Hello, my name is Kätchen, what can I get for you?" I had to practice over and over.

Aunt Minna wanted me to be sure I understood their orders, so I would repeat the order back to the customers to make sure I had it right. She also told me if people are making conversation that I didn't understand, the thing to do was smile and say "yes" in response.

The next day a little before lunch, I was in front of the bar with an order for a soda from a customer. Aunt Minna started to get it, but stopped when she saw a regular customer named Danny walk in. She turned toward him when he came to the bar.

"Hi Ma, I'll have my regular."

"Sure, Danny. Where have you been?"

"Out of town on a job. I'm in kind of a rush, Ma."

Aunt Minna nodded and walked back into the kitchen. Looking over at me, he perked up and sidled over beside me.

"Hey baby, where have you been all my life?" he cooed.

After a moment thinking about the words, I finally understood the question.

"I have been in Germany," I replied.

"Ha, ha, that's pretty funny. I like a girl with a sense of humor. How about you and me, baby, hop into my set of wheels tonight and do a little necking overlooking the breakers?"

Understanding almost nothing of what he said, I looked around for help from Aunt Minna, but she was still in the kitchen. Following her instructions, I smiled and said, "Yes."

"Great! When do you get off?"

"Get off?" I asked in confusion as I got up to get the soda myself.

"Yeah, when do you get off? When are you done working tonight?" he persisted.

"Oh, when I done working tonight," I said finally understanding.

"Yeah, when are you done working tonight?"

"Eight o'clock," I replied, not knowing why he asked.

"Lookin' forward to it," He said with a wink.

I didn't understand this statement either, so I smiled and said, "Yes."

By now, I had the soda I needed. Aunt Minna came back in and put a sack and a bottle of beer on the counter in front of him.

"All ready, Danny," she said.

"Thanks, Ma," he said putting a dollar bill on the counter.

"See ya." he said, turning to me.

I looked at him uncertainly as I paused with the soda at the bar and imitating him said, "See ya."

With a confused look about what just happened, I headed with the soda back to one of the tables.

That night at closing time, Danny came in and sidled over to where I was cleaning up.

"Hey baby, I'm ready whenever you are."

"Ready? Ready for what?" I asked.

"Ready for a little drive and to make a little love."

"What? I cannot go for drive," I said,

"But you said at lunch you wanted to go?"

"What? I said that? I did not understand. I'm sorry, but I cannot go for drive," I replied with surprise.

"Sure you can, baby. All you have to do is climb into the car. It's not hard."

I looked up and saw Aunt Minna watching and listening. She was motioning her head for me to go with him.

"No, I'm sorry. I cannot go, but thank you for the good offer," I said, having no intention of going.

At this point, he could no longer contain himself and started to chuckle.

"Gotcha! I knew you didn't understand. I just thought I'd come up and see if I could talk you into it," he said pointing at me and laughing.

"I don't understand," I said.

"At lunch, I knew you did not understand. I am joking with you," he said, speaking the words slowly.

"Oh, you are playing a joke with me?" I said finally understanding and smiling with relief.

"Yes, but I'd still like to take you for a ride. Let's go."

"No, I'm sorry. Maybe some other day."

"I'll hold you to that," he purred.

"Hold me to that?" I asked, not understanding.

"Yes, I'll take you up on that."

"No, I cannot go up with you on that. Not tonight. Maybe some other day."

"Okay," he said, throwing his hands up with a laugh of frustration.

"Okay," I said imitating his farewell. He waved to Aunt Minna and left.

When Danny was gone, Aunt Minna came over to me.

"Why didn't you go with him? Remember, you are supposed to be good to the customers. Keep them coming back."

"What? I'm supposed to go with customers and make them happy so they come back? What does that mean? Am I supposed to sleep with them too?"

"Well, that probably wouldn't hurt business either," she said with a sly smile.

After considering this statement and determining that I had understood her words correctly, I was not happy.

"Aunt Minna, you brought me over here, and I appreciate it. I'll pay you back in full. I'll do good work for you, be good for your business, be friendly to the customers, but I'm not dating or sleeping with them. That's not part of the bargain."

"Relax. Don't take things so seriously. You're young and don't know much yet. You'll learn there are easier ways to get ahead in life."

To the parts of this statement that I understood, I had no reply. I just sighed and returned to my cleaning.

Later in my room, I read and reread my letters from Mutti. I had none from Rolf directly. He thought it would be unwise to exchange letters directly with me in America.

He suspected it would get him in trouble with the Nazi officials who read and censored mail.

So he wrote to Mutti, and she would include his news and well wishes into the writing of her letters to me. Going in the other direction, she would pass on my news to him in her letters, carefully avoiding the mention of my being in America. It was cumbersome, not very intimate, and took longer to hear from each other, but we thought it was a worthwhile precaution for avoiding trouble.

It wasn't long before I started getting used to my new country, and my English improved. The Americans seemed like nice people. I found it wasn't hard being friendly to the customers. After all, tips were the only pocket money I earned while paying back my aunt.

I told my family how the Americans put money on the table when they leave. The money, called a tip, is thanks for good service. Their reply was, "Why would they do that?"

One busy evening with music playing on our radio, I was returning from a table with the pitcher of water. A young man passing by suddenly swung me and my pitcher around and danced a few steps with me to the lively tune that was playing. I managed to extricate myself from his clutches and wagged my finger at him as I backed away and returned with the pitcher to the bar. No, it wasn't hard being friendly to the customers. I just wasn't as friendly as my aunt wanted me to be.

I stood for a moment at the bar and looked over the scene in the restaurant of people eating and drinking. They seemed to be having a good time. I had never been around Americans before. They seemed to like music, but Germans drinking in a bar like this would be singing together. The Americans didn't sing together, and I missed it.

Chapter 29
Rolf Was Right

BACK IN HAMBURG, Cousin Willie pushed on the apartment door and stood in the doorway weaving as it swung wide open. He stood there in a stupor with his blue eyes half open and blood-shot before taking a few halting steps into the apartment. It was three in the morning, and Aunt Margarete had fortunately left a living room light on.

He was seeing several blurry sofas ahead. Willie picked the middle one and weaved his way toward it. He plopped down on it and was instantly snoring loudly. Mutti had heard him come in and came out from the bedroom.

She saw the door still wide open and stepped quietly over to close it. Going over to Willie on the sofa, she straightened him out a little, took off his shoes and then put the nearby blanket on him.

"Silly boy," she thought, "at least you found your way back and didn't end up on a park bench this time of the year."

She looked him over for a moment and returned to the bedroom. It was early December 1937 and Cousin Willie had made it back again this year for a visit during the Hamburg Dom Winter Fair.

When Willie woke up late the next morning, he had a splitting headache and a dry awful taste in his mouth. He raised himself up and sat on the sofa with his head in his hands. Finally opening his eyes, he discovered he was looking down at two feet standing in front of him. He looked up, and there was Mutti with a glass of water.

"Oh", he said, "thank you, Aunt Margarete, I need it." He took the glass and downed the water.

"You probably could use some breakfast and some coffee too. We have some bread and marmalade or the meats you brought."

"No, no…" he started, then grabbing his head, saying, "Oh, my head." After a moment, he continued, "No, those meats are for you. I'll take some bread and marmalade though and the coffee."

"Okay, come on over to the kitchen table. Uncle Gustav and Ruth are already gone. You were out pretty late last night."

"Yes, I ran into some girls. I was buying the beer, so they wanted to party all night. Of course they were very friendly too. There haven't been enough drunken sailors around Hamburg lately, so I was just trying to do my part," he said with a grin.

"Okay stop. I don't think I want to hear anymore. But one more question, did these girls steal your money like they normally do the drunken sailors?"

At this, Willie suddenly sobered up. He fumbled through his pockets finding nothing. "Damn," he said. He frantically looked around for his shoes. Finding them on the floor near the couch, he searched with his hands inside of each one, finding nothing and then tossing them back down on the floor.

"Damn!" he said with exasperation, looking up. "They got it all."

"Were you looking for this?" Mutti said, pulling some folded bills from her pocket and holding them up.

Seeing the bills, he let out a sigh of relief and reached up.

"They fell out of one of your shoes last night when I took them off," she said handing the money to Willie.

"Thank goodness, I still have money to get home. I almost had to borrow some."

"Willie," Mutti said, "when will you learn?"

"I was just having a little fun, blowing off a little steam, Aunt Margarete," he said looking bleary eyed and running his fingers through his messed up hair. "I need to. Things are crazy at the Junkers plant. We're under great pressure to have Stukas rolling out of the factory every day."

"Stukas?" Mutti asked.

Willie slowly stood up and started to make his way unsteadily toward the kitchen table.

"Yes, Stukas. It's an airplane, a dive bomber. We're building them for the Luftwaffe. It's funny. It used to be so hush, hush, but now they bring foreign diplomats into the plant for tours. I guess to impress or scare them. The plane dives really well."

He paused a moment thinking, then continued, "Maybe too well. If a pilot pulls back too hard when he comes out of the dive, the blood is forced down from his brain. Then he passes out and crashes. We're working on a way to keep it from happening."

Mutti listened as she brought the bread and marmalade to the table. "Oh, my goodness. And are you making a lot of these dive bombers?"

"Our plant is working full time producing them, and we have hundreds on order. We're also working on a medium range bomber, but it isn't in production yet."

Mutti was carrying a cup of coffee to the table, but stopped with a look of dismay.

"Oh, dear. It's true then. It sounds like Rolf is right. We are preparing for war."

"It would seem so," Willie said matter-of-factly, sitting down at the table. His head was throbbing terribly as he stared down at the food in front of him.

Chapter 30
My Sponsor

AT AUNT MINNA'S restaurant, business in the evenings had picked up since my arrival. I'd like to think my cooking had something to do with it. I tried hard to make sure the cooked meats were tender not overcooked, and the potatoes were buttery. A few extra seasonings added here and there made the dishes even tastier.

The customers seemed to like my cooking and friendly service, and were coming back more often. Business on Friday and Saturday nights got so busy that Aunt Minna decided to hire another girl part time to help out on those nights.

The girl named Olive was a good worker and friendly with the customers. Although I got along well with her, we never became close friends. Even though we were about the same age, I think she thought of me more as a boss than a co-worker. I wanted to tell her to "du" me instead of "Sie" me, but the English language didn't provide for it.

I began to realize that just like Aunt Minna had predicted when I arrived, I was pretty much running the place already.

One afternoon after our lunch rush, I was clearing dishes and wiping tables. I looked over at the well-dressed English gentleman with a large mustache that stuck straight out on each side. He was sitting by himself at a table, sipping tea, smoking his pipe, and reading a newspaper.

The gentleman, Percy Smyth-Haverlock, was an old friend of my aunt and a regular here in the afternoons. He was a very congenial man who always had some interesting story to tell. He had told me early on to call him Percy, so when I sauntered over to his table, I said, "Hello Percy, how are you doing? Can I get you anything?"

"Why yes, my dear. I could use another pot of your fine tea and a few cookies to go with it. I say, Kätchen, I believe you are the only one in this otherwise lovely area who knows how to make a proper pot of tea. One has to get the tea pot very hot before adding the hot water and tea. Yes, one must heat the pot properly first. That's the ticket. Good girl. Yes, yes, another pot will do nicely."

"Coming right up," I said, smiling at his praise. Back in the kitchen, I put a big kettle of hot water on for the tea. Meanwhile, Percy sat contentedly reading his newspaper and smoking his pipe.

Percy had known my Aunt Minna for many years, even back in South Africa. He told me in the strictest confidence that before immigrating here to America she ran a house of prostitution there. That bit of information certainly explained a lot for me.

As we had promised, Magda, Hanni, and I kept in touch. Aunt Minna's restaurant was closed on Sundays, so we were able to get together occasionally on Sundays when I was free. We tried to meet at a café near a park where we could walk and hike.

At our first meeting, Hanni told us that she and her parents were Jewish and had left Germany before things became worse. They had sworn her to secrecy during the voyage as a precaution, not wanting anything to ruin their departure from Nazi Germany. I told her that her parents had been very smart to leave.

When we wanted a break from talking and catching up on one another's experiences, Hanni and I would sing our old favorite German folk songs and Magda would join in too. Growing up, we school girls would take field trips to the parks and forests, where we would sing folk songs like *Waldeslust* (*Love of the Woods*).

In the arid climate of California, the woods in the parks were Eucalyptus groves. So we three young girls would stroll arm-in-arm along a dusty path though the Eucalyptus trees singing *Waldeslust*, which must have seemed pretty odd to other people there in the park.

As the end of my nine month obligation to my aunt neared, I began to think about what I should do. While my aunt had treated me well, we had had our differences and had never really become close. I would never be able to accumulate much money working at her restaurant for $25 a month plus half of my tips. Being an independent sort, I wanted to strike out on my own.

One night after the evening rush, only a few couples were sitting at the tables drinking and talking. Aunt Minna was sitting behind the bar looking at a magazine, and I was sitting on a stool in front of the bar. I decided it was a good time to broach the subject.

"Aunt Minna, my nine months here are over in two weeks. You'll be paid back then."

At hearing this, Aunt Minna gazed up from her magazine with a look of concern.

"Yes, I guess that's true. You've been a good girl, Kätchen. So I'll start paying you $25 per month. I think that's what we agreed before."

I stared down at the bar and didn't say anything. She watched me, rose from her chair and said, "Okay, you've learned quite a bit since you started here and you've proved to be a good cook. I guess you deserve a raise. Let's make it $25.75 per month. That's a three percent raise after less than a year, which seems to me more than fair in these times."

She grew more concerned when I still didn't answer. Finally I said, "Aunt Minna, I appreciate what you have done for me, but now that I've finished paying you back, I want to start out on my own."

"What? Why would you want to do that?" she blurted out. "Haven't I been good to you? Didn't I go through a lot of trouble to bring you over here?"

"Yes, you've been good to me, Aunt…" I started.

"Well then, you should show a little gratitude and stay here!" she interrupted with an angry tone.

I started over, "Yes, you've been good to me, Aunt Minna. I'm just saying I want to get out on my own. You have Olive working here part time now. You can put her on full time."

With anger, "Have you forgotten I am your sponsor? Do you know what that means? That's like a guardian. It means I'm responsible for you until you're an adult, and you have to do what I say until then. If you don't, I can have you sent back to Germany!"

As I stared at her in speechless surprise, she added in a more soothing tone, "Now don't make me do something like that, something I don't really want to do."

With anger, I shot back, "That's not right. I was to work for you until I paid you back. No one said I'd have to work for you until I'm twenty one. I just turned nineteen. That's two more years!"

Still in her soothing tone, she added, "I'm sorry, dear, but that's what it means. Now don't get all worked up. It'll be good for you. Just two years, then you can start out on your own. You'll thank me then for keeping you on here. You'll see."

At this point I had nothing more to say. My broaching of the subject had not gone well. This was the first I had heard that she could send me back to Germany if she wanted. I turned away from her feeling very vexed. I decided it would do no more good to argue with her. I needed to find out if what she said was true.

Two days later, I told Aunt Minna that I needed the afternoon off to see a doctor about a pain in my side that was bothering me. She consented but reminded me to be back in time to prepare foods for the dinner menu.

In fact, I had no pain in my side. With a determined look, I climbed on a bus and headed north to visit the Immigration Office on the pier in San Francisco, where I had first met Aunt Minna. After a number of bus transfers, I finally made it.

Walking into the waiting room of the immigration office, I was surprised to find it uncrowded and quiet. To a woman at a desk behind a counter, I said, "Hello, I recently emigrated here from Germany and I have questions concerning my sponsor's controls over me."

The woman replied, "I take it you don't have an appointment?"

"No, Ma'am, I don't."

"Just a minute. Mr. Winston should be able to answer your questions. I'll see if he's available. What is your name?"

"Kätchen. Kätchen Thielke," I said.

She returned in a minute, informing me, "Mr. Winston will be able to see you in about fifteen minutes. Why don't you have a seat until then?"

I thanked her and took a seat. Fifteen minutes later in Mr. Winston's office, I told him my situation. He answered my questions with ease as if reading from a prepared script. Apparently, I was not the first immigrant to ask about sponsor controls. It seemed to be human nature for sponsors to try any means to keep their cheap labor working for them.

Aunt Minna had not told the truth. As my sponsor, she was only responsible for supporting me financially should I not have my own income. She had no control over me and could not have me sent back to Germany. I was relieved to hear that answer, but at the same time I was disappointed to find Aunt Minna had lied to me.

When I arrived back to the restaurant that evening, Aunt Minna was mad at me for getting back so late. She had needed to prepare dinner by herself in my absence. I told her I was sorry my doctor's appointment had taken longer than expected.

I helped out with dinner as if nothing was different, but she must have sensed that something was amiss.

"Your side doesn't appear to be hurting?" she asked pointedly.

"Yes, it turned out to be nothing," I replied without explaining further.

She quickly forgot about being mad at me and seemed to be watching me expecting something more was about to happen, the other shoe about to drop, so to speak.

During the slow time after the dinner rush, I told Aunt Minna where I had been and what I had found out.

She was, at first, dumbstruck and then expressed regret for saying what she had said. In the heat of the moment, she had said the first thing to come to her mind, not knowing if it was true. She was using the old ploy that if you say something loud enough and with enough conviction, people will believe it. I had been a big help to her, and she was only trying to keep me there.

After hearing her, I wasn't mad at her anymore. I told her I would stay on an additional month to give her more time to get ready for my leaving. While we were different people, I did appreciate what she had done for me. So, we parted on good terms in the end.

Ten months after arriving at my aunt's restaurant, I emerged from the front door carrying my suitcase. Aunt Minna, Olive, Pepe, and a few regulars followed. I said my goodbyes, hugged Aunt Minna, waved goodbye, and began walking down the road. Aunt Minna waved and sadly walked back inside.

Chapter 31
Bomber Duty

THE TWO ENGINES of the German Luftwaffe plane roared as the Heinkel-111 bomber taxied along the concrete taxiway and turned toward the unloading area in front of the supply building at the airbase.

Following the directions of the ground crew, the pilot taxied to a designated spot, stopped, and killed the engines. As the engines sputtered to a stop, a hatch opened on the bottom of the plane's fuselage back under the wings. Legs appeared, and a crewman crawled out. It was Rolf.

Without much room under the plane and the wings, Rolf was stooping low when he moved forward to talk with one of the ground crew. The two big propellers were now stopped.

Soon several low cargo wagons were pulled out to a spot behind the wing by the fuselage. Rolf and a fellow air crewman began lowering boxes down out of the hatch, hauling them out from under the wing, and loading them onto the cargo wagons.

Sometimes, they would use the cockpit hatch above and carry cargo down from the wing. Either way, the plane was not very well designed for moving cargo, even though it was supposedly designed as a commercial cargo and passenger plane. But Hitler had only told the Allies that because such development was allowed by post-war treaty limitations. In fact, it was covertly and illegally developed to be a state-of-the-art military bomber, which was not allowed. So when they used it for cargo handling, it was a lot of work for the crew.

It was June of 1938, eleven months since Rolf had said goodbye to me at the train station. We had written each other regularly via Mutti. These letters to me and the ones to his own mother were welcome breaks from the tedious life of a bomber crewman. The periods of training, exercises, and transport duties normally kept them busy. Whenever not busy with those activities, he was assigned guard and kitchen duties on base.

They had flown cargo, and occasionally passengers, to all parts of Germany. They also had been flying to Austria since its takeover by Germany several months earlier. After being in the Luftwaffe two years, he had been promoted once.

Rolf was by now accustomed to life in the Luftwaffe. While some duties didn't appeal to him, he was happy, in general. He still would rather be cabinetmaking with his father and planned to get out as soon as his service time was up. But he liked the comradery and at times even considered all the flying and training to be exciting. He pulled his own weight in their work and got along well with his fellow air crewmen. While he didn't drink as much as the others, he did sometimes join them in their barracks revelry.

He had been assigned to Heinkel-111 bombers for about eighteen months. The aircraft was a medium range bomber designed to fly faster than the fighters trying to shoot it down, thereby only needing to be lightly armed with defensive machine guns. The plane had performed well when the Luftwaffe had tested it out in the Spanish civil war. So the Heinkel-111 crews were all proud to be flying in them.

Even so, Rolf had considerable misgivings about his assigned gun station on the bottom of the plane, which the crewmen called the "pot." What genius would design a gun station that must be lowered down outside the skin of the plane in order to fire the gun? He guessed it was necessary for Hitler's ruse to hide the military intent of the plane.

To man his gun station while airborne, he had to crank the "pot" down, then climb down into it so he could fire his machine gun rearward at any enemy planes behind and below. The front side of the "pot" was enclosed, but the back side of it was largely open to give him a wide arc of fire. In addition to being very noisy and cold, he would be very exposed to enemy fire.

While he had yet to be in battle, he felt nonetheless that his "ass" would literally and figuratively be hanging out when he was down there manning his gun. Fortunately, lowering the "pot" outside the skin of the plane added significant drag, which reduced the plane's air speed. Hiding the military intent of the plane was apparently no longer a concern, and his gun station was to be redesigned to improve air speed in new versions of the plane.

Rolf's bomber crew was shortly to be transferred to a new duty station and squadron with the newer Heinkel-111 bombers, which he ardently hoped would have the new design of his gun station. If war came, he had no desire to be sitting in a "pot" hanging below his plane.

Chapter 32
The Bakery

RIGHT AWAY after leaving my aunt's restaurant, I found work in the pastry section of a German bakery in San Carlos. My training consisted of a co-worker showing me their way of making pastries, after which they would check up on me as I made them. I was expected to be experienced enough to learn their way quickly, work quickly, and not need a lot of supervision.

On my second day at work, for example, I was cutting cross sections from a roll of dough with a layer of cinnamon and sugar rolled up in it. I placed the cross sections together into a baking pan. Soon they would be cinnamon rolls. I was making another long roll of dough to be cut when the owner, a white-haired and bearded man, walked up behind me. After observing my work for a minute, he nodded his approval and walked on.

The owner, Mr. Steinhauer, had worked hard all his life, and he expected his employees to work hard too, no exceptions. But hard work suited me fine, and it interested me to learn to make the various kinds of pastries and cakes.

After a day of work at the bakery, I walked along the sidewalk of the hilly suburban street admiring the stucco houses with tile roofs and neat yards. I turned into one, walked up the steep driveway, through the gate to the back yard, and down a set of steps leading to the basement door. I had found a little furnished basement studio apartment, which was not too far from the bakery.

Tired from my workday, I plopped down into an easy chair, glad to finally sit down after standing all day at work. The little apartment was not similar in appearance at all to our apartment back in Hamburg. But each day after work when I opened the door of the apartment, I half-expected to see the apartment in Hamburg and Mutti getting up to welcome me home. I guess it was wishful thinking.

* * *

Meanwhile back at the apartment in Hamburg, Mutti was sitting and knitting in the living room when Ruth came in the door, looking oppressed. Ruth, now fifteen years old, had just finished her first year of middle school. She was starting to look like a young woman with a slim developing figure, light brown hair, and a pretty face. Closing the door behind her, she tottered over to the couch and plopped down on the sofa next to Mutti.

"I'm exhausted, Mutti. Even on our last day of school, we had to march in another parade to a rally. At least I am now on summer break, which means a break from them too. I will be so glad when I don't have to go to them anymore."

"That sounds a lot like what Kätchen used to say," Mutti said with a smile.

"We certainly agree on it. I have no interest in politics and whatever those dreary speakers said today. They drone on and on for hours, and I don't hear a word of it."

"I'm sorry, Ruth. I wish we had the choice of not going, but we don't."

"Ugh," Ruth said.

"Don't worry, Ruth. You've only got one more year of middle school. We can look then into sending you to America."

At hearing this, Ruth became silent for a moment. A year earlier on the pier, she had tried to reassure me about leaving by telling me that she would watch out for Mutti and Vati while I was gone. Ruth was only fourteen at the time, and we had all smiled at her statement. But Ruth had meant it and had resolved not to leave them at any point to immigrate to America. She merely had not told them so, fearing it would upset them.

"I'm sorry, Mutti. I didn't mean to complain so much. I can put up with it. You shouldn't worry about me."

Smiling at her brave little girl, Mutti said, "Ruth, how about if we practice some hand sewing to get your mind off the rally. I'll show you what I am doing on the dress I'm repairing for Frau Stein and you can practice the stitch on another piece. You said you were thinking about being a seamstress after you graduate this year."

"Yes, I hope to design clothes someday, but I'll need to know how to sew well in order to do it. I could use the practice. Okay," she said, standing up.

Putting down her knitting, Mutti stood up too. Together they walked over to where Mutti had her sewing work laid out.

* * *

At the bakery in San Carlos, I worked with a co-worker named Ray in the pastry section. We got along well together. He was a little on the heavy side and in his late twenties. He had been there several years and was my instructor, showing me how to make pastries the way Mr. Steinhauer wanted them. He would check on me when I first started making something new and would help if I had a question.

Today I was working on something they called a "snail". It was a figure eight shaped Danish with a different fruit topping on each end. Meanwhile he was working on some fruit topped torte nearby on the other side of some counters and shelves.

In an adjoining bread-making area, several employees worked making various breads. One of the employees working there named Hilda was also German. She was heavy set, older, and unfriendly looking. I was not around her much. When I was, I felt uncomfortable. She was far too serious for my liking. Sometimes I would glance up and see her looking at me. Then she would quickly look away.

The bakery owner Mr. Steinhauer liked me since I was a good worker. Very seldom did he feel the need to correct my work after watching me during one of his little visits. Despite having emigrated from Germany years before, he was not sentimental at all about his homeland and never talked of it. After all, talking might detract from getting work done.

I was at the bakery five months before any talk of Germany came up. It was Hilda who rushed up to me suddenly one day and said with an excited look, "Have you heard?"

"No, heard what?" I replied, thinking there might have been an accident or something in the bakery.

"Germany has occupied the Sudetenland! Britain and France are afraid of Hitler. They let him do it. He's already taken over Austria. They didn't dare to oppose him then either. You're German, aren't you?"

"Yes, I'm from Germany, but I'm really not interested in politics. Sorry," I said.

Excitedly she said, "But you should be. It's the beginning, the beginning of Germany's thousand year rule."

Then with a start, she stopped talking and glanced around anxiously to see if she had been overheard. She had forgotten herself in her excitement. After a brief look at me, she warily slinked back to the bread-making area.

I had no idea what or where the Sudetenland was and didn't want to know. After our Sudetenland conversation, I was certain that I wanted to have nothing to do with her.

I did my best afterward to stay away from her. Thank goodness I had my girlfriends to meet with occasionally on weekends. We would walk in the parks and stop at a bench to munch on a sandwich and talk. We talked about lots of things, but certainly not about the Sudetenland.

The next month, when we got together, Hanna told us about newspaper reports of the Nazis destroying and burning synagogues and Jewish businesses across Germany in a night of destruction. Since I never read the paper, I had not heard about it. We did not normally discuss such world news, but it was personal news for her since she still had Jewish relations there. Her father and mother had certainly been right to leave Germany. I thought of Frau Zöllmer and was happy for her. Six months before, Mutti had told me in a letter that Frau Zöllmer had been successful in leaving too.

The last day of 1938 was a Saturday, and I had the day off from the bakery. About six months had passed since I had left Aunt Minna's restaurant. During that time, I had stopped by there two or three times a month on Saturdays to visit and help her.

New Year's Eve would be a big night for the restaurant. I knew my aunt would be expecting me to help out. I was happy to help her, since it would be fun and a good opportunity for me to earn a little extra money. Aunt Minna didn't pay me when I helped, but I kept all my tip money as pay.

When I arrived that morning at the restaurant, Aunt Minna was happy to see me as usual. The restaurant needed to be decorated for New Year's Eve during the day while serving customers. We got the streamers hung, balloons blown up, party hats out, tables decorated, and music ready. The bar was well stocked and everything ready by dinner time.

Many of the dinner customers stayed, while others began filtering in later in the evening. Aunt Minna was in high spirits behind the busy bar. The night was a crowded, busy, and noisy one in the restaurant with couples dancing among the tables. Last New Year's Eve, I had been caught in the middle of the crowd at midnight and had not been able to avoid a couple unpleasant kisses from men with breath smelling heavily of alcohol and cigarettes. Not something I wanted to repeat.

So just before midnight, I slipped back into the kitchen and was successful in avoiding them this year. I was nineteen years old, a young girl in the bloom of life. While others were kissing at midnight, I was thinking of Rolf, remembering our times together and kisses. I missed him and had no idea when or if we would ever be together again.

* * *

Back in Hamburg at the bar where my father normally drank, Mutti, Ilse, and several of Mutti's other women friends were sitting in a booth talking and sipping their drinks. It was New Year's Eve, which in Germany was called Silvester, after a pope who died on December 31st of some year long ago in the fourth century. The bar was decorated and crowded with celebrators. Ruth had been out earlier with some girlfriends but not wanting to be out with all the drunken revelers at midnight, was now back at the apartment, probably asleep.

Spirits were high for there was much to celebrate in Germany. There was little unemployment and the defeated Germany of a few years ago was again powerful. Gustav was there singing and drinking with his friends at the bar. He and his friends had been celebrating since early afternoon.

He broke off momentarily from his friends, weaved over to Mutti in the booth, gave her an awkward kiss on the cheek, and then wandered back to his friends at the bar. Mutti watched as he staggered back. She shook her head and looked back at her friends. They looked at her, smiled, and shook their heads too. Mutti and several of them raised their glasses and toasted to their "wonderful" husbands. About then, Mutti was wishing she had stayed home with Ruth.

Their toast made Ilse think fondly of her own husband. They too had come here together before to celebrate Silvester. Unlike the other women here who sarcastically toasted their "wonderful" husbands, her husband had been wonderful to her. She still loved and missed him a great deal.

Chapter 33
Co-worker Hilda

I WAS BUSY making mini-tarts at the bakery a couple months later when Mr. Steinhauer came up behind me and made an announcement.

"Kätchen, the bread making side is having a slow time, so I'm moving Hilda in here for a time to work by you."

"Oh, Mr. Steinhauer," I said with real concern, dropping what I had in my hands, "can't you put her with Ray? I don't have much in common with her. I'm not sure we would get along."

"What's to get along? You work here. She works there. What else is there?" he said, dismissing my concerns. Then he shrugged his shoulders and walked off. Ray had overheard and poked his head out from behind some trays.

"Nice try, Kätchen, but I don't need her over here either. She's all yours," he said with a big grin.

"Oh, hush," I said and looked about for something to throw at Ray. But finding nothing, I had to just give him a "go away" wave. He grinned as I stood frustrated, staring at the tarts in front of me, and dreading the thought of working with Hilda nearby.

The next day, Hilda was beside me on the same counter making pastries. I tried not to look at or talk to her. She was always looking around to see if anyone was nearby. If Ray or others were near, she would not talk. She was scrupulously silent when Mr. Steinhauer periodically came by to observe us working.

When Ray left momentarily to do something, and she thought no one else could hear, she would go on and on in a low voice about how wonderful Hitler and the Nazis were. I told her repeatedly I wasn't interested in politics, but she was undeterred. For two days, I put up with her talk and tried to ignore her.

On the third day, I couldn't take it anymore. When she saw Ray leave to carry a tray of pastries to another area, she started again in a low voice.

"Did you see the newspapers today? Hitler has marched into Bohemia. The Czechs have been mistreating Germans there for some time. They asked him for help. He did it to stop the abuse of the Germans there. It's…"

"Stop! I really don't want to hear about it!" I tried to cut her off in a low voice. "I don't read newspapers and don't care about politics."

She ignored me and continued in her low voice, "It's terrible how the Czechs mistreated the Germans there. The fools. Germany is strong again, and now they have paid for it. Soon we will occupy all of Czechoslovakia. Britain and France are powerless to stop Hitler."

It must have been at this point when Ray came back in unnoticed and began to listen.

"I've told you a thousand times before that I'm not interested in politics. Will you kindly shut! Up!" I told her in a louder voice.

"And I've told you before that you should be!" Hilda responded in a louder voice, "Our führer is a great leader and so handsome too. He has brought Germany from the ruins of the last war and has made it powerful again!"

"I've heard all that talk before, you know," I told her in a raised voice. "I was forced to be in Hitler's parades and rallies when I grew up there. The Nazi speeches did nothing for me then, and your proud talk of Hitler does nothing for me now either! So will you shut up!"

Loudly she continued, "How could you not be proud of our fatherland. Germany, our…" She abruptly stopped when Mr. Steinhauer came in and walked by suspiciously. He had heard our raised voices, but only saw silent workers when he came in. After eyeing us over, he left.

"How could you not be proud of our Fatherland," Hilda continued in a lower voice. "Our German race is going to rule the world for a thousand years. Our führer has predicted it. He is a great man."

I was now mad and told her off.

"Hitler! I've seen your Hitler!" I shouted. "He's short and he's ugly and he screams like a mad man! And he has a stupid moustache! He took my nice old folk song and turned it into one of his ugly Nazi propaganda songs. If Hitler is so great and powerful, why are you here? Why aren't you back there in Germany bowing to your führer and licking his boots!"

At this, she flew into a rage. With bulging bloodshot eyes and exposed teeth, she flung herself at me. She knocked me back into a tall cart holding many trays full of pastries. The cart and us two women toppled to the floor with a loud crash, and the pastries were thrown all over the floor. Hilda was on top of me pulling at my hair and slapping at me.

I struggled with her desperately and fought to get out from under her. I finally managed to get her off balance and pushed her off. I scrambled to my feet and backed away looking for some kind of weapon to defend myself, but found none.

Hilda was up again and readying for another leap when Mr. Steinhauer rushed in after hearing all the noise. "What's going on here! Oof!"

Hilda had leaped again and knocked Mr. Steinhauer, me, and another tall cart of pastries to the floor. Hilda and I wrestled on the floor in the pastry debris as Mr. Steinhauer tried unsuccessfully to get up on the slippery floor.

"Anabelle, call the sheriff!" he called to his wife through the doorway.

Ray had come over when he heard us fighting, but had stood back not sure what he should do. Now he rushed in and tried to help Mr. Steinhauer get up.

"How dare you! Our führer!" Hilda screamed. She was on top of me again trying to punch me in the face. I was able to deflect her fists and, without thinking, grabbed some cream filled pastries, which were strewn all about, and shoved them in her face and eyes.

She screamed at the top of her lungs and was momentarily blinded. I rolled away from her and scrambled to my feet in the slippery mess. Hilda was starting to get up when I grabbed one of the steel pastry trays and hit her over the head as hard as I could, and then a second time. She was momentarily stunned and collapsed to the floor.

I jumped on her back and straddling her, put her arm in an arm lock behind her back. I put all my weight and strength on that arm to keep her there. Hilda regained her senses, struggled, and cried out in pain, but she couldn't get me and my weight off her back and pinned arm. Finally, Hilda's struggling subsided, and she breathed hard from the exertion.

"He has a beautiful moustache," she said groggily. As we laid there, I heard approaching police sirens.

Ray had helped Mr. Steinhauer to his feet. He was covered in pastry mess and looked around in a rage, "Look at this mess! Who is going to pay for this!"

A minute later, the sheriff rushed in with his pistol drawn. He was taken aback by the scene of overturned carts, with smashed pastries and flour strewn everywhere. In the midst of the mess, Hilda and I lay on the floor with me on her back.

Other employees now stood in the background looking on in amazement while Mr. Steinhauer raged at us two on the floor. We were both covered with pastry mess. I held Hilda firmly as I looked up at the sheriff with my face and hair covered with pastry and flour. He looked down at us and couldn't help but laugh.

"Whooeee. What have we here?" he said as a deputy rushed in behind him with gun drawn.

Pointing at us, Mr. Steinhauer raged, "Take them away, Sheriff. You two are fired!" All I could do was sigh, get up, and go with the sheriff.

Chapter 34
Live-In Nanny

THE NEXT DAY, I was scanning the want ads while standing outside a drugstore where I had just bought the newspaper. The sheriff had taken us both away and held us for hours while he sorted things out.

Ray came to the sheriff's office and told him how I had been attacked and that the fight had been over me being tired of hearing her talk about how great Hitler was. The sheriff decided not to charge me, since I had only been defending myself. He let me go although I was prominent in his incident report.

Mr. Steinhauer was not so forgiving. I was out of work and looking for a new job. Unfortunately, jobs were scarce. Going back to work for Aunt Minna would have been like admitting I could not make it on my own, which I still intended to do. I frowned at the job prospects that I saw in the paper, but thought a couple of them looked to be worth investigating.

Later, I was standing in a nicely decorated living room listening to a fashionable lady named Mrs. Gentsch. Her hair and makeup were meticulous. She wore a stylish dress and shoes. She had elegant looking hands, which she seemed to like holding at eye level to show off. She was telling me about her various social clubs and commitments.

Suddenly, a little girl followed by a little boy with a wooden sword burst screaming into the room. The girl, about four years old, tripped on the carpet and fell head long onto the floor, but she quickly recovered.

As the boy, about five years old, closed on her with sword poised to strike, the little girl sprang forward at the little boy's legs and cut them out from under him. He tumbled head long over the top of her and came to a violent stop against the bottom of the sofa. Soon they were both on their feet, running and screaming again. This time, she had the sword, chasing him out of the room.

I was, of course, shocked by their uncontrolled behavior and concerned for their safety. The woman, on the other hand, had not even noticed them and had talked on about her social activities without missing a syllable. I was almost as astounded at her behavior as I was at the behavior of the children.

I could readily see this might be an interesting assignment. I was there interviewing with the lady of the house for the position of live-in nanny and cook for this fashionable family living in the upscale town of Atherton south of San Carlos.

It was one of the few positions available, so I took it. I had to say goodbye to my basement apartment and move my few belongings into the nanny's room of the house.

One of the first things I had to do as nanny was to establish with the kids who was boss. At first, the two kids, Jimmy and Susan, didn't know what to make of me. I seemed to be all business and spoke with a funny accent.

Whenever they started to fight or act up, I put a stop to it right away. I'd get in their face and scold them. I let them know I expected them to start behaving from now on or else. I did this consistently whenever they acted up. I would, of course, bake and display cookies they could have only if they were good.

They quickly learned that I meant what I said. If I told them "no dessert unless you eat your lunch," they knew I meant it. It wasn't long before they were behaving, and I could relax and be less rigid with them. Then, we were good friends, but they knew to mind.

A maid came daily, but I was the only live-in staff for the household. The kitchen was well equipped, and I could get whatever groceries I needed delivered with a telephone call to the local markets. Most of the cooking I did was for the children since Mr. and Mrs. Gentsch ate regularly at restaurants and their clubs.

My room was near the children's bedroom. It was roomy and the furnishings were of high quality, much better than what I was accustomed to. After I put the kids to bed at night, I would retire to my room to work on my English skills or to read and write letters. In Mutti's letters to me, Ruth would sometimes insert miniature drawings of pretty flower arrangements and other artwork. Jimmy and Susan always enjoyed seeing them and would draw their own small pictures, which I would include in my letters back.

Ruth would be graduating from middle school soon. I asked Mutti if we should start the process for Ruth to immigrate here like they had talked about before. Aunt Minna would have to sponsor her since I was not a naturalized citizen. I would go back to working for Aunt Minna if necessary for her to agree to sponsor Ruth. But Mutti wrote that Ruth was not ready to go yet and they would consider it again after she completed her landyear.

* * *

Meanwhile, in the air above Germany, Rolf was dressed in his flight suit with his headset on. He sat in the after compartment of his bomber with Albert, his friend and crewmate. Their bomber always seemed to be flying somewhere or in some kind of training.

It was April of 1939 and his crew had been transferred to a new airbase and squadron, which was flying the newest version of the Heinkel-111 bomber.

On this particular day, Rolf and his crewmates were practicing their bombing accuracy on an exercise range. The bombardier, literally titled the "bomb aimer" in German, was named Rudy. He was in the cockpit kneeling down in the nose of the bomber looking down into his bombsight.

This latest version of the bomber had a new rounded nose, made mostly of Plexiglas panes giving it the look of a round greenhouse on the front of the plane. The new nose greatly improved visibility for the pilot, Captain Metzger, who sat on the left side of the cockpit. The newer more powerful engines filled the cockpit with a loud droning noise.

Rudy was also the plane's navigator and front gunner, but now he was busy performing his bombardier duties. Looking down into his bombsight, he had control of the plane and was flying it to the target.

"Five seconds to target!" he called out into his intercom.

"Away!" he announced when he released two practice bombs, which could be heard leaving the bomb bay located just aft of the cockpit.

In the bomb bay compartment, four bombs were stored in a row vertically in an open rack on each side of the plane. When loaded, the noses of the bombs could be seen sticking up from the top of the racks. In these bomb racks, the plane could carry eight 250 kilogram (551 pound) bombs or greater numbers of smaller bombs. A walkway between the bomb racks allowed access between the cockpit in front and the after compartment.

As Rolf had hoped, this new version of the bomber included the improved design of his bottom gun station.

No longer did he crank a "pot" down to hang out below the bottom skin of the airplane. Most of the floor of the after compartment was a long shallow bathtub-like protrusion on the bottom of the plane for his new gun station. He could either lie down or kneel on the padded bottom to fire the machine gun sticking out the Plexiglas back end of this protrusion.

On the practice bombing runs today, the machine gun was not needed or installed. Rolf kneeled in the bottom of his gun station looking below with binoculars for the impact of the bombs. The practice bombs were inert with dummy warheads, so there would be no explosions.

After a few seconds, Rolf saw the two small plumes of sand and dirt kicked up by the impact of the bombs. Based on the distance marking around the target, he reported the miss distances of the two bombs into the intercom.

After writing the results on the scoring sheet on his clipboard, he looked up from his gun station at Albert, who was the top gunner. He was not up in the metal and canvas chair of his gun station on the top of the plane. Instead he sat on the floor against the fuselage of the plane, looking disappointed after hearing the latest impact report.

"Set up for two more practice bombs. We're turning to make another bomb run. We're not going home until we get a hit. Radio, inform Range Control," said Captain Metzger over the intercom.

"Yes, Captain," replied Albert, who was also the aircraft's radioman. He stood up and stepped over to the radio sets on the fuselage by his gun station. After calling the range and receiving their permission for another practice bomb run, Albert put the microphone down, informed the captain that permission had been received.

Then with an agitated look, he exclaimed, "Dammit, Rolf. I've got a hot date tonight. You would not believe this girl. She has got the greatest body and the bluest eyes."

Putting his hands together and looking skyward, he continued, "Please God, I beg of you, let Rudy hit the target this time."

Then with a look down at Rolf, his expression changed and he said excitedly, "Better yet, Rolf, do your buddy, Albert, who traded guard duty with you when you needed it, a great favor."

"That was two months ago, Albert! How many times do I have to repay you for one favor?" Rolf said laughing.

"Just once more. Just this one more favor, old buddy. Call one of the next bombs a hit no matter where it lands Please Rolf, could you do it for me? The Captain won't notice, and it will make him feel so much better. What do you say?"

Rolf could only laugh, shake his head, and say, "Only if one gets somewhere close, Albert. That's all I can promise."

"Thank you, Rolf! I knew you'd help your old buddy out!"

* * *

It was a beautiful sunny afternoon in Atherton, ideal for taking the kids for a walk in the nearby park. Little Jimmy ran ahead to a flower bed along the path. He stopped in front of the pretty flowers and bent over to pick one.

"No, Jimmy. Don't pick the flowers." At this, he stopped and looked around at me. My efforts with the kids was paying off. All they had needed was a little German discipline. They knew to behave, and we got along real well.

For lunch, I would usually make them little sandwiches along with some fruit. I loved the summers in California when so much delicious fruit was available. They loved a nut paste called peanut butter, which I had never tasted before. I tried it, but it was oily and sugary. It was so unlike the foods I had eaten all my life that I never acquired a taste for it. The kids always wanted a peanut butter and jelly sandwich, but I tried not to give it to them too often, since I thought their parents could afford much better food.

As the summer months of 1939 passed, I got accustomed to my new life with the Gentsch family. Mrs. Gentsch was always busy with her social activities and clubs, and didn't want to get too involved in my duties, which was fine with me. She was happy with my cooking and my treatment of the kids, and even noticed that they now, for some reason, appeared to behave much better.

Their father, Mr. Gentsch, was always away at work or on some kind of business travel, so the kids and I seldom saw him.

Chapter 35
War Begins

ROLF EXITED the briefing room with the crowd of men from the bomber crews. Having just been briefed on the combat mission for tomorrow, excitement filled the air. This one would be actual combat, not another exercise.

Several days before, their bomber squadron had been forward positioned with others to an air base near the Polish border in response to rising tensions between Poland and Germany. While the level of activity at the base was noticeably high, the aircrews had not been told an invasion was imminent. On August 31, 1939, Rolf found himself preparing for his participation in the invasion of Poland early the next morning.

Rolf, Rudy, and Albert walked with their pilot, Captain Metzger, who pulled them aside and said, "Okay, you all heard it. This is the real thing. We're expecting little opposition from the Poles, so it should be a piece of cake. The Polish fighters are biplanes, for God's sake, little better than ones from the Great War twenty years ago. If the Red Baron was still alive today, he could shoot them down!"

They all chuckled at this, and then he continued, "However, we must be on our guard. I expect every one of you to do your jobs to the fullest. Any questions?" The crewmen shook their heads.

"All right then," he said, "I have to go to a pilot briefing now. You all head back to the plane and check to make sure everything is being readied for tomorrow. I'll meet you back there in an hour for a quick status meeting. Plan on getting to bed early. Reveille will be at 0200."

The crewmen all acknowledged this with a salute and "Yes sir, Captain." The Captain saluted back and strode off rapidly to his briefing as his crew headed for their plane.

Early the next morning at daybreak, Rolf knelt in the padded bottom of his gun station, scanning the skies behind and below the plane. His machine gun was fixed in position in its Plexiglas gun port. A number of spare ammo magazines were beside him. He had only to cock the gun to be ready to fire. He looked out to the side and could see other bombers flying with them in their small formation.

Over the intercom Captain Metzger said, "We've been in enemy territory two minutes. If the Poles are smart, they won't try to attack us. Our fighters will make short work of them. But keep your eyes open."

Rolf looked up at Albert in the chair above him at his machine gun station on top of the plane. His head and gun were sticking out from the opening there beyond the top skin of the plane. A fairing sticking up in front of his gun station helped protect him from the wind. But it was still very cold there, exposed as he was to the outside early morning air as the plane flew at high speed at thousands of meters of altitude. Albert was dressed warmly, wearing a heavy coat with its woolly collar up, heavy gloves, and his wool lined leather aviation hat over his headphones. Albert steadily scanned the skies above and behind looking for any enemy fighters foolhardy enough to attack them.

Returning his attention to his own gun station, Rolf began again to scan the skies behind and below the plane.

Up front in the cockpit, Captain Metzger was seated with the flight controls in his hands. He scanned the skies as he maintained his position in bomber formation. The mission was a low altitude bombing run on a rail yard.

The pilot of the lead bomber was the mission commander, the one responsible for navigating the formation to the target and dropping the bombs on it. Radio communications were set up for him to talk directly to all pilots. Captain Metzger was only required to follow the course and altitude changes given, maintain his place in formation and drop his bombs when told.

The bombardier Rudy would have to open the bomb bay doors and release the bombs when they arrived at the target, but now he was stretched out on his stomach up in the Plexiglas nose of the plane manning the forward machine gun.

Rudy scanned the skies in front of the plane and saw a line of small planes up ahead and above. But they were far off, and he couldn't make them out. Captain Metzger noticed them too. Soon Rudy could make out they were biplane fighters diving at them.

"Enemy fighters, ahead to the left and high!" he called out into the intercom as he began firing bursts of machine gun fire at them.

The formation of four biplane fighters swept through the bomber formation, seriously damaging two of the bombers. Up front, Rudy fired at them as they swooped past. Albert and Rolf were only able to get a few shots off at them as they passed behind the plane. Soon other planes could be heard and seen.

In disbelief, Rudy called into the intercom, "Two of our bombers are hit and going down! Here come our fighters!" At his gun station, Rolf looked to the side and saw a Heinkel-111 bomber on fire and losing altitude.

Captain Metzger said on the intercom, "Two enemy fighters, ahead to the left at ten degrees elevation."

Rolf heard the nose gun firing and several seconds later Albert, the top gunner above him, began firing. Rolf heard a number of bullets whistle through their compartment. He saw a plane flash past on the left and got a few rounds off at it before it was gone.

Rolf looked up to see if their own plane had suffered any damage. He saw several holes in the top of the plane, but no other damage. Albert above was looking to the right. Over the intercom he said, "There's a dogfight on our right. The Poles damaged one of our fighters! But we got three of theirs!"

Captain Metzger said over the intercom, "Rudy, one minute to target. Leave the gun and get to your bombsight." Soon the bomb bay doors were heard opening. Rolf wiped the perspiration from his forehead and looked up at Albert, who was putting a new magazine on his machine gun.

Half a minute later, Captain Metzger reported, "Two enemy fighters, to the right ahead and high."

Albert, in his top gun station, craned his head around and spotted them, but again, he would have to wait until they drifted farther aft before his gun could be trained on them.

"Captain, they're getting close, but still too far forward for me to fire on them," Albert reported.

"Roger, fire when you can." Ordinarily, Captain Metzger might want to swing his heading to put the enemy fighter into his gunner's arc of fire, but he was in the middle of the bombing run and needed to stay in formation to the target.

Soon the enemy fighters were within range and began firing. An agonizing second or two later, they came into Albert's arc of fire and he began frantically firing at them in return. Suddenly many rounds hit the after compartment and the plane shook. Bullets pinged about and thumps were heard. Albert coughed and stopped firing.

As Rolf looked up, concerned for his friend Albert. He felt some pain in his own legs and saw blood on his pants from two shrapnel wounds that were not serious.

"Rudy, five seconds to target," announced the Captain.

"Away," he heard Rudy over the intercom say. He could hear the bombs leaving the plane and whistling as they fell to the ground. But Rolf was more concerned about the many bullets they had just taken and about his friend Albert.

"Albert! Are you hurt bad? Albert!" he yelled, looking up at his friend who was bloody and slumped in his chair. Albert didn't answer.

"Captain, Albert is hit! I'm leaving my gun to help him," he reported into the intercom.

"Rolf, make it fast and get on the top gun after you've helped him," Captain Metzger answered.

Rolf hurriedly unplugged his headphone and climbed out of the lower gun station to check his friend above him. He found Albert hanging limply in his chair and bleeding from multiple wounds.

"Albert! Buddy!" He said desperately looking at his face. Rolf checked his pulse and breathing, and saw that he was dead.

Sadly lowering his head for a moment, he thought of his friend. Then after taking a deep breath to collect himself, he returned to his duties. He was needed on the top gun. Rolf quickly unplugged Albert's headset from his gun station, unstrapped him from his chair, and lowered him to the floor where he laid him out and covered him with a blanket. He plugged his headset into the top gun station and reported, "Captain, Albert is dead. I laid him on the floor."

After a pause, Captain Metzger responded, "See if his gun is still usable."

"Yes sir."

As Rolf reached up to see if the gun would still slue around, he heard Captain Metzger in the headset, "Two fighters, right side, twenty degrees elevation!" Rolf hurriedly pushed on the gun swivel, concluding it was still working.

"Gun still usable, climbing into the chair."

"Right side, twenty degrees, Rolf!"

He could hear the dive of the enemy fighters and their guns begin firing. He had just gotten into the chair without strapping in and was swinging the gun around when suddenly bullets pinged all around him. He was hit by shrapnel and took one round through the shoulder. He reeled sideways and fell from the chair to the floor. His head jerking to one side as he fell, when his headset plug was torn from its connection. He lay slumped on the floor.

Half a minute later, Rudy appeared in the doorway and was beside Rolf looking him over.

"Rolf, where are you hit?"

Rolf was still conscious and told him, "My left shoulder and maybe other places too, I don't know." Rudy checked Rolf over, sat him up against the fuselage of the plane, and put gauze dressings on several of his wounds.

"Rolf, you're lucky. Only the shoulder wound is a bad one. Keep pressure on it to stop the bleeding and it should be okay. I have to get back to the nose gun. I'll be back in a bit." Rolf nodded weakly and sat back holding the dressing to his shoulder.

"Thanks, Rudy."

"I'll be back in a bit, Rolf. Don't worry," Rudy said as he stood up and looked around at the damage. He paused for a moment looking at Albert's body and then disappeared through the doorway toward the cockpit.

Rolf resignedly stared at the bullet-riddled fuselage of the plane as he heard the nose gun firing at some aircraft zooming by, and then more aircraft and more machine gun fire.

He thought of what had happened and he marveled at the bravery of the Polish pilots who attacked formidable modern German aircraft with their outdated biplanes. They had done so at great risk, with little chance of success, and probably few had survived. He noticed the nose gun had stopped firing. Soon Rudy appeared again.

"Don't worry Rolf. I think the few remaining fighters have gone. We're on our way back and should be home soon. We'll get you to the hospital there."

He went to Albert's body, lifted the blanket from his head, and checked his pulse. Shaking his head, he put the blanket back over his head.

"Poor Albert, he was a good kid. What a shame."

"Yes, a really good kid and friend."

They both looked sadly at Albert's body for a moment. Then looking around at the damage, Rudy said with a sigh, "The plane seems to be holding together. We should be able to make it back with no trouble. Are you doing okay?"

"I think so."

"Do you need a shot of morphine?"

"No, I'm okay for now."

"Good. I'll check on you again soon," Rudy told him and quickly disappeared again.

Rolf looked down at his shoulder. He pushed down on the dressing to give it more pressure, but winced when it proved to be painful.

He took a breath and looked around at the damage. Light streamed through the many new holes in the fuselage.

Rolf looked over at Albert's body again. Rolf thought about his friend back in the barracks joking and laughing, their work together moving cargo, and his many girlfriends. His family lived only thirty miles from base and Rolf had gone home with him for Christmas last year. He thought of Albert's family who had been so nice to him. He would have to write them a letter expressing his sympathy. His buddy Albert was such a great guy, so full of life, but now he lay there lifeless. Rolf felt very sad for Albert and his soon-to-be-grieving family.

He closed his eyes and tried not to move.

* * *

At the Gentsch household, I laid in bed in my room unable to sleep. I closed my eyes and tried not to think about it. There was no avoiding the news that war in Europe had started. The newspapers and radio had been filled with reports of Germany's invasion of Poland. Rolf had been right. Germany had been preparing for a war that they now apparently wanted to begin.

I thought of Ruth and the possibility of her immigrating. Maybe there was still time to make the arrangements and get her out. I would write to tell Mutti that I would talk to Aunt Minna about it and check to see if immigration quotas were available.

Then I realized that it was already too late. It would look very bad for someone to want to leave Germany now that they are fighting a war. They would be considered a disloyal traitor. Plus even if she already had a passport and immigration visa, she could no longer simply book passage on a German freighter and come to America like before. We were too late. I felt terrible for her, like I had let her down. It was one more reason to cry when the war started.

I sent them a letter the day after I heard the news. In my letter to them, I told Ruth that I deeply regretted and was sorry for not having gotten her out. I also asked them if now that the war had started, was there anything that they needed that I could send them.

Three weeks after the start of the war, I received a letter from Mutti, which relayed news from Rolf telling me that he had been wounded on the first day of fighting. Of course, he had made it sound like a few scratches, but they thought he would be in the hospital for several weeks and in rehabilitation for another month. Mutti didn't mention my letter, so they had not gotten it yet.

I received another letter from Mutti three weeks later that said that Rolf was recovering well. He was out of the hospital and in rehabilitation. They had received my letter. In response, Ruth told me not to beat myself up about her not having immigrated. Her being there with Mutti and Vati was probably for the best anyway. Mutti told me that things in Hamburg still seemed normal. They could not think of anything that they needed me to send them right now. They would be keeping it in mind though and let me know should some need arise. It was a comforting thought for them to know that they could depend on me for help should they need it.

In her next letter two weeks later, Mutti said that Rolf was almost done with rehabilitation. He was expected to recover fully from his wounds. Unfortunately, once he recovered, he would be fit for duty again. He had been told he would be assigned light duty with a training command for a month after completing his rehabilitation. She also said that Vati had thought about what items might soon be in short supply with the British now blockading imports. He suggested that coffee and chocolate would be useful not only for them to consume, but also possibly as valuable trading items. Would it be possible to send some?

As soon as I read her letter, I told Mrs. Gentsch about my need to go to the store right away to buy the items to send to my family.

She said, "Why do that? Just call the market like normal and order it. You can pay me back later at some point."

I gave her a hug in thanks and went to the phone. The next day, I sent Mutti a case of twelve one pound cans of ground coffee. I had decided that before sending more things, I would send just the coffee as a test package to see if they got it.

Three weeks later, I received another letter from Mutti. Rolf was now on his light duty assignment with a training command. Things still seemed normal in Hamburg. No mention was made of receiving coffee.

That was the last news I heard from her before mail service between Germany and America unexpectedly and suddenly stopped in November 1939. America was a neutral country and not at war with Germany, but for some reason, mail service for private citizens ended. I lost all communications with my family and Rolf in Germany, and they lost any possibility of me helping them.

Chapter 36
Back in Action

THREE MONTHS after being severely wounded, Rolf was assigned to a new Heinkel-111 bomber crew, again at the lower gun station. His new crew thought highly of him since he was a battle tested and decorated combat veteran who had acted bravely and coolly under fire. At least, those were some of the words on his medal citation.

After two months with his new crew, he felt like he was one of them and very much liked his crewmates and pilot officer. Oddly in those two months, they had not flown a single combat mission. No one in the Luftwaffe had. The air campaign in Poland had lasted only a few weeks in September. In the five months since then, there had been a strange lack of warfare anywhere in Europe.

Rolf wasn't complaining. He certainly was not itching for more combat, but the lack of combat was unexpected given the hue and cry at the start of the war. Instead, there had been a frenzied pace of supply flights, readiness preparations and training, but no combat missions.

One night when Rolf was lying on his bunk propped up and writing a letter to his mother, one of the others living there in the barracks came to him and said, "Rolf, Captain Huber is outside and wants to talk to you." Rolf quickly jumped up and strode out to see him, not having any idea of what he might want.

Captain Huber, the pilot and commander of his new aircrew, was outside waiting. Rolf saluted him and said, "Good evening, Captain. You wanted to see me?"

"Yes, Rolf. I wanted to talk with you for a minute." He motioned for Rolf to come with him.

As they walked, he said, "Rolf, there's a need for more pilots for all the new bombers being built and the bomber group is looking for names of flight crew personnel who we would recommend to become pilots. You're still pretty junior in rank, but I'd like to submit your name."

"Me, sir?" Rolf said with surprise.

"Yes, you, Rolf. You're an outstanding crewman and do well when I let you take the controls. I know you'd be a good pilot," he said with a smile.

Heinkel-111 procedures called for the Navigator-Bombardier to be the copilot and fly the plane in an emergency if the pilot was killed or incapacitated. But Captain Huber encouraged his entire crew to learn, so there would be more than one emergency pilot onboard.

When the opportunity presented itself on routine hops and good weather, he offered to let others take over the controls. Rolf was the only one who liked doing it and was surprisingly good at it. He had even completed a few take-offs and landings. On long flights when Captain Huber needed a break, Rolf would take over for him. He had become the Captain's unofficial back-up pilot.

Dorfman, the Navigator-Bombardier, who was technically the copilot, didn't like flying the plane. He didn't feel very good at it or about it, so he happily let Rolf do it. Dorfman had been interested in astronomy and navigation since a boy and had volunteered for training as a navigator. Unfortunately for him, the navigator on this particular aircraft was also the co-pilot, bombardier, and nose gunner.

Rolf thought about it for a moment. He would be promoted and in charge of his own bomber crew. No, he was in the Luftwaffe because he had to be, not because he was ambitious to rise in the ranks and be in charge, or because he believed in "world domination for a thousand years." It didn't take much considering before replying.

"Thank you, Captain Huber, for the kind words. I like flying, but I'm too much of a common country boy. I'd be out of place rubbing elbows with the officer pilots."

"Nonsense. You'll be fine. It would mean more pay."

"I do appreciate your offer and recommendation, sir. But I'd better stick to being a gunner."

"Okay, Rolf. Let me know if you change your mind," said Captain Huber, a little disappointed.

"Thank you, sir. I will." Rolf stiffened to attention and saluted. The Captain smiled and walked away.

A little over three months later, Rolf knelt in the padded bottom of his gun station and rapidly scanned the skies behind and below for fighters. He could hear machine gun fire from nearby bombers and the zoom of fighters, but none were immediate threats or within his gun's range.

Warfare had begun in earnest in the west with a German offensive into the Netherlands, Belgium, and France. The Dutch city of Rotterdam had been holding out, and Rolf was part of a large bomber formation on its way to bomb the defenses of the city.

"Two fighters, right side, fifteen degrees elevation," said Dieter, the top gunner, into the intercom as he began firing. Rolf heard the machine guns of the fighters firing, but only heard a few pings of bullets hitting the plane.

"Rolf, on the right side, buddy, you might get a shot as they pass," Dieter said. But the enemy fighters had veered off to evade several German fighters and were out of range.

Rolf noticed the enemy fighters were no longer biplanes, but they were still outclassed and regularly shot down by the more capable German fighter planes.

"One minute to target." Rolf heard over the intercom as he continued to scan the skies. His gun station on the bottom of the plane gave him a good view of the landscape below, which changed rapidly from farmland to an urban setting of buildings and houses.

Some anti-aircraft rounds began bursting in the air nearby but not close. He heard the bomb bay doors open. "Five seconds to target," and then "Away."

As he heard the bombs leaving, Rolf could see explosions on the ground below from the bombs of the planes ahead of them. The buildings and streets erupted as the patterns of exploding bombs left a wide path of destruction in what appeared to be the center of the city.

Rolf looked briefly again at the skies for fighters, but could not help looking back to watch the destruction happening below. Their targets in the past had been military targets or transportation hubs. This was the first time they had bombed a populated city, and he hoped it had been evacuated.

He thought of Kätchen and how her ship had stopped for a day in one of the big ports along here, but he couldn't remember which one. He watched below as dense patterns of explosions replaced the attractive city blocks that had been there only moments before.

* * *

I tried hard not to read the newspapers, but the war in Europe had started to heat up. When walking with Jimmy and Susan, it was difficult to ignore the headlines of a paper when you passed by, so I had to avoid walking past newsstands and drugstores. One morning, I was walking with my two kids through a residential neighborhood on our way to the park. As we approached, I tried to look away, but I could not avoid reading the large headlines of a newspaper lying on a driveway up ahead. I stopped suddenly when I read "Nazis Bomb Rotterdam. 30,000 killed."

"Hey, why are we stopping?" little Jimmy said, but my mind was so far away I didn't hear him. I detoured into the driveway, picked up the paper and read the front page article, which said a large raid of German bombers had mercilessly bombed the city without warning, killing 30,000 innocent civilians. The Dutch had bravely defended the city and had shot down many of the attacking bombers.

"Nana, let's go," little Susan said.

"What? Oh. Yes. Sure, Sweetie. Let's go," I said numbly, putting the paper down and rejoining the kids.

Had I known at the time that 800-900 civilians were actually killed in the bombing, not 30,000 as reported, I probably would have been just as horrified.

* * *

In late June of 1940, just over a month after the attack on Rotterdam, Gustav and his friends were in their bar celebrating the news of France's surrender. The Netherlands and Belgium had previously fallen. Jubilantly drinking beer after beer, they slapped one another on the back, waved newspapers, shouted, cheered, and toasted the troops.

"I can't believe it!" Gustav declared. "We struggled for five Godforsaken years in the last war and never succeeded. And now we take France in six weeks! Can you believe it?" They all cheered loudly.

Bruno quieted everyone down and shouted with emotion, "In 1918, Germany was defeated and forced to sign the armistice ending the war. That hated document was signed by us in a railroad car in a forest, and the terms of peace have been a humiliation and burden for every German ever since!" The crowd booed and roared with indignation.

"And now the French have surrendered!" The crowd cheered loudly.

"And where did Hitler make the French sign their surrender document? In the exact same spot in the forest! The exact same spot, mind you! The same spot where we were forced to sign the armistice in 1918!" Again the crowd cheered loudly.

Bruno continued excitedly, "And they sat in the same chairs in the same railroad car! Hitler had it taken out of their museum and brought to the exact same spot! God, I can't think of revenge possibly being any sweeter!" Everyone in the bar was by this time cheering wildly.

One of them waved his arms to get attention and shouted. "Wait a minute. Everyone quiet. This calls for a toast to the Führer!"

"Yes, yes, to the Führer! Our great leader!" they all chimed in. They all raised their beer steins high, drank heartily and cheered.

Gustav was not a Hitler or Nazi enthusiast, but Germans were understandably euphoric over the phenomenal success of their army and their rapid victory over the French, especially the ones who had been part of the previous defeat. So Gustav and his friends celebrated like many others in Germany.

"Next, it's the British!" another shouted and they cheered.

When the cheering subsided, Gustav said to Bruno, "After their disaster at Dunkirk last month, Churchill and the British will surrender soon."

"If they have any brains!" Bruno said, and they laughed and cheered and started to sing a German marching song.

Chapter 37
Battle of Britain

BUT THE BRITISH did not surrender. So Hitler ordered preparations to begin for an invasion of Britain, which was to take place several months later in the autumn of 1940. Such an invasion could not succeed unless Germany controlled the skies over the invasion forces.

In August of 1940, as the preparations for the invasion of Britain progressed on the ground in occupied France, the Luftwaffe began a bombing campaign to win control of the skies by destroying the airbases and planes of British Royal Air Force (the RAF). Rolf's bomber squadron was part of this bombing campaign.

Rolf was quickly swinging his machine gun, firing bursts as the enemy fighters quickly came into view. They mostly came from above and were hard to hit from the bottom gun station. They would swoop by quickly and were soon out of range. He saw German fighters chasing some of them and heard the noise of the fighters dogfighting all around.

His plane was part of a large formation of bombers over Britain heading for its target. The nose and top gunners were firing machine gun bursts. Over the intercom, Captain Huber said, "Fighters, ahead on the right, twenty degrees."

Rolf was then tossed back and forth at his gun station as the pilot jinked the plane about to be less of a smooth steady target. Rolf looked out and saw two nearby bombers on fire and falling out of formation.

He heard, "Rolf, coming by left side." He swung his gun around and waited for the plane to flash by from above. He heard the engine of the fighter and began firing where he thought it would show up, but it appeared off a bit from where he thought. He might have hit it with a few bullets, but it zoomed off apparently undamaged.

For weeks, Rolf's bomber flew missions daily, weather permitting, to bomb the RAF's airfields. They were losing bombers every mission to the British fighters, who were proving to be a stubborn and capable enemy. Rolf's bomber had suffered numerous hits numerous times, and the crew had suffered minor shrapnel wounds.

Even with heavy damage to the RAF airfields, the RAF's fighters still managed to get aloft and be vectored out in numbers to attack their bomber formations. The defensive guns on the Heinkel-111 bombers seemed less and less capable of defending against the fighter attacks.

Rolf and the others onboard felt a heavy reliance on the German fighters for protection. They would appear from above whenever the bombers came under attack and engage the British fighters in desperate dogfights.

As the daily missions continued, it seemed to Rolf that the diving German fighters were able to protect them less and less. Rolf felt safer when German fighters began to fly with and escort the bomber formations, but soon these escorting fighters were being shot down as much as the bombers.

It seemed to him that the tide of battle had turned against them.

* * *

Needing a break, I had decided to go to the movies at the movie theater on El Camino Real, a main street in Atherton. I didn't go to very many movies, but a brand new comedy called *I Love You Again* was out, and I needed a little comic relief.

The comic relief I needed was not from my work environment, but from my worries about Rolf. We had lost contact nine months earlier and I knew nothing about his current whereabouts or condition. If he hadn't been killed already, he was now surely involved in the combat over Britain.

"Dear God, please keep him safe," was all I could think, and I wasn't even religious. It had been very taxing on me, and I needed a break.

I had arranged with Mrs. Gentsch to watch the kids that night. She was beginning to show some signs of motherly interest in her children after all, and it gratified me to think I had contributed to it. She and I got along well. She seemed to appreciate how the kids behaved and how the house was running.

Sitting inside the theater as people filtered in, I was looking forward to the movie and its short reprieve from my worrying. The lights in the theater began to dim, and the projector lit the screen. A popcorn bag with legs and a soda cup with legs began dancing a cha-cha to a Latin beat. It was one of those silly refreshment advertisements before the movie. It ended with all the animated moviegoers running to the refreshment stand to buy popcorn and sodas.

I wasn't sure if there would be a cartoon before the movie, but I settled back in the chair anticipating the start of the movie or a cartoon. Instead, a newsreel began about the Battle of Britain.

I saw stricken and motionless as I watched scenes of men in bunkers on the English coast scanning the skies with binoculars pointing at large formations of bombers, then RAF pilots running to their fighters and taking off on the grass runways. The narrator told how the British were valiantly fighting off the efforts of Nazi Germany to bomb and invade them.

When they showed gun camera footage of an RAF fighter's bullets tearing through a German bomber, which then burst into flames, I let out a big sob and lurched up to go. Crying and sobbing, I hurriedly clambered past the people in the row who looked up at me in amazement and annoyance.

When I made it to the aisle, I ran out of the theater. As I stood outside on the sidewalk sobbing, the people passing by stopped and asked me if I was okay. I couldn't answer.

Chapter 38
Shot Down

ROLF KNELT DOWN in the back of the cockpit between Captain Huber in the pilot's seat and Navigator-Bombardier Dorfman sitting in his jump seat to the right of the pilot.

Rolf looked with awe at the huge formation of bombers and escort fighters visible all around through the Plexiglas dome of the cockpit. The English coastline was approaching below, and Dorfman was busy looking at his maps.

"Wow, we've been bombing the British for over a month now, and this is our biggest formation yet," Rolf said.

"Yes, it's an all-out effort to break the back of the RAF and to break the spirit of the British," Captain Huber said.

"We've been bombing London instead of the airfields for a week now," Dorfman said. "They've suffered a lot of destruction. I wonder how much more they can take?"

"Or us?" he added.

All three exchanged a knowing glance of agreement. He had said what they all were thinking.

"Well, about time to get ready," Captain Huber said. "Everyone to your stations."

Dorfman put down his map and started to crawl up to his gun in the nose of the plane. Rolf turned and made his way back through the bomb bay to the after compartment.

Dieter was already there in his chair at his top gun station. His chair hung down close to the forward hatch partially blocking it. Rolf gave his chair a friendly push as he scooted around it and passed. In response, Dieter playfully reached down and grabbed at Rolf, but missed.

Dieter grinned and said, "You should be nicer to me, Rolf. You may need me someday."

"I need you every time we're up here. Give them hell today, Dieter."

"I intend to. I feel sorry for them already," he said with a grin.

Dieter and Rolf were good friends. Dieter never failed to amaze Rolf with his cheerfulness and ever present toothy grin, even as they flew into the teeth of the enemy and potential death.

Rolf had never seen a better specimen of German manhood and youth. Dieter was handsome with blonde hair and blue eyes, just over six feet tall, with a strong and agile physique, a former ice hockey player. His cheerfulness, confidence, and easy way were infectious and made him very likeable, especially to the girls.

But now, none of that mattered. What mattered was his skill at shooting down Hurricanes and Spitfires, the enemy fighters.

"You give them hell too, Rolf," he said.

Rolf, who was feeling the stress of the moment more, managed a weak smile up at Dieter. Then Rolf sat down on the floor with his legs down in his bathtub-like gun station. His aviation hat with its headphones and his parachute were there by his side. He put them on quickly and climbed down into his gun station.

Rolf knelt down in front of his machine gun and checked it out to make sure it was loaded and ready. He ensured he had several extra magazines of ammunition beside him. He plugged in his headset to the box at his gun station.

"Fighters are probably on their way and should be here soon. Everyone get ready and make your rounds count," he heard the Captain announce on the intercom.

Rolf took a deep breath to calm his nerves and reported into the headset that his gun station was manned and ready. He scanned the skies a few times. All he could see was the

English countryside below and the many German bombers and escort fighters all around. Soon gunfire could be heard in the distance.

"Sounds like they have arrived," Captain Huber said over the intercom.

Dorfman reported, "Group of fighters coming in, ahead on the left, high."

As he fired his nose gun at them, the line of diving fighters split up and attacked individual bombers as they passed. Several fighters passed forward of them and the bomber ahead started on fire and fell out of formation.

With the stricken bomber so close ahead, Dorfman excitedly reported, "They got the bomber ahead of us!"

"I see it. Pay attention to the fighters," replied Captain Huber. He was already adjusting his maneuvering and jinking to avoid it.

Dorfman called out, "More fighters, left side, high!" Both Dorfman on the nose gun and several seconds later Dieter on the top gun started firing.

Dieter shouted, "Rolf, one coming by on the left side."

Rolf swung the gun around and began firing as the fighter flashed by. Smoke started streaming from the fighter as it peeled off.

Rolf said excitedly, "I got him. He's smoking."

Captain Huber responded over the intercom, "Good going, Rolf. Everyone stay sharp. There's plenty more. Short bursts. You may need all of your ammo."

Dieter reported, "Fighters, aft of the right side, twenty degrees," as he began firing his gun. Rolf saw some fighters passing below and fired at them.

In the nose of the cockpit, Dorfman fired burst after burst at the passing fighters when his gun stopped firing.

"Damn!" he said as he quickly removed the ammunition magazine and reached for a nearby new one.

Captain Huber reported, "Fighters, ahead on the right, fifteen degrees."

Dorfman popped the new magazine on his machine gun, cocked it, and began firing at the incoming fighters. Bullets suddenly raked the wings of their bomber and many began hitting the cockpit.

Shattered Plexiglas flew in all directions inside the cockpit. A number of instruments and equipment were struck by bullets and flew to pieces, showering more debris.

Captain Huber and Dorfman were hit by the glass and debris but amazingly not by bullets. Captain Huber winced in pain from the wounds to his arms, back, and shoulders.

He tested his flight controls and was amazed to find they still seemed to be working. He looked around assessing the cockpit damage. He saw Dorfman moving slowly and he asked him if he was hit, but Dorfman didn't respond. His intercom was out. Captain Huber shouted to him, "Dorfman, are you hit?"

Dorfman looked back at him from his prone position at the nose gun, gave him an okay gesture, and resumed his grip on the machine gun. Both Captain Huber and Dorfman showed blood from a number of shrapnel wounds, but none seemed serious enough to need immediate medical attention.

Captain Huber continued his survey of damage and saw oil streaming from the right engine, which he immediately shut down. Not able to continue the mission on only one of his two engines, he scanned the skies quickly and saw a bank of low clouds nearby to the left. Without delay, he banked the plane steeply and dove for the shelter of the low clouds.

"We've lost an engine. I'm diving for some clouds. Stay at your stations," he said into the intercom in a painful voice.

Rolf, at his gun station in the after compartment, had heard the bullets hitting up front, and now the plane was suddenly in a steep bank and dive. He fearfully looked up at Dieter above him who appeared unhurt. Dieter was looking back at him, but without the normal toothy grin.

"Captain, are you and Dorfman hit? Do you need help?" Rolf asked into the intercom.

"We got hit by shrapnel, but I think we're okay. We've lost the right engine. But if we can make the cloud bank down there, we can get back across the channel. Stay at your stations," he replied.

"Yes, sir," Rolf responded.

Still in the dive, Captain Huber remembered the emergency release lever to jettison their bombs. It was located above his head and to the right. Flying with his left hand on the flight controls and looking straight ahead as the plane dove, he tried to raise his right arm to reach for the release lever, but was stopped by intense pain in his right arm and shoulder. He looked down at the torn and bloody right arm of his flight suit and tried again to raise his arm, again without success.

"Dorfman!" he shouted over wind noise. "Come back and pull the emergency release to jettison the bombs. My right arm is injured, and I can't reach up to get it."

Dorfman looked back at the pilot and nodded. As fast as his injured body would allow, he began to work his way back from his prone position in the nose.

They had good reason to be diving for the clouds, for within seconds, Dieter called out, "Two fighters in pursuit, to the right behind us! They'll be in range soon."

The crippled German bomber dove for the nearby clouds with the two fighters rapidly closing on it from behind. Soon the fighters were within machine gun range, and Dieter opened fire. The fighters also began firing, but only seconds before the bomber disappeared into the low clouds.

The two fighters veered off sharply and climbed above the clouds to watch and wait for the bomber to emerge.

Captain Huber leveled the bomber off. He had zero visibility but was able to keep the plane flying level and hidden in the clouds.

He looked over at the right engine, which was covered with black oil but was not on fire. "We still have one good engine, and we're safe here for a time in the clouds," he thought to himself with a little bit of relief.

Meanwhile, Dorfman had managed to painfully turn and start to crawl back toward his seat, which was below the emergency bomb release. His right arm was also hurting. He would have to use his left hand, he thought. Looking up, he was startled to discover the emergency release lever had taken a direct hit and was no longer there.

"Captain, the lever is shot off. We can't jettison the bombs from here. I'll have to go back to the bomb bay and manually release them there."

"Okay. Do it," Captain Huber told him.

"Yes, sir," Dorfman replied.

Worried about his pilot, Dorfman saw that he was in pain, but still seemed able to handle the flight controls.

"A good thing," Dorfman thought, "I'm not in such good shape to fly either."

As he rose stiffly to climb past the pilot, the plane burst suddenly from the safety of the clouds into bright sunlight. Dorfman and the Captain anxiously scanned the skies.

Immediately, Dieter reported, "Fighter, at close range right behind us at ten degrees!" and he began firing his machine gun.

Captain Huber would try to make it to another cloud a distance off, but exposed as they were, he began his evasive maneuvering again. Meanwhile, Dorfman was lurching back and forth beside him in the cockpit as he tried to make his way back to his nose gun.

Below at his gun station, Rolf was also tossing back and forth. Still, he looked for the fighters, but had none in his view. Looking up for a second, he saw Dieter above him swaying about in his chair firing nearly continuously. He also heard the machine guns of the fighter firing. A number of bullets pinged through their compartment and more bullets could be heard hitting forward in the cockpit and wings.

The airframe shook as the bomber jerked and buffeted for a few moments and then recovered. Dieter suddenly stopped firing.

"The fighter veered off!" he shouted.

The pilot of the enemy fighter, seeing the bomber was finished, had banked away to watch and confirm the outcome of his attack.

Rolf was alarmed that the evasive maneuvering of the plane had stopped. Fearing the pilot was dead, he called into his headset, "Captain, are you all right!"

There was no answer, and the intercom sounded dead.

Dieter, in his top gun station with his head above the top of the plane, craned around looking to see how badly the plane was damaged.

He yelled down to Rolf, "We're hit up front! The left engine's on fire!" Rolf was already up from his gun station below and rushing past Dieter's chair forward to the cockpit. Dieter scrambled out of his chair and was right behind Rolf.

When Rolf got to the back of the cockpit, he saw severe damage. Much of the Plexiglas nose was shattered and open to the rushing air. Captain Huber sat in the pilot seat with numerous bloody cuts and tears in his flight suit. Although his head was slumped forward on his chest, he still seemed to be flying the plane, keeping it level with two bloody hands draped on the flight controls. Even so, the plane was losing altitude rapidly.

Dorfman was on his hands and knees, crawling back from the nose where he had fallen. He dragged his right leg, which had a bleeding bullet wound.

"Captain, are you all right!" Rolf shouted over the wind noise.

"Rolf, quick! Cut the fuel to the left engine!" Rolf quickly reached over and pulled the lever.

"Good," shouted the pilot. "We're too low to bail out. We'll have to crash land. The controls still seem to work. I'm hit, but I can fly. I think I can still get us down. Get Dorfman back aft and brace for shock."

Dieter had already slid by Rolf and had started hauling Dorfman back from the nose.

"Hurry! We don't have much time!" Captain Huber shouted to be heard. Rolf helped Dieter get Dorfman through the doorway and they disappeared aft while Rolf stayed with Captain Huber. They were over open farmland, and the fields below were rapidly approaching.

Rolf was again alarmed when he saw the pilot's head slumped forward so much. He thought Captain Huber might have passed out.

"Captain, are you okay? What can I do to help you? Can you fly well enough?" shouted Rolf.

"I'm having trouble holding my head up. Brace yourself there and hold my head up so I can see."

"Yes, Captain," Rolf said as he quickly wedged himself behind the pilot's seat, put his hands on each side of the pilot's head, and raised his head up from his chest.

"That's enough," the pilot said, wincing with pain.

The flames from the left engine were now out, and the plane glided with no engines toward the open field. With the ground rapidly approaching, Rolf yelled back through the bomb bay to Dieter and Dorfman, "Brace for impact!"

Only then did Rolf notice the noses of the bombs in their racks. He suddenly realized with a sinking heart that their bombs, all eight 250 kilogram bombs, were still onboard. At that terrible instant, he was sure they would all be killed.

"Rolf! My right arm is weak! Help me hold the right side of the controls!"

This shout brought him out of his shock. Turning forward again, Rolf saw the Captain struggling.

With one hand holding up the pilot's head, he leaned forward quickly and grasped the right side of the controls.

I'm trying to fly it level to the ground! Just follow my pressure on the controls. Good!"

Seconds later, the plane struck the ground and amazingly plowed smoothly along the ground without bouncing. Captain Huber had managed to make a nearly perfect pancake landing in a level field of grain.

Rolf had lurched forward at impact, but was able to pull himself back and hunch behind the right side of the pilot as the plane skidded and buffeted along the ground at rapid speed. The wings and the fuselage are holding together, he noted thankfully.

Fortunately, the bottom of the plane did not catch on anything to make it flip over or go sideways. Unfortunately though, they did not have a lot of field left after impact. The patch of small trees that edged the field were rapidly approaching. Within seconds, the plane skidded off the field and plowed into the trees.

Hunched beside the pilot's seat, Rolf watched in horror as they struck, and everything went dark.

Chapter 39
Getting Clear

THE NOSE AND ENGINES of the plane were heavily damaged by the violent impact into the trees, but miraculously, the fuselage and wings remained intact. The left wing and engine had plowed up over some broken trees leaving the plane resting with its left side tilted up.

The wreckage of the plane sat there quietly for several moments before a hatch on the bottom of the plane was kicked open, and Dieter jumped out. He struggled to help Dorfman out of the same hatch. Finally they were out from underneath the plane and got to their feet.

Dieter bent to put Dorfman over his shoulder, picked him up, and carried him, half running, along the tree line away from the wreckage. He put Dorfman down on the ground about fifty meters from the plane and ran back to the wreckage.

When he arrived back at the plane, he headed for the right wing so he could get to the right access hatch of the cockpit. A large farmhand carrying a shovel had also arrived at the wreckage and met Dieter at the back of the right wing.

They stood looking at each other for a second. Dieter said, "Men!" pointing to the cockpit. Then he ran onto the damaged right wing, now at ground level, and raced to the access hatch of the heavily damaged cockpit. The front of the cockpit was covered with a tangle of tree branches, but the access hatch was still clear. He could see Captain Huber inside still strapped in and slumped forward in the pilot's seat as he worked to force open the access hatch.

The farmhand was suddenly beside him and helping to pry open the hatch with his shovel. They finally wrenched the hatch open, and Dieter climbed inside. He immediately noticed Rolf lying in a lifeless tangle forward in the nose of the plane. It was a momentary shock for him, but he recovered himself when he heard Captain Huber beside him groan.

Dieter quickly unstrapped Captain Huber and lifted him out of the seat. He hoisted him up and passed him to the farmhand who was standing in the open hatch motioning for him to pass him out. The farmhand lifted Captain Huber out of the hatch, picked him up over his shoulder, and carried him off the wing and out to where Dorfman lay.

Meanwhile, inside the cockpit, Dieter looked again at Rolf who had been thrown forward by the impact and lay bloody and motionless in the shattered nose of the plane. Dieter crawled forward to him. As gently as he could, he pulled him free from the debris and branches in the nose.

Rolf looked to be dead as Dieter hauled him back to the cockpit hatch. Another farmhand stood in the hatch looking with amazement into the cockpit. Dieter lifted Rolf up and out of the hatch. The farmhand took Rolf and carried him away.

Sad at the loss of his friend, Dieter looked around the cockpit of the bomber one last time. He climbed up and out of the hatch. From the wing, he stepped down onto the ground where the first farmhand again stood.

"Any more inside? More men inside?" the farmhand asked pointing at the plane. Dieter shook his head.

The farmhand picked up his shovel from the ground nearby where it had fallen and held it in a threatening manner.

"Okay, Fritz. On with you then. And no funny business if you know what's good for ya," he ordered. He motioned with the shovel for Dieter to go. Dieter nodded his compliance and walked back to join the others, with the farmhand close behind him.

The others lay under a tree at the edge of the field with several farm hands guarding them. Captain Huber lay lifeless on his back with a jacket stuffed under his head as a pillow. Dieter knelt down beside him, looked him over, and saw he was still alive. He was covered with many bloody cuts from shrapnel, but didn't appear to have any bullet wounds or deep seriously bleeding cuts.

Dieter looked over at Dorfman, who was sitting up and loosening the tourniquet on his wounded leg to allow blood flow for a moment. Dieter had used his own belt to tie around Dorfman's leg in the brief moments before the crash. Dieter took a handkerchief and held it on the bullet wound to help stop the bleeding. Dieter and Dorfman looked over at Rolf who was covered with blood from multiple cuts and didn't appear to be breathing.

"Poor Rolf, he's dead, isn't he?" Dieter said in a low voice.

"He appears to be. The farmhand there checked him and said he was dead, but he could be mistaken. You ought to check him, Dieter," Dorfman said.

"Yes, I agree," Dieter said, starting to rise.

But a police car approached rapidly and skidded to a stop in the dirt nearby before he was able to do so. Dieter lowered back down and sat with his hands visible. A police lieutenant and sergeant burst from the car with their revolvers drawn and briskly approached.

To one of the guarding farmhands, the police lieutenant asked, "Is this all of them? None got away?"

"This is all. None got away that we saw. This bloke here," said the farmhand pointing at Dieter, "he said there aren't no more inside. I think that one on the end is dead."

The police lieutenant glanced briefly at the lifeless body of Rolf.

"I took this pistol and belt off that one when I laid 'im down," a second farmhand said, pointing at Captain Huber on the ground.

"I think he's the pilot," the farmhand said as he stepped forward and handed a gun belt to the sergeant.

"Good work," said the police lieutenant and then he turned to Dieter.

"On your feet. Hands on your head." he said motioning with his revolver. Dieter slowly stood up and put his hands on his head, as directed.

"You speak English then?"

"Yes, a little."

"Any more weapons?" the lieutenant asked him pointing to the handgun held by the sergeant.

"No. What use are they down here?" Dieter replied.

"Quite right. Good thinking. But we better have a check anyway," the lieutenant responded, motioning the police sergeant forward. The sergeant frisked Dieter and found no weapons.

"Sergeant, check the others for weapons too and get their names from their dog tags for the report so we can keep track of where they are sent."

"Yes, sir," replied the sergeant as he holstered his revolver. Pulling out a notepad and a stubby pencil, he walked briskly over to where Captain Huber lay.

An ambulance now pulled up by the police car. Two orderlies got out, opened the back door of the ambulance, and brought out several stretchers. They examined Captain Huber briefly, put him on the stretcher, carried him to the ambulance, and put him inside.

A crowd of townspeople began arriving to look over the enemy airmen. Some hurried over to the plane to look at it.

A few in the crowd jeered at the prisoners, calling them "Filthy Jerry Swine." Meanwhile, the orderlies attended to Dorfman's leg and put him on a stretcher.

Finished with his weapons search and name check, the police sergeant looked up and yelled for the people to stay away from the plane. But they still gathered and walked around it, curious to get an up close look at the enemy warplane. With a scowl, he returned to the lieutenant and Dieter.

"Is it correct, you said there are no more men on board?" the police lieutenant asked Dieter.

"No more men," Dieter replied.

Glancing toward the plane, he saw the people starting to climb on the wings and look into the cockpit.

"No more men, just the bombs, and they had a rough trip," he added after turning back to the lieutenant.

"Good lord!" the police lieutenant exclaimed.

"Sergeant! Get those people away from that plane!"

The sergeant ran off toward the plane yelling loudly for the people to get away.

"Blimey!" exclaimed one of the farmhands. "And me standing on the wing right there next to 'em. Wait 'til I tell 'em at the pub!"

After the orderlies put Dorfman in the ambulance, they came back to Rolf, who lay motionless on the ground. They seemed in a hurry to be off. One checked him quickly for a pulse.

"This Jerry is now a good Jerry. He's dead," he said without emotion.

Dieter swelled with rage at hearing this and was about to leap at the orderly. The police lieutenant seeing this and pointing his gun, warned him firmly, "Steady! Stay where you are!"

Dieter checked his anger and stood glaring at the orderly. With his eyes and gun still on Dieter, the lieutenant said to the orderly, "That's enough of that. Now get on with it."

"What? I only…" the orderly started to protest, but the lieutenant cut him off.

"I said get on with it!"

Without saying anything more, the orderlies hoisted Rolf's body roughly onto a stretcher and covered him with a sheet. They put him in the back of the ambulance with the others and closed the back door.

As the ambulance pulled away, the sergeant returned and reported, "I told some men to keep people away from the plane until the RAF comes to take charge of it."

"Very good, Sergeant. Put some handcuffs on this one. We'll take him back to the station."

When the sergeant had Dieter's hands cuffed behind his back, the police lieutenant holstered his revolver. The sergeant took Dieter's arm and walked him back to the car, while the lieutenant followed. They put Dieter in the back seat, climbed into their car, and drove off.

Chapter 40
The Coroner

THE CORONER WAS SITTING at his desk finishing up the paperwork for Mrs. Archibald. She had been riding her bike on the narrow country lane on her way into town to get groceries like she did every day. The narrow paved lane had thick high hedges on each side and was actually only wide enough for one vehicle. There were turnouts so oncoming cars could get by each other.

The military truck was delivering supplies to the old flying club outside of town, which was being set up as an emergency landing field for the RAF. After getting lost, the driver was late and in a hurry. He had somehow ended up on her lane and was driving too fast when he came around the blind sharp curve and hit poor Mrs. Archibald. She was another innocent casualty of the war.

The coroner put down his pen, thinking what a nice lady she had been and how she didn't deserve such a terrible end. Through the windows in front of his desk, he saw the ambulance pull up to the morgue's entrance and two orderlies emerge. He stood up and walked over to see what new casualty had arrived. When he reached the entrance, the two orderlies were carrying in a body on a stretcher with a sheet covering it.

"Afternoon, sir. Dead Jerry from the bomber crash in Henry White's field. We already delivered two others to the hospital, but this one's for you."

"I see. Put him on the examination table, please."

The coroner watched the orderlies put the stretcher on the floor by the table. With one orderly on each end, they roughly hoisted the body up on the table. The coroner noticed the body still seemed very limber.

"How long has he been dead?" he asked.

"The plane crashed probably about two hours ago."

"Hmm," the coroner said and he walked over to look at the body. The orderlies seemed in a hurry and were already starting to leave.

"Thank you, sir. He has his dog tags on 'im. We're in a bit of a rush, so we'll be on our way." And they were out the door.

The coroner lifted the sheet to see the dead man. His eyes widened when the head twitched to the side and back. He rushed out and caught the orderlies as they were getting in the ambulance.

"You two buffoons get back in there and take that man to the hospital. He isn't dead."

"Blimey! He seemed dead enough out in Henry White's field?" the driver said as he grudgingly trudged to the back of the ambulance and brought the stretcher out again. The orderlies followed the coroner back inside.

At the table, the orderly lifted the sheet and looked at Rolf's face.

"He looks dead," he said.

"I tell you he is alive, not dead. He doesn't belong here in the morgue with a sheet on him. He belongs in a hospital. Do you understand?" the angry coroner said with contempt, pulling the sheet from Rolf.

"Aye, Governor," the orderly said reluctantly. He started to lift him and paused.

"Ya know, Governor, we've been pretty busy today thanks to these buggers. Maybe we should leave him here. He'll be dead soon enough, and it'll save us another trip to the hospital."

"Take him to the hospital! Damn you! And be quick about it!" the coroner shouted in a fury.

"Aye, Governor. Right away." They hurriedly put Rolf back on the stretcher and rushed out.

Outside as they were loading Rolf back into the ambulance, the coroner firmly told them, "I'm ringing up the hospital to tell them you are coming! They will be expecting you. Now be on your way!"

This, he thought would hopefully keep them from stopping at a pub on the way to the hospital. The two orderlies rushed to finish loading, jumped in the ambulance, and were off in a hurry. As the coroner watched the ambulance race off, he shook his head.

"Most unprofessional!" he said with disgust. Then turning, he went back into the morgue to ring up the hospital.

Chapter 41
Notification

SEVERAL WEEKS LATER in Germany, Rolf's mother opened the top half of a split kitchen door and admired the nice sunny weather they were having. She decided to leave the top of the door open and swung it all the way back into the house. About to get her mail, she thought to herself, "Please God, let my Hans and Rolf be safe."

Reluctantly, she reached around to the mail box attached on the house next to the door. She pulled out several letters from the box and glanced through them as she started toward the kitchen table to sit down.

Suddenly she stopped, frozen in her tracks, staring at the official looking envelope from the government. She feared the worst, that it was notification of the death of her husband or her son. She felt a little faint, so she walked to the kitchen table and sat down in a chair.

She slowly opened the government envelope, unfolded the letter inside and began to read. She had only read a sentence or two when she stopped, put her hands to her face, and began to cry.

"Mama! What's wrong?" called Rolf's little sister, Lotti, in the next room when she heard her crying. She jumped up and ran to her mother. In the kitchen, she saw her mother crying at the table with the letter in her hand.

"Mama, what is it? Has something happened to Papa or Rolf?"

Rolf's mother looked up sadly and took Lotti's hand. "Rolf's plane was shot down and he was killed."

Lotti burst into tears and hugged her mother as they cried together. Through her tears, Rolf's mother said, "Let's pray there's been some mistake."

* * *

Mutti sat motionless in a chair in the living room of the apartment in Hamburg. She stared thunderstruck at the letter in her hand. She had just read the letter from Rolf's mother and learned that Rolf had been killed. She could still vividly picture him from his visits to the apartment. How young he was and how handsome he had looked in his uniform.

"Poor Rolf," she thought sadly to herself. "He had warned Kätchen he might be killed and he was right about that too. Probably killed in some fiery plane crash. How terrible it must have been for him. He was such a nice young man. My poor Kätchen. They would have been so happy together. She'll be devastated. All of Kätchen's hopes for a future together with Rolf are now gone. How heartbroken she'll be when she finds out."

Mutti pictured me in America, maybe still living with the family taking care of the two children. If there had been mail service to America, she would have sent me a letter with the terrible news. She imagined me smiling and happily opening the letter from home. As I read, I would start to look alarmed and then suddenly drop the letter in shock and start sobbing uncontrolledly, as the little girl and boy watched in amazement.

"With no mail service, I don't have to tell her the awful news yet," she thought. "But someday, mail service will be restored. I dread the very thought of it. The task in the future of shattering all of Kätchen's hopes and dreams will be a terrible weight upon me for years."

Mutti pulled out a handkerchief and started to cry into it.

With Mutti not able to send a letter, I knew nothing of Rolf's reported death. I continued to cook and watch the children. I kept my hopes up that Rolf was still alive and well. I tried to keep thinking he would somehow survive the war, and we would someday be able to finally get married.

Chapter 42
Answered Prayers

ROLF LAY MOTIONLESS in a hospital bed in a large open ward. His eyes were closed, and he had been unconscious ever since the crash. His head was heavily bandaged. He had lost a lot of blood, and a bag of plasma hung beside his bed with a tube running to the needle in his arm.

In the next bed, a patient named Harry was recovering from surgery to remove a ruptured appendix. Feeling much better, he was propped up and reading a magazine.

Rolf let out a small grunt, and Harry looked up from his magazine. Harry had been there for two days, and the German in the next bed had been completely quiet and motionless the entire time. Harry thought he had just heard him grunt.

He watched as Rolf's finger twitched slightly, and then Rolf slowly opened his eyes and looked around. Harry saw a nurse several beds down and called to her, "Nurse, the German is coming to."

Rolf couldn't see much when he first opened his eyes. He began to realize he was lying in a bed and the light-colored blurry area in front of him was probably a ceiling. After blinking his eyes several times, his vision became a little clearer. Ooh, his head hurt.

Looking at the blurry images around him, he recognized that he was in a hospital. He tried to speak, but nothing came out. Suddenly, the blurry face of a nurse appeared in front of him. "Don't try to talk. I'll get the doctor," she said before disappearing.

Looking down at his left arm, he tried to move his fingers. They were stiff, but seemed to work. He moved his wrist up and down. Rotating his forearm, he felt a stabbing pain and had to stop. His left arm must have been injured. He wondered if his right side was any better, but before he could try out his right arm, the doctor arrived and started to examine his eyes. He had a little light, which he shined in them. The nurse was back too.

"Nurse, give him some water." The nurse had a glass of water ready. As she raised up his head to drink, he winced with pain. After a pause, she raised his head a little more, enough to put the glass to his mouth. After sipping some water, she lowered his head back to the pillow.

"You're in a hospital. Do you understand?" the doctor asked. Rolf nodded slightly.

"You were in a plane crash and have multiple broken bones and injuries, including a fractured skull. You've been unconscious, asleep, for five days. Do you understand?"

Rolf's English skills were not good enough to understand everything, but he grasped the general meaning. He was just waking up from the plane crash days ago. He wanted to say he understood to the doctor, but couldn't seem to get any words out.

"Don't try to talk right now. Just rest and get better," the doctor told him, picking up the clipboard hanging on the bottom frame of the bed and beginning to write.

The nurse offered him the glass again and he drank more down. The cool, wet feel of the water in his dry mouth and throat was wonderful. He had been without food or water for the last five days. He closed his eyes again and drifted off to sleep.

For several days, Rolf lay in bed awakening at times but mostly sleeping. When awake, the nurses were able to give him water to drink and a mush to eat. If he had remained comatose much longer than the five days as he had, he might have died of starvation and thirst, since there was no way of giving him food or water while comatose.

But thankfully, he had awakened in time. This period of intermittent wakefulness lasted another two weeks. One morning, he awoke and suddenly felt much better. After that day, he stayed awake most of the day and slept at night. His blurred vision was better, and he could talk again. Although he still suffered headaches from his head injuries, his numerous broken bones and cuts seemed to be healing. The doctor thought he had more color now and looked to be on the mend.

No longer in danger, he was transferred from the intensive care ward to another ward for recovering prisoners, where an armed guard stood at its doorway. A nurse was making rounds and stopped at Rolf's bed to check on him.

"Well, you are looking better today. How do you feel?"

"Better, a little, I think. Please, can I write to my family in Germany? Tell them I am here."

"We thought you were getting well enough and would soon be asking about it. The Red Cross has a card you can fill out to notify your family you are alive and a prisoner of war. Are you strong enough?"

"Yes, please."

"Okay then. I'll let Betty know. She's our Red Cross representative. She will help you with the card and the Red Cross will get it to your family in Germany."

"It will be much relief to me. Thank you," Rolf said in his broken English as he started to choke up with happiness and relief.

* * *

Several weeks later, Rolf's mother had just read the first lines of the Red Cross card when she burst into tears of happiness. She was incapable of doing anything but stand there in the middle of the kitchen hunched over crying.

After a moment she called out, "Lotti! Gregor! Rolf is alive! He's a prisoner in England. He wasn't killed!"

Rolf's sister, Lotti, flew into the room happy and crying. She nearly knocked her mother over hugging her. Soon Rolf's little brother, Gregor, flew in and all three hugged.

"Rolf is alive. I'm so happy," Lotti said.

They held one another tightly, laughing and crying. Rolf's smiling mother looked at their happy faces and said, "Our prayers have been answered."

* * *

Several days later, Mutti stood in the living room of the apartment sadly looking at the unopened letter. After hearing of Rolf's death, she had written back to Rolf's mother telling her how she shared her grief and felt like she had also lost a son, which was not an exaggeration. What a fine young man he was. What a shame he and Kätchen would not have their happy life together as they had hoped. It had been a difficult letter to write.

Now she had just received another letter from Rolf's mother. His mother would probably thank her for her sympathy and tell her some things Rolf had told her about him and Kätchen. It was probably going to be a sad letter and she knew it would start her crying.

So with a heavy heart, she opened the letter and started to read it. After an initial look of astonishment and then tears of happiness, she broke into a huge smile and spun around giddily kissing and hugging the letter.

She was so elated and relieved! Rolf was alive and in a hospital in England! He hadn't been killed after all! She was so glad she was not able to write Kätchen, thereby sparing her the unnecessary grief she had experienced herself.

It had been devastating news to all of them. She and Ruth had cried a good deal at the terrible news. Ruth, who worked in a dressmaker's shop, had to stay home for a day to recover somewhat from her grief. Gustav felt too sad to be good company for his drinking friends, so he hadn't been back to his club yet. The thought of someday having to tell Kätchen and destroy all her dreams was a heavy burden for him.

Mutti grabbed her sweater from the chair and ran excitedly out the door of the apartment. She had to tell Gustav and Ruth the good news.

* * *

The doctors seemed to be happy with the progress Rolf was making. With the help of a nurse, he was able to lift himself up so he could sit up in bed. His thinking was more clear now, although he still had headaches. Last week, he had met with the Red Cross representative to send the notification to his mother.

The idea of also sending a Red Cross notification to Kätchen was now on his mind. She was, in effect, his wife and should be notified that he was a prisoner of war. He had briefly debated in his mind over whether to do it, but had quickly decided that it is better for her to know.

He raised a hand to get the attention of a nearby nurse. When she came over, he asked her if she would have Betty, the Red Cross representative, come to see him again.

* * *

Three weeks later, it was almost lunchtime, and I was trying to decide what to make for Jimmy and Susan when the doorbell rang. I walked over to open it and was surprised to see Pepe standing there. Now fifteen years old, he still worked part time for Aunt Minna at the restaurant. My immediate thought was something had happened to my aunt.

"Hello, Pepe, what are you doing here?"

"Hello, Senorita Kätchen, the señora at the restaurant, your Tia Minna, she sent me to give you this," he said handing me a small envelope with a note on it.

I took it and read the note from Aunt Minna. She just received this letter and thought I should see it right away.

I looked at the letter. It was from the Red Cross in Washington, DC. I knew immediately that it must be bad news about Rolf or my family. I felt a little faint.

Pepe saw me reeling and rushed to my side to hold me up. He helped me into the living room and onto the couch, then sat next to me propping me up until I recovered. Pepe looked up and saw little Susan standing in a doorway wide-eyed.

"Mama, mama, there's a black man in the house. Mama, Mama," yelled little Susan as she disappeared.

Reviving, I yelled out, "No, Mrs. Gentsch, Susan, it's okay. It's Pepe from the restaurant."

"Maybe I should go," Pepe said standing up.

"No, wait. Let me open this first."

Susan and Jimmy had in the meantime appeared in the doorway and were staring at Pepe. Mrs. Gentsch came in too and was startled when she saw him.

"Kätchen, is everything all right? Who is this?"

"Mrs. Gentsch, this is Pepe from Aunt Minna's restaurant. He brought me this letter she got in the mail for me."

I stared down at it and said, "It's from the Red Cross in Washington, DC. They are probably forwarding a Red Cross message from overseas."

Sadly I added, "I'm afraid it is probably bad news."

"Oh, dear," said Mrs. Gentsch.

I took a deep breath trying to steel myself for what surely would be terrible news. But it didn't work. I started to cry as I sat looking at it. Rolf or one of my family had been killed or had died. I didn't recall hearing lately about bombings of Hamburg, so I suspected and dreaded it said Rolf had been killed.

I was sure that soon all my hopes and dreams would turn to dust. It would do no good to postpone the knowledge of it. I already felt his loss terribly. I might as well open it.

Still crying, I numbly opened the envelope as the others looked on. I pulled the notification card out from it and wiped the tears from my eyes. I unfolded it with trembling hands and began to read. When I saw Rolf's name, my heart sank and I dropped the paper. I began to sob uncontrollably, falling over on my side with my face in my hands.

Mrs. Gentsch and the kids stared, not knowing what to do or say.

The notification had fallen to the floor. Pepe picked it up and looked at it.

"Poor, Kätchen. What does it say?" asked Mrs. Gentsch.

"It is about Rolf. He is her boyfriend," he said as I continued to sob.

"It says he is a prisoner of war."

I suddenly stopped crying and slowly took my hands from my face. With a wide-eyed startled look, I gasped, "What? What did you say?"

Not waiting for his answer, I sprang upright and reached for the notification. He handed it to me, and I began to read.

I burst out overjoyed, "Oh, my God! I thought he was killed, but it says he is a prisoner of war in England!"

Now overjoyed and crying with happiness, I continued, "It says he was captured on the fifteenth of September and is recovering from his injuries in a hospital!"

Seeing my excitement and happiness, Susan and Jimmy excitedly rushed over to hug me, cheering, "Yeah! Yeah! Rolf is a prisoner!"

"That was two months ago. Is that all it says? Nothing else?" asked Mrs. Gentsch.

"That's all it says. His plane must have been shot down, and he was injured somehow. It doesn't say."

"I'm so relieved," I said shedding more tears of happiness. "I hope he isn't hurt too badly, but at least he is alive and out of the war."

Mrs. Gentsch came over and sat down with me to give me a hug. Jimmy and Susan joined in.

Looking up and seeing Pepe smiling at my good news, I asked Susan to get me a piece of paper and pencil. Both she and Jimmy raced out of the room to get them. When they returned, I wrote a quick note back to Aunt Minna thanking her and telling her the good news. She too worried about Rolf for my sake and would be greatly relieved.

I thanked and hugged Pepe for bringing me such wonderful news. Soon, he was away and headed back to the restaurant.

Chapter 43
Prison Camp

IN TIME, ROLF was well enough to leave the hospital and was sent to one of the crowded prisoner of war camps run by the RAF. His fractures and injuries were not fully healed yet, but his fractured hip was mended and strong enough for him to walk with a cane. A car from the prison camp had been sent to pick him up. In his condition, only the soldier driving the car was needed to guard and escort him.

Arriving back at the prison camp, the driver pulled to a stop, got out, and walked around the car to open the door for his invalid prisoner. Rolf put his legs out of the car onto the ground. The driver helped him get upright on his legs. He grasped his cane and positioned it in front of him. With the cane for support, he took a few feeble steps away from the car and his guard closed the car door behind. He was wearing his flight suit, repaired after the crash and with insignias or badges removed. All of his worldly possessions fit in its pockets.

The prison camp enclosure before him was to be his new home. It was far different from the hospital where he had been for the last several months. He had expected to see the high barbed wire fences, guard towers, and crowds of milling prisoners. But instead of wooden barracks inside, he saw rows and rows of round corrugated steel huts.

As he looked at the strange scene, he wondered what life would be like inside a prison camp or if he would know anyone there. The British had been good to him already, so he didn't anticipate any cruel treatment from them.

After getting photographed and processed at the prison camp duty office, one of the guards escorted him to the main gate of the prison camp enclosure. Some prisoners gathered inside near the gate to see the curious new arrival. He was told he would get his bunk assignment at Hut Number One inside where he needed to check in.

The guard at the gate looked Rolf over and directed one of the nearby prisoners to give him some assistance. The prisoner inside nodded and came forward. The gate was opened, and Rolf gingerly walked in.

"This way," the prisoner told him and started with him through the crowd.

Suddenly from back in the crowd, Rolf heard an astonished shout, "Rolf! Rolf! Is it really you?"

Looking to see who it was, he saw Dieter wide-eyed and pushing his way excitedly through the crowd.

"Dieter!" Rolf said happily.

Standing in front of Rolf and overjoyed at seeing his friend alive, Dieter looked him over in astonishment.

"Rolf, it really is you! I can't believe it! We thought we lost you!"

Seeing that Rolf was still fragile and recovering, he carefully put a hand on his shoulder. He was now over his initial shock and grinning happily.

"Rolf, I'm so glad to see you. I still can't believe it!" he said.

Rolf gave his arm a pat in return. He too was smiling and ecstatic to see his friend.

"Dieter! You survived too," Rolf said with happiness.

"Me? Survived too? I barely had a scratch! You're the one who was dead!"

"I can't believe you're alive. How did it happen?" Dieter asked incredulously, looked him over again.

"I don't know. All I know is that I was in and out of a coma in a hospital for about three weeks after the crash. I've been recovering there ever since."

A crowd of prisoners had gathered around them enjoying the happy reunion scene, a bit of good news for a change. They wanted to congratulate them with pats on the back, and Dieter had to tell them to stay back a bit to give Rolf some room.

"How about the Captain and Dorfman?" Rolf asked as they started to slowly move away from the crowded front gate area.

"They made it. They were wounded and in the hospital for a time, but they made it too."

"Wow, we all made it," Rolf said. "How about that. I didn't think any of us would, and we all did!"

"They're here somewhere too," Dieter said, excitedly looked around.

"Captain Huber! Dorfman! Where are you?" he shouted.

He heard no answer, but heard the names being relayed ahead by others. Dieter was bursting with happiness and excitement as he cleared a path for Rolf through the prisoners.

"I still can't believe it! They won't either! They will both be happy to see you, but especially the Captain. He took your death pretty hard. He credited you with saving us," Dieter said as they made their way along the huts.

"Captain Huber! Dorfman!" Dieter excitedly shouted ahead again.

"Dieter! We're here. What is it?" he heard Dorfman shout up ahead.

"Captain Huber, Dorfman! I have a surprise! You won't believe it!"

Rolf and Dieter emerged from the other prisoners to see Captain Huber and Dorfman walking carefully toward them to find out what was the matter. They stopped in shock when they saw Rolf and then beamed with delight.

"Rolf? My God! I can't believe it. You survived!" Dorfman exclaimed. They both hurried forward, and came together shaking hands and carefully celebrating.

"Rolf, you're alive! Thank God! How can it be?" Captain Huber said thankfully, but then looking down at the cane, he asked, "But you are badly hurt."

"Don't worry, Captain. The doctors said I'm supposed to fully recover. But I wouldn't even be alive, Captain, none of us would be if it hadn't been for that perfect landing you made."

To Dieter and Dorfman, he said, "You two were in the back and didn't see it."

"No, we could tell it was a good one back there too," Dorfman said.

"But more importantly, the bombs liked it," Dieter chimed in, and they laughed.

"It was the best landing I've ever made, but I couldn't have managed it without your help, Rolf," Captain Huber said. "Unfortunately, we ran out of field. Here, I had asked you to stay up front to help me fly, and then you got killed for your efforts. Or so we thought. Thank God you're alive! It's a big weight off my mind."

Captain Huber looked at his crew with admiration in the midst of a crowd of happy onlookers and said earnestly, "Finally we have something to celebrate and no beer to do it with. Damn!"

After more laughter, handshakes and careful back slaps, Dorfman said, "How about we get you to a bunk so you can get off your feet?"

"That would be good, thanks," Rolf said.

"This way, Rolf," said Dorfman, pointing. They gingerly started off in that direction as they continued to happily talk. Dieter was out in front actively clearing the path ahead through the many prisoners.

"Make way! Coming through! Give us some room!"

* * *

As I walked along the sidewalk on the way to the post office, I said the happy words again to myself for the hundredth time, "Rolf is safe." It was such a relief to know he was alive and no longer in the war. Before the notification, I had no idea if he was alive or dead. While it was a relief to finally hear something, my next hope was that he hadn't been wounded or injured too badly. Having no idea if prisoners of war were allowed to send letters, I was impatiently waiting to hear from him again.

I may have been thinking about a letter from Rolf, but the letter in my hand was from the immigration service. It was not a comforting feeling to receive an official letter from Washington, DC, so I was a little concerned as I entered the post office.

After a short wait in line inside, I handed the letter to the clerk behind the counter and said, "I recently received this letter. It says I must register here with you."

The man took the letter and read it.

"Did I do something wrong?" I asked.

"No, Miss Thile' kee. Is that how to say your name?"

"No, it's pronounced like Teel' ka."

"Teel'ka, I wasn't even close. No, Miss Thielke, it's a new law. Starting in September 1940, all aliens have to register at their local post offices. The first letter of your last name is near the end of the alphabet, so you are just now getting your letter, only a couple months late. Can I see some identification please?"

"I brought my passport with me like the letter said."

He nodded and took it. He flinched and frowned when he saw the Nazi swastika on it. He looked at my picture in it, looked at me, entered my name in a book. He filled out a form and pulled out an ink pad. After getting my thumbprints, he handed me a tissue to wipe the ink off my thumbs.

"We only have to do thumbprints just this first time, but from now on, you have to register here at the beginning of every month. Do you understand?"

"Yes."

"Okay, so we'll see you again at the first of next month."

I nodded and left. I didn't know if this registering was directly related to the war in Europe, but I was beginning to suspect the war was going to have some official, not just personal, repercussions for me here in America too.

* * *

One evening soon after Rolf's arrival at the prison of war camp, Dieter and Dorfman stood beside Rolf who was lying in his bunk. Around them in the round corrugated steel hut were multiple rows of two-high bunk beds where groups of prisoners played cards and talked.

Rolf still suffered from periodic headaches like the one bothering him now, but talking with his friends would take his mind from it.

"When I was up in the cockpit and called back for you two to brace for shock, I saw the bombs still sitting there in their racks. I thought for sure we were all going to die. I still have bad dreams about that moment. But somehow we all made it. I still can't believe it," Rolf told them.

"Thankfully, the bombs don't arm themselves until they are released. So that helped, but they still could have gone off in a strong impact or fire," Dorfman said.

Dieter chimed in, "You can't believe we made it? I thought for sure you were dead when I saw you lying in a heap in the nose of the plane."

"So it was you, Dieter, who got me out of the plane?"

"Yup, me and some big farmer," Dieter replied with a grin.

Dorfman related, "We were lying by the trees after getting out of the plane. I was loosening the tourniquet on my leg when the farmhand carried you over. He checked you after laying you down and said you were dead. I thought we should check you ourselves though. After Dieter came and helped me, he was getting up to check you, but the police came before he could."

"I admit Rolf looked pretty dead, but you'd think those damned fools in the ambulance should have figured out he wasn't," Dieter said with contempt.

"I suspect they didn't have much sympathy for the guys dropping bombs on them," Dorfman offered.

"They were a couple idiots," Dieter said.

"You're probably right, Dieter," Dorfman conceded. "They were in a hurry to get to the pub or something, no matter who was lying there."

"But somehow I ended up at the hospital," Rolf said.

"I don't know how," Dorfman puzzled. "You were with the Captain and I in the ambulance that took us to the hospital. You were lifeless and covered with a sheet the whole time. I wanted to check you myself, but you were too far away. After taking the Captain and me inside, the ambulance left the hospital to take you to the morgue."

"I was taken right to a police station, so I don't know how you got there," Dieter inserted.

Dorfman continued, "We never saw you later at the hospital. So naturally, we thought you were dead."

"How long were you there?" asked Rolf.

"Less than two weeks in their prisoner ward."

"Then you were already gone by the time I made it to the prisoner ward. That explains why you didn't see me."

"I wonder how they finally discovered you were still alive?" asked Dorfman.

"I'm sure it wasn't those two orderly jokers. I hope someday to run into them again," Dieter mused with a determined look.

"Look at you, Dieter, where is the usual smile?" Rolf asked jokingly.

"I'll be smiling if I ever run into those two jokers again," he said with a grin.

Only a few days later, Rolf, Dieter, and Dorfman had to say goodbye to Captain Huber, who was being transferred to a prison camp for officers. Apparently he had been sent to this camp with them only temporarily. Their pilot officer had been good to them and had watched out for their interests as a good officer should. He had earned their respect and affection, and his flying skills had saved their lives when their plane went down. With great emotion and sadness, they shook hands with and saluted him when he departed.

Chapter 44
The North Atlantic

ROLF COULD FEEL the rolling of the ship as he lay in his bunk in the cargo hold of the British merchant ship. The weather in the North Atlantic on the first two days of their voyage had not been stormy. While the rolling and pitching weren't violent, it made getting around in their make-shift living quarters a challenge for Rolf in his injured condition.

He had been in the RAF prisoner of war camp for only a month or two before the British had decided to transport some of their prisoners of war from the overcrowded camps in England to camps in Canada.

Large convoys of merchant cargo ships from Canada had been braving the dangerous waters of the North Atlantic for some time to bring badly needed supplies to the British Isles. Some ships in the convoys returning to Canada were now being loaded with hundreds of prisoners of war. An upper cargo hold on a returning merchant ship was temporarily fitted with bunks five high, as well as all the associated extra systems and supplies necessary to support the prisoners during the two week transit to Canada.

Confined in their cargo hold, Rolf and the other prisoners tried to fill their time at sea as best they could. They carried out assigned cooking and cleaning duties, exercised, talked, played cards, sang songs, wrote in journals, read books, anything to keep their minds off a wartime transit of the North Atlantic in winter.

All the prisoners were enlisted Luftwaffe airmen from the RAF prisoner of war camps. The prisoners were expected to take care of themselves while in transit, all the cooking, cleaning, etc. The highest ranking enlisted man was in charge of running the day to day work, and ensuring military order and discipline were being maintained. The men were expected to carry out orders of their seniors, perform assigned duties, and muster in a timely, military manner. The senior man in charge ran a tight ship, so to speak, and the spaces were kept clean and orderly.

Since Rolf was still recovering from his injuries, he was assigned a second bunk in the stack of five because it was the easiest level to access. As he lay in his bunk, he was chatting with Dieter and another prisoner named Emil, standing beside his bunk.

"So why don't they paint 'P O W' in big letters on the side of the ship?" Emil asked.

"And how would you know if it was true?" Dieter chided him. "Face it, Emil. You're going to have to risk getting torpedoed by our U-boats (German submarines) and going down with the ship like the rest of us."

"But to be sunk and killed by our own U-boats!" Emil protested, "Getting killed accidentally by our own forces in war is bad enough, but to be killed intentionally by them is ridiculous. What am I supposed to think as I go under the icy water for the last time?"

"The enemy has one less cargo ship?" Rolf offered.

"I don't think that would give me everlasting peace," Emil frowned.

"War is hell, Emil," Dieter said cheerily. "At least the U-boat captain will get another medal. Our highly esteemed Führer himself might pin a big fat colorful one on him."

Looking around with concern, Rolf said, "Dieter, you shouldn't talk about Hitler that way. You'll get in trouble with the Nazi fanatics among us."

Dieter shrugged.

"Yes, let's talk about something else," said Emil. "I wonder what it's going to be like where we're going. The

British didn't treat us too badly. It was crowded, and the food wasn't great."

"I hear British food is like that, whether you are a prisoner of war or not," Dieter said drolly.

"The British didn't beat or starve us," Emil continued. "I don't know anything about Canada or Canadians. I wonder how they will treat us?"

"Well," Dieter said, "they believe we Germans crucified their prisoners during the last war, so how do you think they will treat us?"

"What? They do? Sounds like they probably hate us," Emil said with concern.

"Don't be surprised, Emil, if the Canadians want to pay us back a bit when we get there, a little tit for tat. Nope, I wouldn't be surprised," Dieter told him, tongue in cheek.

"We didn't really crucify their prisoners in the last war, did we?" Emil asked Rolf.

"I don't know," Rolf replied.

"Who knows what ill treatment the Canadians may have in store for us. And with any luck, our own U-boats won't save them the trouble."

"Oh, that isn't funny, Dieter!" Emil said looking pale.

Seeing his jesting had frightened the poor guy, Dieter felt bad.

"I'm sorry, Emil," Dieter said, "I was just kidding with you, of course. The Canadians probably aren't bad people. I mean, after all, they invented ice hockey! They can't be all bad. So, Emil, buck up! Try to relax and not worry. Everything will be fine."

Emil managed a weak smile, was a little less pale, but he still looked worried.

"Take heart, Emil," Rolf told him. "Luck is with us. If we survived being shot down over England, we can survive this trip to Canada too."

Chapter 45
The Coming Storm

ROLF COULD HEAR a prisoner throwing up in the washroom. He felt a little woozy himself, but not quite sick to his stomach. He was lying in his bunk late at night as the ship rocked heavily in a storm.

He was actually glad to see the heavy weather. Despite their joking with Emil about getting torpedoed by German U-boats, it was a very real danger and threat. He thought the storm with its clouds, rain, and swells would help conceal them from the roving packs of U-boats, improving their chances of getting safely across the Atlantic.

If they did get hit by a torpedo, there would be very little chance of their survival in the icy waters of the North Atlantic in early March. If they were able to make it up from the hold to the main deck and into the water, he would only have a few minutes to make it to a boat or life raft before dying of hypothermia.

But Rolf himself was still stiff and recovering from his injuries. While the chance of survival for the other prisoners was very small, he basically had zero chance of survival if they were torpedoed. He lay in bed trying not to think about it.

He tried instead to think about me chasing after my two little kids. He pictured me standing in front of a stove cooking their meal for them, gazing ahead with a worried look as I thought about him. He was sure the Red Cross notification and its news would be a relief for me. Unfortunately, he had not been allowed to say much on the notification or to send any letters since.

He had addressed the notification to my aunt's restaurant, the only address in America that he knew. No longer having the napkin on which he had written it down long ago, he hoped he had remembered the address correctly, and I had received it.

If he made it to Canada, maybe he would be allowed to send letters from the camps there. He wondered what it was going to be like. He knew nothing about Canada.

* * *

When I walked in the front door of Aunt Minna's restaurant, she was busy cleaning up behind the bar. She perked up when she turned around and saw me. It was Saturday, the first of March 1941, and Mrs. Gentsch had given me the day off. Aunt Minna was always happy when I came to help her out. I liked doing it too. I got to see her again, do some real cooking, and visit with the regular customers who I knew and liked. It was also a good way to take my mind off things.

After exchanging greetings with Aunt Minna, we went back into the kitchen. I put on my apron as she went over the planned dinner special for the night.

Maybe for a while, I would be thinking about cooking the roast just right and not wondering what it was like for Rolf as a prisoner of war. I would be taking food and drink orders to customers and not wondering how the war was affecting my family in Germany. I hadn't heard from them in sixteen months since mail service was cut off. If busy, maybe I wouldn't be wondering if Ruth, now eighteen years old, had a boyfriend or was married.

Even so, there were still times when I would pause and stare off into space for a moment thinking of them.

* * *

Mutti and Ruth walked together along on the sidewalk and came to the door of Vati's club. Ruth opened it, and they both walked in. Immediately, there was an uproar at the bar where Gustav and his friends were drinking.

"Look out, Gustav. The wife is here. Watch what you say about her!" his friends shouted loudly so Mutti could hear, as they chucked him on the shoulder laughing. It was something they did every single time Mutti came in.

Gustav turned and smiled at seeing Mutti and Ruth, and went to meet them. After giving them a kiss on the cheek, he went with them to a booth by the window. They had come to join him for the afternoon.

The bartender came over with Mutti's and Ruth's usual drinks, namely coffee and Alster Water. Gustav and Mutti listened as Ruth told about her day at the dressmaker's shop. She had been a dressmaker's assistant for about six months, ever since graduating from a sewing trade school, conducted in a local dressmaking shop. She was still only doing uninteresting sewing work while the more experienced people did the creative work. Mutti and Gustav were still proud of her. They knew she had the artistic talent to become a successful clothes designer someday when she got the chance.

The war had thus far not been a terrible hardship for them. Meat, butter, bread, and other food basics were still available although many were rationed. Some things such as materials for dress making were becoming harder to get, but there were no significant hardships due to shortages.

Gustav's job at the restaurant still provided an income for them. At fifty four years of age, he did not fear being recalled to fight in the war. The three of them still lived in their apartment. Thus far, the British had conducted less than a dozen small bombing raids on Hamburg, mostly aimed at the shipyards and oil refineries on the south side of the city. The bombing raids had been largely ineffective with little loss of life.

Despite its lack of immediate personal hardship for them, the war still greatly affected them. Life would be much better and less stressful without the war. A few of their friends and neighbors had lost sons in the fighting.

They had worried a great deal about Rolf, but now he was safe as a prisoner of war. They worried about Cousin Fritzi who had been drafted into the army. Cousin Willie still worked in the aircraft plant, so they had less worry for him. So far, the war's worst effect on my family had been the perceived need to send me away to safety in America and then to lose touch with me when mail service ended.

Gustav and his friends at the bar had not been able to celebrate the defeat of the British, which they had expected with such certainty. The British RAF had successfully fought off the German Luftwaffe's air offensive, so Hitler postponed indefinitely the German invasion of Britain.

Hitler's failure to defeat the British, his first big unsuccessful campaign, had privately been very unsettling for them and probably others. German forces seemed, however, to be successfully advancing on a number of fronts in the Balkans and North Africa. Still, Hitler and his armies were no longer considered invincible.

Sitting there in the booth, they talked about me. It was hard for them to imagine I lived in a country that was not even at war. Although the war had not had a severe immediate impact on them, the uncertainty of it made them thankful that they had sent me to America.

* * *

Rolf looked up in surprise when he heard the merchant ship's general quarters alarm go off. He was just getting his tray in the breakfast line. He glanced uneasily at Dieter beside him as the loud speakers announced, "General

Quarters! General Quarters! All hands man your battle stations!"

They had heard "General Quarters" announced before a number of times when the ship conducted training drills, but they didn't usually hold drills this time of the day during breakfast.

"Shit!" Dieter swore as they put down their trays quickly and worked their way through the excited scramble of prisoners. The ship made a sharp turn and heeled over causing loose gear on the bunks to tumble to the deck.

The violent maneuvering of the ship seemed to confirm their thoughts that this was the real thing, causing a sense of dread among the prisoners. After some effort, Rolf and Dieter got to their bunks where they put on their coats and knitted caps. Dorfman was there too getting on his coat.

The prisoners were locked in the cargo hold and there was nothing they could do but listen and try to stay calm. Without portholes, they had no way of seeing what was happening outside. They needed to be prepared to abandon ship if it came to that. But it would not be possible until their access hatch was unlocked, enabling them to get out and up to the main deck.

The loud speaker system repeated general quarters and announced a surfaced submarine sighting. There was much excited talking in the hold and one of the senior prisoners hollered for everyone to quiet down.

The ship made a sharp turn in the opposite direction and heeled steeply over to the other side causing more loose gear to tumble and crash to the deck. They hurried to the life jacket locker where lifejackets were being hastily distributed. One was handed to Rolf and he began donning it. Normally, they would be put on outside on deck, but they would don them down here to save time.

They heard the boom of the ship's three inch gun on the bow not far forward of them. Every ten seconds or so, it would fire with a boom. Soon other smaller caliber guns began a more rapid fire. The prisoners could only listen and wait anxiously. Rolf had managed with the help of others nearby to get on his life jacket. He tried to be calm as he and the other prisoners listened intently in silence.

Suddenly, a loud explosion rocked the cargo hold. The lights went out and the ship shook violently. Bunks, storage lockers, and other gear were torn loose from foundations and tumbled down. Many of the prisoners were knocked down in the dark by the shock of the explosion. Some were hit by and pinned beneath overturned bunks and other gear.

There had been an initial outcry of shock and surprise by many, followed by moments of stunned silence as the ship continued to vibrate. Then the moans and cries of injured men were heard as well as the sounds of the men stirring and groping in the dark to assist one another.

Finding himself still alive in the dark after the explosion, Rolf had to face the dreadful, numbing reality that his worst fears had been realized. He could only conclude that their ship had been torpedoed, and he realistically didn't have much longer to live.

The End

If you have enjoyed the story of Kätchen and her family so far, their story during the terrible remainder of the war and its aftermath continues in *Kätchen's Continued Story - A German Girl Like Me, Book 2.*

Made in the USA
Monee, IL
24 June 2021

72260271R00171